PENGU
SUICID

Rex Burns has written s ... ...
The Alvarez Journal, winner of an Edgar Award, *The Farnsworth Score*, *Speak for the Dead*, *Angle of Attack*, *The Avenging Angel*, *Strip Search* and *Ground Money*, and sees the series as a continuing fictional biography. In addition he has published several other novels, including *Suicide Season*, which introduces private detective Devlin Kirk. He writes reviews for newspapers and teaches at the University of Colorado at Denver.

SUICIDE
SEASON

REX BURNS

PENGUIN BOOKS

PENGUIN BOOKS

Published by the Penguin Group
27 Wrights Lane, London W8 5TZ, England
Viking Penguin Inc., 40 West 23rd Street, New York, New York 10010, USA
Penguin Books Australia Ltd, Ringwood, Victoria, Australia
Penguin Books Canada Ltd, 2801 John Street, Markham, Ontario, Canada L3R 1B4
Penguin Books (NZ) Ltd, 182–190 Wairau Road, Auckland 10, New Zealand

Penguin Books Ltd, Registered Offices: Harmondsworth, Middlesex, England

First published in the USA by Viking Penguin Inc. and simultaneously in Canada 1987
Published in Penguin Books 1988

10 9 8 7 6 5 4 3 2 1

Printed and bound in Great Britain by
Cox & Wyman Ltd, Reading
Set in Caledonia

To "Susie" Mangum

SUICIDE
SEASON

CHAPTER 1

Michael Loomis—Professor Loomis—shut down his Audi Quattro with the same precision he used to dismember critics of his theory on short-range economic growth: first the windshield wipers and lights to leave us in the dark, then he choked off the radio's voice, killed the throb of the motor, and gave a hefty pull on the emergency brake to leave nothing to chance.

"Please realize, Devlin," his face was a blurry shadow as he turned toward me. "This could be a very big opportunity for you."

"I appreciate that, Professor. But I'd like to meet the client and hear what he wants before taking the job."

"You won't be judging Mr. McAllister. He will judge you." The shadow turned into a profile and stared through the windshield. "And please understand, my boy: I'm not doing this just because your father and I were friends, but because I know that despite your youth and relative inexperience, you are very capable at your—ah—profession."

Outside, the darkness was made blacker by the steady drizzle of an early September rain that threatened to congeal into sleet, and through it I made out the scattered lights of a sprawling mansion. My apartment would probably fit into one of its rooms and still leave space to park my rebuilt Austin-Healy 3000. And in fact, the 3000 would probably be more at home here than anything else in my rooms, including me. It promised to be the kind of job most security agencies would drool over, the kind a new agency like Kirk and Associates could only dream about for that mythical time called Someday. Yet here I was, and I wasn't all that happy; the professor had a way of making it seem like I would owe him if McAllister hired me. We needed the work—any new agency needed anything it could get. But I didn't need one with strings, and the reservations I'd felt earlier when I talked to Loomis on the telephone came back stronger as I stared through the rain.

A pair of electric carriage lamps flicked on to show a semicircular porch penning the doorway behind an arc of columns. The porch roof was too high to keep the rain from blowing in but it wasn't built for practicality, and I wouldn't have been surprised to see a Truman balcony nesting somewhere in those tall columns. It was no surprise at all to find a screaming eagle pinched between the wooden horns of the door's scrolled pediment. "I won't embarrass you by washing my socks in the punch bowl. But I want to make up my own mind about who I work for, Professor. That's one of the reasons I'm in this racket."

The glow from the porch lights deepened the two lines that ran down from the corners of his mouth toward his chin. They made his jaw seem to move with the stiff mobility of a ventriloquist's dummy. "You could have had the same freedom by being an attorney, as your father wanted."

Leave it to Loomis to bring up my father and that whole wad of soreness and regret about law school and his dream for me. I'd dropped out because of boredom, but my father never really understood that. He worked too hard to know what boredom was; his life had been one of early struggle and long and careful effort to give his only son all those things he never had. But he couldn't give me what I really wanted: something called adventure. How to say that my life felt dry and wasted when I faced another mountain of books? How to put that restless aching, that yearning to be out from under into words that wouldn't sound trite and corny? Or, worse, immature. It sounded as impractical as that time in high school when I loaded up a backpack and started to walk east across America because it hurt with a deep pang to know there were all those places to see and I hadn't been there yet.

"It's the age, Devlin," my father had said. "All the turmoil, the chaos in the streets and on television. You were at the top of your college class—you're in a first-rate law school. Just finish your degree—three short years—then you can do what you want to and you'll have a career to fall back on."

But I hadn't. Instead I applied to the FBI, who wouldn't have me—no law degree—and the Secret Service, and while I was waiting to hear, I became a cop. To get law-enforcement experience, I told my father, and—though I didn't admit it aloud—to do some good for somebody. The waiting turned into three years during which time I did what good I could, but it wasn't much. And though I had spurned my father's dream for me, he never reminded me that I could have finished law school by the time the Service accepted me. But he didn't have to, and after that it was too late. I wasn't home often, after that. I wasn't home when he needed me most.

"I like being disreputable. That's a kind of freedom no lawyer can afford."

"This is not a subject for levity, Devlin. You have the same stubbornness as your father. If he'd listened to me, your future would have been far more secure than it is, and he would . . . well, that unfortunate business wouldn't have occurred."

"My father was a good man. And he did the best he could with what life dealt him." With the windshield washers stopped, the little semicircles of cleared glass began to fill up first with the flattened explosions of heavy raindrops and then with the jerky, zigzag tracks of the fragments. "He gave me a fine education and he didn't complain when I went my own way. We'd better go in—I see Big Mac waiting for us."

Loomis, like a lot of professional talkers, wanted the last word, and through the crackle of rain and the slam of car doors, I heard something muttered about the younger generation's disrespect for older and wiser heads. It brought a short-lived prick of remorse—the good professor was only trying to help the son of his ex-partner, and the son didn't seem at all grateful. But I was sick and tired of the awkwardness and hesitation that came when my father's death was mentioned. Which, with Loomis, seemed often.

It wasn't McAllister who waited in the cold for us, but his man: a proper butler trained in the British manner but with an American accent. Living expenses, fringes, and a salary probably above forty thousand a year. That was a lot to pay for an automatic door opener, and I nudged my sliding scale to the top. Despite the brave words to Loomis—and as Bunch had reminded me earlier—we needed at least one client who would pay his bill with more than promises. And the professor was right: with or without strings, this was a big opportunity. Not only would the pay be good, but it was also the kind of job that could lead to work for other major businesses and corporations. And the bigger the corporation, the bigger their need for security.

The butler led us through an anteroom into a dimly lit inner sanctum whose dominant feature was a fireplace large enough for even me to stand in. A single heavy log smoldered against the sooty back wall while a forest of smaller trees crackled in front and, in a deep chair set for pensive contemplation of the fire, sat a stocky man. He seemed to be in his fifties, but when he stood to shake hands, he had an energy and force that belied the graying hair and the carved wrinkles in his neck and at the corners of his eyes.

"Mike! Good to see you. Sorry about the weather—that's the one thing I can't control. Not yet, anyway." He turned from Loomis to squeeze my hand in a brief test of strength. "And you're Mr. Devlin."

"Kirk, sir. Devlin's my first name."

"Ah, sorry, young man."

"It's a common mistake."

"I don't make common mistakes, Kirk. When I make them, I make uncommonly big ones." He waved toward another pair of chairs, less thronelike than his own. The butler, efficient and silent, was rolling a portable bar from a far corner of the room. "Sit, gentlemen. A bit of pleasure before business?"

If I'd been wrong in expecting McAllister to be reedy and tweedy because he had a butler, I wasn't wrong about the purpose of this pause for hospitality. He measured me while the butler quickly served Loomis his usual Scotch and asked what I would have. The drinks came from unmarked decanters, but my tongue recognized the smooth, buttery heat of Wild Turkey, and I chewed it for a long, pleasant minute before swallowing. Unlike a lot of people who used anonymity to get by with something, McAllister apparently wanted his ostentation based on fact, and he had the money and the pride to do it right.

"How tall are you, Kirk?"

"Six-three."

"Mike tells me you went to Stanford. What'd you study there?"

"History, sir. I was prelaw."

"But you don't have your law degree?"

"Not my interest."

"I see. Play football there?"

"No, sir."

He didn't try to hide his disappointment. "You should have. You look big enough."

"I was on the crew."

"Oh. Rowing." He waved the butler away with a tiny gesture and toyed a moment with his glass of plain soda water. "Has the professor said anything to you? About what I'm after?"

"No, sir."

"You asked me not to, Owen."

"Yes, yes—I know." He leaned forward into the glow of the fire, silent for a moment and staring at the slow waver of the flames. A spray of raindrops rattled across a bank of french doors that, I guessed, opened to a patio outside. At one of the far walls, made larger by the low light from the fireplace, stood a scattering of book-shelves and hunting trophies. The books were broad bands of colorful matched sets with gilt titles that caught the firelight; the trophies included a massive, waxy trout curved in a frozen leap, an elk head's spreading antlers and glassy gaze, the entire lean shape of a pronghorn poised to run. McAllister, it seemed, was a collector: trophies, mansions, companies, and all the people he needed to serve them.

"How old are you, Kirk?"

"Twenty-eight."

"What's your experience? How long have you been in private security?"

"I'm just getting started with my own agency. But I've had extensive training as a Secret Service agent, and before that three years in public law enforcement. As I'm sure Professor Loomis has told you."

"Devlin tends to be a bit abrupt, Owen. It's a young man's impatience. But he does know his—"

"That's okay, Mike. He's right. I just wanted to hear it from you, Kirk. If I didn't have a problem, I wouldn't need a detective. And I wouldn't call one without learning something about him first. The main thing—not that experience doesn't count—but the main thing is that the professor says he trusts you. Trust is damned important to me." He sipped his drink and held it in his mouth a second or two. "In this instance, trust is also vital. That, and discretion. It's an extremely sensitive issue."

I nodded and waited. Measured in dollars, McAllister's importance was probably as big as he thought it was. Certainly, he spent a lot to impress his interests on others. And, after all, I had accepted the man's whiskey.

"Do you work alone?"

"I have an associate. He's an experienced and capable man."

McAllister glanced at Loomis, his red, shaggy eyebrows lifting slightly to show the gleam of pale eyes. "Know anything about him?"

"Homer Bunchcroft. I believe he spent some time in local law enforcement. I've never met the man, but neither have I heard any adverse commentary about him."

"He prefers 'Bunch' and he was a Denver police detective for eight years."

"Devlin assures me that he, and not this 'Bunch,' will be in charge, Owen."

"Why don't you just tell me what the problem is, Mr.

McAllister. I'll be the one to tell you whether or not I accept the job."

Another burst of rain crackled across the glass and McAllister's mouth tightened as his eyes settled on mine in a spurt of quick anger. Beside me, I heard Loomis give a muted groan and the only other sound was the flutter of the fire. Then, unsmiling, McAllister nodded. "All right—let's get to business, then. I've heard a few things about one of my division managers. I want him investigated. But I want it accomplished very quietly so that if the rumors are false, no harm's been done."

"What kind of rumors?"

McAllister hesitated. "I don't want to say too much if you're not interested."

Bunch had told me he'd wad me up like an outhouse catalogue if I let this one get away. "We specialize in company security and executive protection. Is this a security issue?"

"Security? It sure as hell is a security issue. Yes, sir."

"Then it sounds like our kind of job. We're interested."

"All right." He lifted his glass in a brief toast. "That's fine. Now, what's happened—and if I leave anything out, Mike, you tell me—is that in the past six months, two major proposals have been torpedoed. The Lake Center development project, and the Columbine Industrial Park project. These were big deals, Kirk, even for me. Each one was a hundred-million proposition. It cost a hell of a lot just to get the proposals done, let alone what the start-up costs would have been. Of course McAllister Enterprises would have made a bundle or two once the projects were rolling, but that's what America's all about, right? Or damn well should be. Anyway, the damned things never got off the ground." His eyes turned to mine, telling me to ask what happened.

So I did.

"Each proposal had a major computation error. The result was that the costs were underestimated by a couple million each. That would have been all right—we would have caught it soon enough and factored it in later in the project. You work on deals this involved and mistakes get made, computers or no computers. Right, Professor?"

"That seems to be the case, Owen. Though it's not my field of expertise."

"Right. But what shot us out of the saddle, Devlin, was an outfit called the Aegis Group. Each time, exactly one day after our proposals were submitted, they stepped in with theirs—and without the computation error. Their final figures were higher, but they—or somebody—pointed out the errors in ours. Aegis got both those projects. They've already broken ground on both of them. Each one's going to make a fortune—a bunch of fortunes!" McAllister dipped his head to the glass and sipped and I saw that he was pressing his arm against the chair to keep it from quivering. He turned his eyes from the fire to me, the reflection of the flame still in them. "I don't know where those people came from. But I know goddamned well where they got their data. After it happened a second time, I managed to get a copy of their Columbine proposal, Kirk. It's ours. Our figures, touched up here and there. Our categories, our numbers, our everything except that goddamned error. They stole our work, and the bastards stole our projects."

A proposal that complex would be as individual as a fingerprint, and McAllister was right to suspect espionage. "How did you get their proposal?"

"Never mind. I got it, that's all."

"And you think the false figures were fed in on purpose?"

"Don't you? When I saw the Aegis proposal, I had a

team of accountants go over our own with a micro-scope, and it still took us two days to find it. Aegis knew where to take it out and where to plug in the right figures and run off a new computation. And somebody knew enough to tell the lenders where to look. Hell yes, it was on purpose—it was sabotage!"

"I take it the proposals were drawn up on your corporate computers?"

"Right. Combine the best equipment and the best people, you get the best work."

"The copyright laws on intangible property—and that includes software—are pretty vague, Mr. McAllister. Even if we do find something, that's no guarantee you'll have a court case."

"Let's leave that part of it to my lawyers, Kirk. You find the evidence of Aegis poking around in my business and who the hell let them poke around. I'll take care of the litigation end."

"Don't forget the telephone call, Owen."

"Yeah. Right. This morning I got a call—my assistant got a call—saying that one of my division directors, Austin Haas, had been approached by an Aegis repre-sentative about six months ago."

"And?"

"And nothing. That's all. Christ, what else do I need?"

"No time of meeting or evidence? Nothing more than an anonymous call about Haas?"

"That's why I'm hiring you—to find out if there's anything to it. But do it in a way that doesn't rock the boat. Loyalty's a two-way street; my people know I expect it and they know I give it. But this. . . . Damn it—if there's nothing there, I don't want Haas to get his feathers ruffled. He's a good man and I don't want to ruin his reputation or lose him to somebody else be-cause of an anonymous tip. And I don't want the rest of my people to find out that I'm . . . spying on one of them, goddamn it. But if Haas is on the Aegis payroll, I'll by God kill him!" McAllister leaned back against his chair and the corners of his mouth clenched into something close to a smile. "Or at least figure a way to make him wish he was dead."

"How many people besides Haas had access to the completed proposals?"

"Uh huh. Good. You're right: only a handful. Each section worked on its part and then a few of us pulled the whole thing together and ran a final check of the figures before drawing up the proposal's narrative. Haas was one of that few."

"I'd like a list."

"You only investigate Haas. I told you I don't want my people upset."

"Suppose he's not the one? Suppose someone else on that list wants you to think he is?"

"I'm not that stupid, Kirk—somebody could be setting Haas up. But I'll worry about that when and if you clear him. If I wanted my whole damned staff screened, I'd use my own security people. But I want this kept quiet and narrowly focused. I don't want Haas's reputation shot down for no reason, and I don't want my people to think I'm running a general inquisition. That's why I'm bringing in an outsider. The only person who'll know what you're really after is me. Nobody else is to know what you're doing. Any questions about that?"

"No, sir."

So Kirk and Associates had the big break. Beside me, Professor Loomis gave a muffled grunt of satisfaction, and, at the edge of hearing and beneath a gust of rain on the glass, the flames fluttered in a soft, furry chuckle.

CHAPTER 2

We spent another hour on the details, and McAllister handed me a thick folder holding Haas's life as viewed by McAllister Enterprises. The usual material was there—dates and places, assignments and achievements. The man himself, of course, would escape his paper profile. But that undefined part was the most interesting. In a lot of ways, the work was like trying to define a thing by saying what it wasn't—you could come close; sometimes you could even draw a circle around it. But the thing itself waited secretly until finally you found the right word or only the right metaphor, perhaps, to state what it was. And sometimes that never came.

But Bunch and I tried, buoyed by the fact that a healthy portion of our fee had come up front. We fondled the money briefly as it went through our fingers to pay off debts that loomed larger and larger as Kirk and Associates nickel-and-dimed its way toward a bankrupt's early grave. Taking Uncle Wyn's investment with it as well as the monument I secretly wanted to build—the thing I could point to in my mind and say, "See, Dad? I didn't let you down."

It was the kind of work where you could spend a lot of time looking out the window, and that tended to make the chief backer nervous. Uncle Wyn wasn't happy to see me or Bunch swiveled around to prop our feet on the iron rail that fenced off the office's large, arched window while we stared out across the flat roofs of neighboring warehouses and office buildings toward the gleam of snowfields in the distant mountains. But he wasn't happy, either, at the thought that Bunch and I occasionally looked into windows from the outside. We had tried to convince my uncle that what we did had some redeeming social value and was worth the money he'd invested. But neither Bunch nor I could make him believe that our occupation wasn't slightly pornographic.

"Hey, listen, some porno I like." Bunch sat on the tired stenographer's chair in front of the glass, his hams spilling over the Naugahyde and pinched by the cuffs of running shorts that on anyone else would have been baggy.

"That's the kind we call erotic."

"You call it erotic. Susan, she calls it dirty. Me, I call it fun." He scrubbed with a towel at the mat of hair on his chest and then sniffed it. "God I smell good. Sweat. Sunshine. A light coat of carbon monoxide. I love it."

"You jog through that traffic, you'll lose more years of life than you save," said Uncle Wyn. Like Bunch, he was in the middle of his morning routine. Which, today, meant a visit to the office to check on his investment.

"No, no—I'm contributing to evolution. Five, six more generations, and my descendants will have these carburetors instead of lungs. And it all started with me." He hocked something out of his throat and stood to spit through an open window panel into the street three floors below. "They'll think it was a pigeon. Speaking of which, did you tell your uncle about our big client?"

I told him about McAllister.

"The McAllister? Carnival Ball Owen McAllister— the guy that's into movies and oil and real estate and whatever?"

"That's the one."

"He wants to hire you two?"

"Has hired us, Uncle." I held up the check with its string of numbers. "If things go right, Kirk and Associates is on its way."

Uncle Wyn, his arthritic leg stiffly out in front of the chair, leaned forward to read the check. "Jesus H. It's for real."

"That's just the retainer," said Bunch. "Wait till he gets our final bill."

"I never met the man, but he's solid. His name's worth a lot on the street," Uncle Wyn said. "How did Loomis know him?"

"I'm not sure. But they call each other Mike and Owen."

Uncle Wyn grunted. "I was surprised you'd even talk to that guy."

"It wasn't his fault. And he lost money, too."

"Crap," said Uncle Wyn.

"Loomis didn't lose as much as your old man, Dev. And he got it back damned fast. And he didn't blow himself away, either."

"You want to talk about this case or not?"

"Sure, Dev. But you know what Susan says?"

"What makes you think I give a damn what Susan says?"

"Mr. Kirk, you know what Susan says about your nephew? She says he keeps it inside too much. He never talks about it, you know? She says it's going to blow up some day—that he's got to ventilate it."

"Ventilate?"

"Yeah. It's psychology talk for mental farting."

"Susan has enough patients without worrying about me. Or about my flatulence."

"Don't get huffy. You always use big words when you get huffy. And then our communication, as they say, breaks down."

"Let's communicate about McAllister."

Uncle Wyn heaved to his feet, levering his stiff leg up neatly with the cane. "For a change, you boys got real work to do—congratulations. Me, I got the Cubs game coming on. So good luck with your big chance."

"Hey, when your lenders wish you luck, you know they mean it."

I closed the door behind my uncle; his uneven tread on the landing was a pale echo of the years he had spent sprinting across the grass of a baseball diamond.

"He's a tough old bird, your uncle."

"He keeps an eye on his investments, that's for sure."

"Naw, he just wants to look after his favorite and only nephew."

"You tell him that when we miss a payment."

"I hope I never have to. Fill me in on McAllister."

After Loomis dropped me off last night, with a final reminder of how important this account could be toward establishing the reputation of Kirk and Associates, I spent an hour going through Haas's personnel file and then following up with some time in the library on points that the official documents only hinted at. Of course all I found in the newspapers was what received public notice at the time—a biographical note when Haas served as a director of the United Way drive a few years back, a squib from a social column about one of his trips to the Caribbean with his attractive wife Margaret and his two lovely children Austin, Jr., and Shauna. These are little things, but they help fill in the background; and, on very rare occasions they can turn into something important. But after a lot of reading, I didn't see how.

"And this guy Haas is the one who did it?"

"That's what we're supposed to find out. Very quietly."

Bunch, who couldn't stay in one place more than five minutes when he was awake, moved to the office window and gazed down at the semis and vans and delivery cars that choked Wazee Street this time of day. "We'll want a twenty-four-hour on Haas."

That meant hiring some freelancers for routine surveillance, and I began listing the p.i.'s that could be trusted to do decent work. It was a short list. "McAllister gave me permission to tap Haas's office phone." I spun a key across the desk to Bunch. "Here's a pass key; might as well do it this afternoon after the offices close."

"How about his home phone?"

"That too."

"How hard is it going to be?"

"I'm glad you asked."

"That's what I was afraid of." Bunch began pulling on his soaked sweat shirt, the muscles of his arms knotting as he shrugged into it. "All right—I'll check it out. You want me to go ahead and make the plant if I can?" The sleeves had been cut off, and the waist, so that the thick, hard flesh of his belly showed.

"Yeah. McAllister might give us twenty-four hours before he starts calling about results."

"I never met one of those rich guys who didn't want things done yesterday."

"When did you ever meet someone like McAllister?"

"That's what I said: I never met one."

He left me trying to puzzle that out. The tread of his large running shoes made the ancient floor of the remodeled warehouse creak as he started down the metal stairs. In the office above, a piano began thumping de-

liberately up and down the scale, its muffled chords like
a final shred of summer: open windows on a hot afternoon and some kid in the neighborhood pinned under
the eyes of a piano teacher. And the day outside looked
like it still had some summer in it, too; the sky's blue was
bleached by heat, and the hard, cloudless glare made
the worn brick of the warehouses and factories in the
district seem sharp and brittle. But beneath the appear-
ance of heat, the sun had a lower angle—a shorter intensity, a longer shadow, something that hinted at how
brief these bright days would be and how soon winter
would close around the city. My father had liked this
time of year; it reinforced his melancholy, he said, with
a sort of visual carpe diem. Then he'd apologize for
being morbid. "Some people find greater happiness in
being unhappy, Dev. Don't let an old man's self-indul-
gent gloom rub off on you." But I suppose that it already
had. I couldn't remember a time since my mother's
death when I was eleven that my father hadn't carried
around the faint aroma of sadness. Even in the midst of
hilarity—one of my birthdays, for example—a moment
would always come, no matter how brief or secret,
when his laughter had a forced note and the thought
deep in his eyes was how much my mother would have
enjoyed seeing this. That sadness must have increased
especially when I left him to go away to college and,
later, to Treasury School and then to Bellesville and all
the assignments the Service likes to ship its agents to.
But I had been too busy too notice. My father's scorn
for suicide—"We're in this life to do penance, and a
man shouldn't quit on a duty just because he doesn't
like it"—and the busy pace he kept telling me about
when we'd talk on the telephone made me ignore the
little hints that must have been there. He did not want
to burden me with his sadness, and I did not want to be
burdened. It was that failure to him that Susan wanted
me to "ventilate" and which I was still trying to under-

stand—the feeling of guilt for being too blind when he must have been asking me for help; the feeling of unclean selfishness for having been too wrapped up in my own life to see what was happening to his. It was a lousy way to repay a father for all that he'd done for his son.

But even though we labor confused and blind, we must labor nonetheless. "That's where the faith comes in, Dev. We do the best we can at the time, and the rest of it is up to whatever gods care to be bothered with us." That's what he would have said. And, "Forget it—it wasn't your fault; it was my decision, and the best one all-around." Trying to be generous toward me even in death.

The large old window—the arched top of a brick frame that reached down to the ground floor—showed the flat roofs across the street, and past them the tree-tops rising from the river. In the glare-faded distance, beyond the low ridges of sprawling suburbs, the forested peaks of the Front Range washed against the ragged outline of the more distant Rampart Range with its blue snowfields, landmarks that had been there long before the city itself and that would be long after I was gone, too. "Lift up your eyes, Dev, lift them to the mountains. Isn't that a sight? It makes a man thank God he's alive!"

I pulled away from the window. "God doesn't know we're alive," Bunch would have answered. "And if He does, He doesn't give a shit."

Up to a certain level, background checks are fairly routine. For a credit history, a call to the Credit Bureau or an inquiry on stationery with the Devlin Mortgage Company logo for veracity. Credit card numbers and a larcenous skill with the computer—provided by Bunch —opened up credit accounts and bank accounts, and that in turn led to income tax returns, license information, a list of previous addresses, even a fairly up-to-date medical history. People are willing to trade a lot of privacy for a good credit rating. And, of course, McAllister Enterprises employment and personnel records provided a fund of information and further leads. What the paper trail wouldn't reveal was a bank account not mentioned anywhere in the credit or tax records, an account that provided shelter for the legendary ill-gotten gains. And from what McAllister had said as well as from what little I'd been given access to concerning the two stolen projects, we were talking a lot of gains. Deals that big meant payoffs with an impressive number of zeros to the left of the decimal. And since people with money have a tendency to spend it, it doesn't take a genius at subtraction to find out if someone's spending more than the records show he's making. IRS does it all the time.

Haas's account with the First Bank of Denver was an orderly one, the month's paycheck automatically deposited on the thirtieth and the withholding figures matching the records in his company dossier. With the right strings of numbers to cite, it wasn't hard to find a voice on the telephone that would be happy to discuss Mr. Haas's current balance.

"Well, you've got your numbers and I've got mine, and I still can't find the discrepancy. Can you send me a printout of my last year's transactions?"

"No trouble at all, Mr. Haas. I'll send it to the address on your account."

"Fine—no, wait. Why not just send it directly to my accountant. I'll tell him it's coming."

"Yes, sir. His name and address?"

"Devlin Accounting Agency, 1557 Wazee, 80202. Thanks a lot."

A series of like telephone calls to various credit accounts took up the rest of the morning and promised a steady flow of mail for the next few days. I'd just finished a call to the regional Visa office requesting a record of the last year's purchases when the telephone rang as soon as I set it down.

"Jesus, Dev, you been living on that thing. I tried to get through a dozen times."

"After this case, we'll get a second line. We can afford it then. What do you have?"

"I looked at the Haas place. I think we ought to talk before I go any further."

"What's the matter?"

"It's going to be rough. It's right in the middle of Belcaro Estates. That's one of these walled-off areas—you know, Cherry Hills, Polo Grounds, that kind of thing: private roads leading in and a private gatekeeper to keep the peasants out."

"Can't you go in as a deliveryman?"

"I already did. That's how I found the place. It looks like a bunch of barns stuck together out in the middle of a field. All the houses look like that—clumps of barns standing off by themselves and a wall around it all. A few shrubs, not much in the way of trees—it's too new to have any—and the utilities are all underground. Be harder than hell to get a parallel transmitter on their phones without getting spotted."

"It's a new house?"

"Couple years old, I guess. The whole development's new. One of those with a golf course on the other side of your swimming pool. Where the hell do people get the money to live like that?"

"That's what we want to find out. What's the house worth?"

"Four, maybe five hundred thou. And that's one of the cheapies. There's a couple must go for a million or two. They got the goddamn golf course in the living room."

"Can we get to it tonight?"

"That's what I'm thinking. Look, I'm supposed to

meet Susan at the Chute. You go on over and we'll lay some plans that even you can't screw up. It'll take me a half-hour to get there, so keep your hands off my woman."

"If she keeps hers off me. Why do you take her to a place like that?"

"Hey—I feel comfortable there. It's like home."

For Bunch, that meant other people were spitting on the floor, too. Chute Number One was a cowboy bar just off Colorado Boulevard, nondescript from the outside and the inside didn't even try for that. Some of the customers may have been genuine cowboys—if so, they were the ones who stayed by themselves and looked out of place. The others thought they were and wanted everyone else to think so, too. A long bar filled one wall and a line of plywood booths filled the other; in the floor space, tables were jammed as tightly as possible, and toward the back a pair of pool tables glowed green in the cigarette smoke that swirled under their hooded lights. Over it all, a woman's electronic wail sang something about how hard it was to love a man who loved to roam. A lot of people shared Bunch's affection for the place, and as usual, it was crowded.

It took a moment to blink away the sun-blindness, then I saw Susan's blond hair, smooth as a single stroke of silk, catch the light at a table toward the back. She was by herself, but glances from the clusters of men seated around her said she wouldn't be alone for long.

"Can I buy you a drink, lady?"

"Dev—it's good to see you!"

If there was a Colorado look, Susan had it: healthy glow, a face that had no cuteness about it, but a beauty that was in the clean symmetry of lines and planes and a smile that—literally—gleamed of all outdoors. All matched by a lithe, tanned body that did nice things to the thin summer dress covering it. Bunch was very fortunate, all the more so as she was a one-man woman,

which was fine with me because no matter how polite
and friendly we were when we met, we usually parted
arguing.

"The animal said he'd be here in about twenty minutes. He told me I could do anything I wanted with you
until then."

"Ha! What happened to your raven-haired beauty—
the one who's jealous of blondes?"

"Renee?" I pretended to dredge up the name. "Ah
yes, Renee." "She couldn't understand my work schedule: canceling dates at the last minute, out at all hours,
muffled telephone calls. She thought I was seeing another woman." It hadn't been all that neat. Pretty
messy, in fact. She had wanted more than I was willing
to give, and what had started out as a lot of fun for both
of us somehow changed into a burden for me and a
sadness for her. There had been no other woman—the
last thing in the world I wanted right now was to be
serious about a woman—and that included Renee. But
another woman was something she could understand
and be jealous of, just as—after a glass or two too much
wine—she had once admitted to Susan her jealousy of
blondes. So I let her believe it. And that was the end of
that.

"Weren't you?"

"What kind of question's that? And besides, it's none
of your business."

A shadow thinned the already dim light on the table
and I looked up expecting to see the waitress. But it was
a pair of wide, sloping shoulders in a plaid flannel shirt
topped by a face that was mostly jaw.

"You folks having a good time?"

"Delightful."

He pulled out a chair and wedged himself against the
table to smile at Susan and prop a heavy arm in my face.
"What's your name, little lady?"

"If you're selling something, we're not buying."

The head turned to show a pale, hot eye topped by a bushy black eyebrow. Two small white scars made tiny streaks through the hairs. "I'm not selling nothing, dude. But I just might give you something. Free."

"It's all right, Dev."

"You hear that? The little lady says it's all right."

"She's making a mistake."

"Well now, that's up to her. Why don't you just take on off before you make a mistake, too."

"It's not me she's worried about."

That took some seconds to work into the cerebellum, then he leaned back and gave me his undivided attention.

"Dev, please."

In the springtime, young bulls get hot and randy, but a short beer and a long look at Susan could make it rutting season all year round. For all her degrees in psychology, Susan didn't seem to understand that— Bunch was all she wanted, and she assumed her lack of interest in anyone else was plain. Nor did she understand the two-by-four rule of gentlemanly discourse: try to get two in before you get one back. The jaw began to move: "You come in here wearing a goddamn coat and tie . . . you come in here to slum around and have a few laughs at the cowboys? By God, I'll give you laughs!"

He didn't hesitate; while he talked, he swung a heavy elbow at my head and followed with a lunging right that thudded off my forearm. Somewhere beyond the crash of breaking glass I heard Susan's muffled scream, and beneath that a deep-chested bellow of pleasure as the figure loomed up against the ceiling and bore down, arms a blur of angry flesh.

I came up under him, a fistful of shirt over one shoulder and his flailing legs on the other. A quick twist and the heavy body flew in a high arc to crash against the table and send it wobbly and skewed into the scramble of cowboys dodging out of the way. A clubbing fist jarred my ear with a metallic ring and a second one swung hard toward my groin, smacking into the quickly lifted thigh and pushing me back against a wall of outstretched hands that shoved me forward. Everything except the man in front of me was blotted out by a gush of anger born of pain and, far deeper, hatred of the man's arrogance.

Head down between his shoulders and knotty fists high, he came at me with the awkward grace of someone who has training enough to know the basics and strength enough not to worry about refinements.

"You son-of-a-bitch, I'm gonna kill you!"

Through the redness of my vision, I saw him try. A fist aimed for my head and a pointed boot swung at anything it could reach. I caught the leg on my crossed wrists and grabbed its heel, twisting and lifting to spread his body and snap a side-kick where his Wranglers advertised their reinforced inseam. The man didn't scream but he did grunt and stagger back in a painful crouch and the outraged, blind fury of a moment past was replaced by a cold wash of pain and then calculating rage. Something was going on around me, the shouts of voices, yells of encouragement and scorn. But it made no impression other than a distant buzz beneath the rushing sound that was my anger throbbing in my ears. The whole universe narrowed down to that man getting slowly to his feet and to the eyes that measured the distance between him and what he would go for next. I feinted a left and he jabbed stiff fingers toward my eyes and raked clawing nails past my ear as he brought a knee up hard into my stomach and clubbed at my face again. I grabbed a wrist that my hand couldn't close around; up-turn-pull-bend, the basic throw drilled into rote by hours of practice at Bellesville, and as his head rotated past he cursed me for not staying in one place to fight like a white man.

Down as hard as I could flip to stun him and then almost automatically go for his elbow. He screamed a hoarse shout as I levered his arm across my knee and bore down, but before I heard the snap of living bone, a pair of arms wrapped around me to haul back. I drove an elbow into the thick flesh and a startled, hot breath grunted at my ear, "Dev—Dev, hold it. It's me: Bunch!"

"Let me go—let me go!"

"He's down, Dev. You'll kill him. He's down."

The man, making little gasping sounds through gritted teeth, held his arm tightly against his body and curled in a scooting circle of pain among the spilled beer and broken bottles. Slowly the shouting circle of faces came into focus and I straightened and felt Bunch's arms slack a bit.

"You okay now? Can I let you go now?"

"You can let go."

"He's down."

"I see him. You can let go."

The arms fell away as the grunting man fought up to his knees, eyes tight with pain. "My arm—my fucking arm . . ."

"Devlin, if this is your lunch break, what do you do for supper?"

"You picked this place."

"Leave some for next time."

Two men helped the injured warrior to his feet and led him hunched tight as a snail toward the door. A balding man in a bartender's apron stepped forward to survey the broken glasses and test the table leg. Then he turned to me. "Winner pays for damages. House rules. That'll be twenty-five dollars."

"The winner?" Bunch kicked a broken Coors bottle. "In a civilized country, the loser's supposed to pay!"

"The losers don't usually hear me. That'll be twenty-five dollars. Payable now."

"But I didn't start it. He did!"

"Don't make no difference. Winner pays. Twenty-five dollars."

"Hell," said Bunch. "It's not worth winning if you got to pay for it."

"Then maybe folks'll realize there ain't no winners and stop tearing up my place. That'll be—"

"I know," I said. "Twenty-five dollars. Here."

Bright and tiny behind wire-rimmed glasses, the eyes glanced sharply at the bills. "Right. Thank you. You folks want another round?"

"Who with?" asked Bunch.

"Never mind—we're just leaving."

We sat in the car for a few minutes while a tensely quiet Susan dabbed a tissue at the blood seeping out of my cheek.

"Damn good thing he didn't get his teeth in that ear. He'd still be hanging there—or have it chewed off by now. That's the trouble with your kind of fighting, Dev. All those holds and throws. It lets a man get too close. A punching technique, now, that keeps them off." Bunch filled the back seat and leaned forward to study the scratch. "It's not deep but it'll fester a bit. Finger-nails are as bad as teeth for carrying dirt."

"They weren't any dirtier than his breath—ouch!" I pulled away from the sharp thrust of the tissue. "What's that for?"

"Because you enjoyed hurting that man."

"What?"

"I saw your eyes when you had his arm. You were actually enjoying it."

"The only thing I enjoyed was being where I was in-stead of where he was. And don't forget—he started it."

"Hell, Susan, that was just a little scuffle. That guy'll be back in an hour looking for another party. That's what they call fun."

"I could see that." Her voice took on the reflective tone that meant she was moving her observations from categories to theory, the kind of generalization that always grated on me. "But his enjoyment was more . . . reflexive. It was exciting to him, like driving fast or jumping from heights. You were more calculating. You knew exactly what you were doing, how to do it, and how much to hurt him."

"Good for Dev, I say. A guy who keeps his cool in a fight generally wins it."

"But it was a savage cool—a vicious one." She wadded the tissue into the car's trash bag. "That man was only a convenient target for all the rage and frustration you still haven't gotten rid of."

"I wasn't tangled up with a theory, Susan. I was fighting a man who tried to kill me—and came damn close to it. All because I told him he couldn't do what he wanted. I don't feel one twinge of guilt for trying to break his arm—I should have tried for his neck."

"Naw—you were right to go for the arm, Dev. I don't think he had a neck."

"It's not the fighting, Dev. That's excusable. It's the cold pleasure I saw in your eyes when you were trying to break his arm. I find that disturbing."

"I was pleased to be winning. If you find that disturbing or inexcusable, that's too bad. And thoroughly unprofessional for a dispassionate observer of human nature like yourself."

"To be scientific in method doesn't mean I have to reject ethics."

"All right, you two, that's enough. Don't get started again—I'm hungry."

"It was unethical of me to fight back? Is that what you're saying?"

"I'm telling you for your own sake to get professional help. You need to come to terms with your father's suicide before you kill someone."

"Hunger. Eat. Food. Now."

I knew she wasn't entirely wrong, and this wasn't the

first fight she'd seen me in. But it wasn't the calculating wish to hurt that she had seen. It was blind rage—the berserker explosion of a kind of savage joy in attacking something tangible. Looking back, it wasn't hurt that I had wanted to inflict, but destruction. The beast that slumbers within, a crack in the fragile crust of civilization—my father used to joke about the primitive behavior of human offspring, especially at the age of puberty, and then draw analogies to political movements or religious fanaticism. But Susan didn't have the answers for what was the cause of rage in me or in society, and I resented being made a case study by her or by anyone else. For all her theorizing, she missed the simple, basic fact that once a man's committed to a fight, he'd better finish it or be finished.

Bunch thumped the car seat to jar us toward a restaurant where the noon flow was beginning to ebb and we could have a quiet table.

"You guys cooled off now?"

"I wasn't angry," said Susan. "Just professionally interested."

"And I wasn't interested. Just professionally angry."

"Glad to hear it. Now we can enjoy our food. And drink—waitress!"

Susan and I ate and finished and watched Bunch continue to eat while he told about the Haas home. "It'll be no trouble getting into the grounds—we can go over the wall. The trouble's the underground phone cables —a single post serves three houses, and I don't have the code for which wire's which."

"The call-in trick?"

"Yeah. Probably our best shot. Eleven? Eleven thirty?"

"What's the call-in trick?" asked Susan.

"I get set up on the post and hook up the wires. Devlin calls their number and I see which wire lights up. Then we plant the bug and run. Don't even have to go near the house itself."

"I call at a prearranged time. Late at night's best, when the other wires are least likely to be active."

"And they don't suspect anything?"

"What's to suspect about a wrong number? Even unlisted phones get wrong numbers."

"Did you get his office phone?" I asked.

"Sweat not. The security in that building is lousy. McAllister's key opened everything including the executive toilet, and the rent-a-cop was off sleeping somewhere. All we have to do is dial in and listen to the tape." Bunch winked at Susan. "I got a new toy— I can tap a phone and then call up and listen to the tape from anywhere in the world. And reset it, too. Works just like calling in to screen your answering machine."

"Can't they trace something like that?"

"They got to find it first. Then they could put a countertap on it, and if I was dumb enough to use our own phone—which I'm not—they could trace back." He explained, "The beauty of this little jewel is that we use the telephone company's own wires instead of our own. They can find it with a sweep—it's your basic parasite rig that steals the phone company's electricity—but McAllister's not going to sweep, right?"

"That's what he promised me."

"Then we got no sweat."

At least that's what we hoped. When I called at eleven thirty that night, Haas himself answered the telephone, politely angry at being disturbed. At first I refused to believe it was the wrong number and that Haas wasn't my old drinking buddy Swede. Then I apologized at length to give Bunch as much time as possible to locate the right wire. When we met in the shadows of a lilac hedge a couple of blocks from the

walled enclosure, Bunch grinned and gave a thumbs-
up.

"She works. But now comes the bad news. The only
place for a remote's in a culvert. And I don't trust it—
too many kids and bicycles going through."

"We have to sit on it?"

He shrugged. "The transmitter only has a mile range.
And there's really no place to put a remote. Look
around."

Bunch was right. The Haas home sat near the middle
of the enclosure, a half mile from the nearest wall, and
beyond that was a tangle of homes and condominiums
—nothing with a small room or office for rent by the
week. We would have to monitor the tap from the van,
setting up the recorder in the vehicle's windowless interior and driving it periodically from point to point
within the radius of the transmitter. It meant frequent
checks of the vehicle—even in the sunny acres surrounding Belcaro Estates, cars were vandalized. And it
meant tedious nights of uncomfortable slouching on
the front seat of an alternative vehicle when it was used
for variety. It meant that we brought in extra help to
spell us—p.i.'s who were generally glad to pick up a few
hours a week on surveillance—and it meant that we
became familiar with Haas's voice and those of his wife
and son whose fifth birthday was coming up and who
loved to answer the telephone whenever it rang. Finally, it meant that, half asleep in the car and sheltered
from the clear autumn moonlight by the restless dark
of a wind-tossed cottonwood, I heard the call as soon as
the police did: a woman's tense but efficient voice asking the police to please hurry because her husband had
just shot himself.

CHAPTER 3

From the ridge of high land where the van was parked, I could see the flashing emergency lights zigzag through the late night flicker of traffic and dark streets. Discreetly without sirens but urgent in motion, the rescue unit led a blue-and-white quickly past the lit gate. Then, drawn like flies to the smell of blood, other vehicles began to converge: homicide detectives, forensics detectives, another team of uniformed police, a couple of civilian cars with, I supposed, the doctor or medical examiner and—inevitably—the press. It was too late for the television crews—the ten o'clock news hour was long past—but I recognized the careening Honda Civic that paused momentarily at the gatehouse and then sped through, the guard's voice trailing it with a distant "Hey! Stop!" I waited another few minutes, but the ambulance did not leave in its rush for the emergency room; instead it sat. The motionless, erratic flash of the lights told me that the victim was in no hurry to go anywhere. Finally, I dropped the car in gear and turned away.

Using the radiophone in the van to roust Bunch, I asked him to meet me at the office. Anyone overhearing that transmission wouldn't know what it was about, and Bunch didn't ask questions. He said only, "I'll be there." But to explain it to McAllister, I used a pay phone.

Raymond the butler didn't want to disturb the master at this hour.

"He told me to call at any time. Please put me through."

"I shall be happy to give him your message in the morning, Mr. Kirk."

"This is an emergency and he'll have questions about it. It's something he'd better hear now. Right now."

". . . One moment, sir."

If McAllister had been asleep at 2 A.M., his voice didn't reveal it. It was terse, energetic, and wide awake. "What is it, Devlin?"

"It's Haas, Mr. McAllister. His wife just called the police. She says he shot himself."

"My God! Is he dead?"

"I think so, but I'm not certain. I just monitored the call. The police got there about five minutes ago."

The line was silent for a moment. "Did he find out about you?"

"Not that I know of. It's always a possibility. But if he did, he kept it pretty well hidden."

"Have you come up with anything?"

"Not on his house phone. We haven't checked the last tape from his office phone."

"Can you find out what the police know about it?"

"That's my partner's area. I'm meeting him in a few minutes."

"Let me know what he says immediately." The line was silent but McAllister didn't hang up. "If it was a suicide, well, I guess that's an admission of guilt, isn't it?"

"Not necessarily. But possible. Do you want us to close the case or shall we stay on it?"

Another long pause. "There's no sense attacking the poor bastard now, I suppose. No—damn it—you meet me here in half an hour. I'm going to see Margaret. You might as well come with me." The telephone clicked off as his voice called for Raymond.

Bunch was waiting when I clanged up the open stairs that rose from the small lobby in an angled spiral. During the day, the sound was hardly noticeable because the foot traffic was so constant that it blended with the steady noise of trucks outside. But at night, when the offices in the old remodeled warehouse were closed and the streetlights outside shone on the empty, worn paving stones, the black iron rang under each step and echoed back from the dim corners of hallway and atrium to emphasize the loneliness of the hour.

"You wearing your mother's army boots again?" Bunch sat at the worn and scarred desk, the single lamp throwing his shadow broadly across the wall. Through the window, reflected from the brick surfaces of other walls, the glow of Union Station and the post office terminal filled the night sky. From somewhere beyond the district in the tangle of railroad tracks that filled the river bottom came the dull crash of a freight car being humped.

"Haas shot himself. The police are over there now."

"No shit? Well, what the hell, it happens in the best of families. How'd you find out?"

"His wife called nine-one-one."

"Is he dead?"

"Nothing said, but the ambulance was in no hurry. And she didn't ask for an ambulance—just for the cops. Can you find out what they have?"

"Depends on whose case it is. But I should be able to come up with something."

In his eight years as a cop, Bunch had moved up quickly to make detective sergeant before he finally burned out—perhaps because he had been so good. First it was the growing knowledge that his job wasn't to help people but to wipe up the city's human garbage after they were beyond help. Then it was the ever-increasing paperwork whose only purpose was to cover ass—yours and especially your superiors'. Then it was the court system, which took a cop's good, hard work and threw it away on technicalities and plea bargains so that the scumbag was back on the street faster than the arresting cop. Finally it was the politics, intensified by a conflict between those who joined the police union and those who didn't, which divided the department and set cops against each other. He had quit playing professional football after three years because he grew sick of the routines of training camp and season, and especially because—despite all the color and noise—there seemed no real point to it except a few hours entertainment for John Q. once a week. He had quit to do some good as a cop. Now he was among the growing numbers of ex-cops in the private police business. "Screw it—I got more freedom out here. I do a better job, too; I've put away more people as a p.i. than I ever did in uniform." And because he didn't care who took official credit for a collar, he often turned the arrest over to friends in the detective bureau. In exchange, of course, for help when it was needed.

He dialed a number from memory and asked for Sergeant Kiefer. "Okay, would you ask him to call when he gets a chance? Thanks." Bunch gave the duty watch the office number and hung up. "The good news is Keifer's on duty. He'll fill us in. The bad news is he's out on call—probably over there now, and God only knows how long it'll be before he gets back. End of shift, probably."

"How about staying on it? McAllister wants me to go with him to see Haas's wife."

"Tonight?"

"I have to be over there in fifteen minutes."

It took slightly longer and McAllister, who didn't like to wait, was pacing a small circle on the porch under his wooden eagle. "Glad you finally got here, Kirk. Leave that damned van of yours—Raymond will drive."

He was silent most of the way as the limousine moved smoothly through the steely flicker of passing street lamps. Raymond slowed a bit for empty red lights and stop signs, but McAllister didn't seem to notice until finally he sighed and opened the small bar mounted behind the partitioned driver's seat. "Something to drink?"

"No, sir."

He poured himself a glass of mineral water and watched the liquid sway with the spongy lean of the heavy car. "It wasn't worth shooting himself, Devlin. Not even for as much money as they must have paid him."

"Maybe it was the shame. I've known a suicide or two for that reason."

"And I've never known a commercial real-estate salesman to have any shame, let alone to die from it. But perhaps you're right." He drank deeply. "I wouldn't have guessed Haas was the kind to have that weakness, but perhaps you're right."

We hesitated briefly at the gatehouse; the guard caught a glimpse of the car's length and its license plates and quickly waved us through—something I wanted to remember for future gate crashings. The ambulance had gone, but a number of vehicles still clustered in front of the large home sitting on its own spread of prairie; a few lights burned in the bulky shadows of neighboring houses, but the only sound was an occasional distant whisper of traffic from I-25 when the wind shifted.

"Well, let's get to it. You wait here, Raymond."

"Yes, sir."

I followed him up the winding flagstone walk and noticed a few young trees, their trunks staked as if anchored against some evil wind. The old money had grown up with their trees; the new money was just planting theirs. And some wouldn't grow up with the trees at all. I rang the doorbell—McAllister waited for that service—and a uniformed officer answered, glancing at our jackets for identification badges.

"Who are you?"

"Owen McAllister. A friend of the family."

"Nobody's allowed in unless they're on official business. This is a crime scene."

"I said I'm Owen McAllister. I'm here to see Mrs. Haas. She will need some help."

He puzzled for a moment over whether to shut the door in our faces. Then he caught a glimpse of the limousine and finally stepped back. "Stay right here and I'll get the sergeant. It's a crime scene, so you got to stay right here."

The detective was short and nattily dressed and would have seemed more at home wearing a letterman's sweater and smoking a pipe in some campus beer joint. But Sergeant Kiefer was thoroughly professional and very jealous of his role, and never more cheerful than when peering at a body. And despite thinking of me as a mere civilian, he was willing to admit that he knew me.

"Devlin Kirk! Don't tell me you're the friend of the family."

"No. Mr. McAllister is. Owen McAllister. He's Haas's employer."

The name registered. "Ah. Does Mrs. Haas know you're here, sir?"

"Not yet. We just arrived."

"Ah." He mused on that for a second. "Well, come over here out of the way of the investigation. Please wait in this room. I'll let her know you've come." He led us into a study just off the living room where all the action was. It had more bookshelves than books and a towering mossrock wall that dwarfed one of the house's fireplaces. Ceiling beams, thick carpets, heavily framed windows, all emphasized weight and permanence, but through the casement window with its pattern of diamond panes I could see the thin shadow of one of the small trees.

"How long did Mr. Haas work for you, Mr. McAllister?"

McAllister eyed the detective. " 'Did'? That means he's dead?"

A corner of Keifer's mouth twitched in self-annoyance. "That's what it means. How long was he with you?"

"Almost seven years. He was a good employee."

"And you saw him recently?"

"This afternoon. And, no, he didn't seem depressed or anxious in any way. In fact, he seemed in damned good spirits. Exactly what happened, Officer?"

Kiefer tugged at the pastel shirt cuff that had slipped up beneath his blazer and his eyes glanced hard at me before settling back on McAllister. "It looks like a suicide. Which you seem to know already. Can I ask what brought you here, Mr. McAllister? How did you know something had happened?"

McAllister hesitated, then nodded abruptly at me. "Kirk there. He told me."

"I picked it up on the scanner."

"Ah. The scanner. You just happened to be listening to your CB at two o'clock in the morning?"

"It beats the late-late show."

Kiefer looked steadily up at me. "What's your interest in this?"

"I'm doing some work for Mr. McAllister. When I heard, I figured he'd want to know about Haas."

"I certainly did. And I'd like to see Mrs. Haas. I'm sure she'd appreciate a friendly face."

"And you have no idea why Haas would shoot himself?"

"Not in the least."

It took another couple of seconds to make up his mind, but finally he said, "All right, wait here. I'll ask her if she wants to see you."

She did. McAllister and I followed Kiefer past the busy living room and up a flight of curving stairs to the second-floor family room where Mrs. Haas sat on a heavily upholstered chair and held two solemn children close to her sides. Her bloodless face was a fragile mask whose bone structure still showed the fundamental beauty that had drained from the flesh. Beneath the short, straight nose, her mouth—almost too wide—was a vulnerable line of stiffly clamped lips, and above that her eyes stared at us almost without blinking. The shocked, green eyes had not yet cried, but the strain showed in the taut cords of her neck and in the tense voice that welcomed McAllister. And like an almost visible mist, she and the clinging children were surrounded by an aura of pain and bewilderment.

"I'm so sorry, Margaret. Is there anything I can do— anyone you want me to call?"

Her dark hair, clipped just below the ears, shook briefly. "I've already called the family. They're flying out as soon as they can." Beside her, the girl, forefinger in a round mouth, dug deeper against her mother's ribs and away from the two strangers who, with so many others, had invaded her home. The boy, older, watched with the wide eyes of a child whose adult world has suddenly become incomprehensible and threatening. But his mother wasn't crying. If she wasn't crying, he wouldn't.

"Do you want a doctor? Do you want someone to be with the children?"

"No. We just want to be together right now. I suppose I haven't realized it all yet. Everything seems so . . . so unreal." She pulled the collar of her robe tighter as if a chill blew across her neck. "It's so sudden. I guess I'm —I suppose we're all in a bit of shock."

"Of course you are."

"Can you tell us what happened, Mrs. Haas? Are you up to that?"

Her green eyes looked at me as if just noticing another figure in the room. She was slightly puzzled, but so much of her life had been so suddenly disoriented that one more stranger was almost expected.

"This is Devlin Kirk, Margaret. He works for me."

Numbly, she nodded hello.

"If it's not too difficult, could you tell me what happened?"

"I was asleep. Austin had stayed up to do some work and I had gone to bed. I heard a sound . . . something . . . and I didn't know if I was asleep or awake. Then I knew I was awake and that a noise had done it. I thought it might be the television—sometimes Austin falls asleep. . . . I came downstairs . . . and . . . I opened the study door . . . and he was there." Her arms clutched the children still pressing against her.

"I heard it too." The boy spoke more to McAllister than to me, his voice a solemn assertion that he had shared this thing. "I woke up and heard it too."

"Shh, Austin. There, now." She rocked gently with her son. "I don't want to say any more."

"I understand." The next question was harder and might crack the icy rigidity that held back her tears. But I asked it anyway—it was on McAllister's mind as

well as mine. "Was his behavior any different recently?
Was there anything that might have indicated . . . that
might have shown undue tension?"

"No. When we lost the two projects to the Aegis
Group, he was disappointed. He worked so hard on
them. And he was so upset when we didn't get them.
But not enough to . . . my God, don't you think I would
have noticed something as serious as that?" Her hand
dragged across her pale face, the fingers clutching
tightly around her mouth. "Do you think I should have
seen something? Of course I should have, but there was
nothing! Nothing!"

"There, there, Margaret. Of course there wasn't.
Kirk, go down and see if you can find a shot of brandy.
If you can't, there's some in the car; ask Raymond."

I closed the door on the cluster of figures. From somewhere downstairs came the muffled tread of heavy
shoes and an occasional murmur of voices, punctuated
by the periodic crackle of a radio. Following the curving staircase toward the sounds, I noted the home's
expensive appointments and the absence of those blank
areas that many new houses have when people move in
and haven't yet found the exact thing to fit that corner
or this wall. Here, everything went together and with
the house as well, and for some reason I was certain that
the harmony and control weren't created by the dead
man but by his wife. It was her control and poise that
were reflected in the drapes and carpets and especially
the many paintings and the pieces of furniture that sat
just right, in the scattering of living plants that accen-
tuated the space and airiness of the large rooms. The
house had neither the brittle rigidity nor the carelessness of a suicide. But then my father's house did not
offer a hint of his plans, either.

I peeked into the living room which, despite its size,
now seemed crowded with the bulky shapes of police-
men. Like the rest of the house, it had its arrangement,

the space vaguely marked into three areas by sofas and tables and strategically placed plants that brushed the ceiling and led the eye to this room's towering fireplace. The body was gone, probably pronounced dead at the scene and carried to the morgue for the obligatory autopsy. But the photographer was only now finishing his work, the hot wink of his camera flickering deliberately against the glossy leaves of a large rubber plant. Everything was done deliberately, including the measurement from the chalked outline of the arm to the mark of the fallen pistol.

"What are you after, Kirk?"

"Is that the bar over there?"

Kiefer glanced at it. "Yeah, that's the bar. And this is the crime scene. Go on back upstairs."

The photographer had moved around to the other side of the rubber plant's large tub and aimed again at the rug.

"It's for Mrs. Haas. She's starting to realize what happened. She needs a shot of brandy."

"Brandy." He strode to the wooden cabinet and opened one of the darkly polished doors to peer among the cluster of tall and short bottles. Then he brought one back. "Here. I already asked her if she wanted a doctor or somebody. She said no."

"It's getting to her now."

"Yeah. Too bad. It's a hell of a thing to wake up to. She's a nice-looking woman. Nice kids. Nice house. Too bad."

"Any question about it not being a suicide?"

The bottle paused. "It looks like a suicide: one shot, one set of fingerprints. You have any information I should know?"

"Just asking."

"And I asked how you and McAllister knew about this and you hand me some crap about hearing it on a scanner."

That was better than saying I heard it on an illegal wire tap. "What can I say, Sergeant. That's how it happened."

"Kirk, Bunch and I worked together for a long time, and we still help each other out. We're friends and I'd like to keep it that way. Don't screw me off."

I needed him more than he needed me, and we both knew it. "I don't have any reason to think it wasn't a suicide, Sergeant. In fact, everything I have points toward it. There was a security leak at McAllister's corporation and I've been investigating it. Haas might have been involved."

"Ah? Well, now, tell me more."

"I was hired to check him out and that's what I've been doing. But I've found nothing at all to incriminate him. As far as I know, he had not one thing to do with that leak."

Kiefer finally handed me a bar glass and the squat, black bottle whose label said V.S.O.P. and was sprinkled with stars. "As far as you know. But somebody could have tipped him that you were on him?"

I shook my head. "Not that I know of. Only two people knew what I was doing, and neither of them had any reason to tell Haas. And we were very quiet about it—McAllister insisted on that because he didn't want any rumors getting started." I added, "I'd appreciate you keeping quiet about this, too, for the widow's sake."

"I see." The policeman scratched at his earlobe.

"I've told you what I have."

The eyes glanced at me. "Yeah—okay. Everything we've got is consistent with a self-inflicted gunshot wound from a thirty-two revolver. We'll run a paraffin test as a matter of course, but I don't think it's needed; you can smell the gunpowder on his hand. It looks like he held it up and bang."

"Temple wound?"

"One shot behind the ear. Close range."

"I thought they usually went for the temple. Or the mouth."

"Sometimes. Sometimes they turn their head like this and put the muzzle here."

I could picture it without Keifer's demonstration. Merely substitute one face for another and I saw once more the so obviously dead sprawl of my father in the glossy five-by-eight photographs that were part of the official report. "There's no reason now why Mrs. Haas should know about my investigation."

"She won't hear it from me." Keifer turned as the photographer called to him. "Right—let's wrap it up." Then back to me. "What about domestic problems— anything along that line?"

"Nothing that I turned up."

"Okay. You or Bunch check with me later on—I'll give you a run-down on the lab reports."

I reached the top of the stairs, bottle and glass in hand, and met Margaret Haas shepherding her daughter out of a bathroom. The little girl stumbled sleepily as she dragged against her mother's arms.

"Let me help you." I lifted her on one arm as she pulled away from the stranger and started to whine, suddenly awake again and frightened. "That's okay— Mama's right here. Here she is—see her?"

The slender woman led me past the girl's room to the master bedroom. "Let's put her in here—I'd rather not have her sleep alone."

I placed the small figure on the expanse of white coverlet, and her mother tucked the cloth up to her chin, then sat and stroked the head dwarfed by one of the big pillows. The girl's hair was lighter than her mother's and longer, and draped motionless over the pillow.

Splashing some brandy into the glass, I held it out to Mrs. Haas. "This is for you."

Her hand, pale and slightly trembling, gripped the

glass as she stared at her daughter, whose eyelids sagged shut with exhaustion. A faint tick came from the pillow and I saw the dark splotch of a tear.

"I'll be down the hall."

"Yes. Thank you."

"You finally found some." McAllister and the boy sat together on the small couch.

"Detective Kiefer wanted to ask some questions."

"We'll talk about that later. I've been telling young Austin, here, that he'll have to come work for me in a few years. We'll make a real American capitalist out of him."

I set the brandy on a bureau. "Mrs. Haas is putting the girl to bed."

"Shauna." The boy spoke directly to me for the first time. "She's not just a girl, she's my sister. Shauna." His defiant eyes, brimming with hurt and anger and tears, had found something tangible to focus on, and some part of his disintegrating family that he could defend. "My sister!"

"I forgot Shauna's name, Austin." I smiled. "I'm sorry."

He said nothing but only stared at me and through me toward this threatening thing which he still did not understand and which would not go away, but had begun to loom larger and larger across his future like a widening, empty hole.

"Well I want you and Shauna to come visit," said McAllister. "Do you remember the big picnic last June? When you and Shauna met all the other boys and girls and had such a good time in the pool?"

"Yes."

"Wasn't that a good time? We'll all do that again."

"I got in a fight with that big kid. He tried to duck me."

"Did you now! I didn't see that. Tell me about it."

The boy was still telling his story when Mrs. Haas

came in to say her daughter was asleep. "The police are leaving, too. There's no need for you to stay. It was very kind of you to come over."

"Why don't you and the children stay at my place until your relatives get here. Sarah will be glad to have you."

"That's kind of you, Owen, but we're all right. And I think the children will feel less upset if we stay here."

"Mr. McAllister said he wanted us to come for a visit sometime, Mom. Me and Shauna."

"That's good, dear. And we will go visit soon."

McAllister stood. "If you're certain you'll be all right . . . ?"

"I'm certain."

"I don't like leaving you alone, Margaret. Isn't there someone, some neighbor who can come over?"

"We don't know anyone that well; it's a new neighborhood."

"I can ask Raymond to stay. Or perhaps Devlin, here."

"I think I'd rather be alone, Owen. I'll be all right. Really."

"Well then, Sarah will call in the morning. Please get some rest."

We rode in silence until we had passed the gatehouse and the casual salute of the guard.

"That's a very strong woman," McAllister said finally.

Either strong or brittle. I hoped it was the former. "Did her husband have enough insurance?"

"He had the company's standard coverage, of course, with whatever additional options he chose. And probably some other policies as well." He glanced at me. "Was that a professional question?"

"No. I was just thinking of the payments on a house like that. And the other bills they must have."

"No doubt they have their share. Can't keep up without it."

"That sounds almost smug."

"Smug? Realistic, Devlin: I locate good people, pay good wages, and promise greater reward for harder work. I don't want a person working for me who doesn't want the good things of life. There's not a damn thing wrong with that, young man. And if someone wants to live better than he can afford right then, that's fine, too —makes him work all the harder to pay his bills."

"What happened to the virtue of frugality?"

"Relative term. Always has been. I like my people to enjoy their lives. Makes the golden leash that much stronger. Stock options and good retirement plan: a company can get a man's whole life that way—look what it's done for IBM."

"Do you believe Haas was living better than he could afford?"

"As you've said, it's a big home with big payments. But maybe he traded up, maybe his wife has money, maybe he has family money. I know what you're thinking, but you haven't come up with any proof, have you?"

"No."

"And now it seems pointless to try." He stared out the window at the rows of small, dark homes tucked back from the street under the thinning leaves of early fall. "Damn it! I did what had to be done. There was that telephone call . . . and I did what had to be done."

"There's no indication that we drove the man to suicide. And none that he took the proposals."

"You think it might have been someone else?"

"All I'm saying is there's no evidence one way or another. We have two events: the theft and the telephone call. But they may or may not be connected."

"Then why did he shoot himself?"

I had no answer to that.

The limousine sailed up a small hill toward the crest where the McAllister estate began. "Nonetheless, this investigation's over," he said. "I won't chance anyone else's suicide. And if Haas was innocent, that makes it all the worse, doesn't it?"

"It would if our investigation caused it."

"So we have three events now. Still unconnected? I think the odds are increasing for a connection. But it's time to stop, nonetheless." He was silent for a breath or two. "However, I do want you to evaluate my company's security; it obviously needs improvement. Call me tomorrow—" he glanced at his watch—"this afternoon, and I'll introduce you to Bartlett, my chief of security. As for the Aegis theft . . ." A deep, shrugging breath. "There'll be other times—and other means. Those poor children. . . ."

CHAPTER 4

T he snow had been one of my favorite kinds,
heavy and wet so that it clung to every spur of
brick and cornice and transformed the warehouse district into tiers of frosted cakes. And
the bright glare of the March sun was warm enough
to melt it quickly so it did not have time to be sullied
by the city's grime. Below, dark slashes already cut
the street down to wet asphalt as the morning trucks
lined up for delivery and pickup, and an occasional
shaft of melting snow spiraled down from the sun-
glowed façades across the street. The snows of spring
were far different from those of autumn, more festive,
shorter lived, bringing blessed moisture and the soft
green of leaves and grass, and signaling an end to the
bone-gnawing cold that made it a struggle to walk
outside. It was a welcome change, too, from the dust
and wind and gritty, noisy streets of Riyadh where
Bunch and I had spent the last six weeks. Loomis had
promised me that working for McAllister would be a

fine opportunity, and ever since the Haas case, the luck of Kirk and Associates had changed for the better. Right now, in fact, Bunch was out following up an inquiry from a brokerage firm for a personnel screening. Whether or not the job came as a result of telephone calls to Owen McAllister—"Say, Owen, can you recommend a good firm in executive security"—the good luck was nonetheless tangibly related to our work for McAllister and we accepted it gratefully. Even Uncle Wyn, on one of his visits, had watched with some awe as the old scarred desk was hauled away and the new one with its richly stained wood was carefully set in place.

"A new house for you—new furniture for the office. You're making a real success, Dev. This Peeping Tom business, there must be some real money in it."

"Industrial security, Uncle. Executive protection, electronic defense perimeters, the security of classified and proprietary information. We don't do very much peeping."

"Sure. Right. But it's still good money. Tell you the truth, I never expected to be paid back." He ran a finger along the edge of an oak bookcase that held shelves of legal and technological references. The finger had an awkward twist in it from being broken by a fastball in the minor leagues, one of a number of souvenirs from his years as a catcher. "Douglas would have been proud of you."

"If Dad had hung on for a little while, I could have helped him. Hell, I could have helped him then—so could you. All he had to do was ask."

"Don't blame him, Devlin. Sometimes asking is the hardest of all. Besides, it was that professor—Loomis. He drove him to it."

"How?"

"I don't know how. I only know what I feel. I never liked that guy."

• • •

Liking had nothing to do with a bullet in the brain—so permanent a solution to such temporary problems. And it had nothing to do with bringing back my father or telling him the things I never got around to saying. And of course he would never share any of this, either, which drained something of my satisfaction and brought me even closer to understanding those moments of quiet sadness in his eyes that had punctuated my childhood.

Through the busy rumble in the snowy world beyond the window, I heard the office door open and turned, expecting Bunch. But it wasn't. Well-tailored, and well worth it, the woman smiled and there was something familiar about her black hair and especially the green eyes that studied me. "Mrs. Haas?"

She held out a hand. "I'm flattered that you remember. Owen McAllister told me how to find you. I wasn't certain it was you standing there. I'm afraid I was somewhat disoriented that night."

"Understandably. It was a tragic time." A twinge of pain crossed those eyes and I changed the subject. "How are the children?"

"They're doing all right—as well as can be expected. Thank God, children are resilient."

"In time it will heal over," I lied. She nodded and the brightness that had been with her suddenly dimmed as she remembered. I turned one of the chairs whose leather still had a new and unchafed look. "Please sit down. Would you like some coffee?"

"No, thank you." She sat and stared for a long moment at her slender hands, which were now ringless and gripped the purse that matched her gray suit. Even on the night of her husband's death, despite the shock and dishevelment, she had been an attractive woman. Now that beauty was very clear, and made poignant by her melancholy. "I tried to get in touch with you earlier, but you were—"

"Out of the country. We had a client in Saudi Arabia —an oil company worried about the security of their executives."

"I see."

"I assume this isn't a social visit, Mrs. Haas?"

"Well, I did want to thank you for your help that night."

"That's not necessary."

"And to ask you something." She looked up, her eyes still showing hurt. "I heard that my husband—that Austin—was suspected of taking the Lake Center and the Columbine proposals and selling them to the Aegis Group."

I did not say anything.

"And I hear that you were investigating him."

Leaning back in my chair, I looked at the scattering of items on the new desk: a file for papers, a glass bristling with assorted ball-point pens, a yellow legal tablet with a few scribbled notes, an appointment calendar, the latest copy of *Guns Magazine*.

"It is true, isn't it?"

"That he was a suspect? Yes. Everyone who had access to the plans was a suspect. Everyone had to be. Why do you want to know?"

"There has to be some cause for what he did."

"There was never any evidence that he was guilty."

"Then who was?"

"We don't know. Mr. McAllister closed the case just after your husband's death."

"Because he was sure Austin did it?"

"Not at all. He said the projects weren't worth even the possibility of another death, and he didn't want to take a chance on causing any more pain like yours."

Her long fingers absently stroked the purse in her lap, furring the gray suede and then smoothing it again.

"But you were investigating Austin in particular when it happened, weren't you?"

"That's all in the past now, Mrs. Haas."

"But you were."

"Yes."

"And he could have been guilty?"

"There's no evidence."

"I want you to find out."

"What?"

"I want you to determine if he was innocent or guilty."

"Mrs. Haas, there's no purpose in this. Why not leave it alone?"

"Suppose he was innocent?"

"He probably was. I've told you, there was no—"

"We both know what it implies when a man shoots himself while he's under suspicion. The children have already asked why their father did it. I don't have any reason to give them. And I don't want someone else telling them it was because he was a thief."

"Who told you about your husband?"

"A friend who'd heard some gossip among the company wives. It's only a matter of time before their children hear it—and then mine."

"I see. . . ." I tapped the legal pad in line with the edge of the blotter. "Suppose—only supposing now—that he was guilty?"

The fingers stroked again before she looked up without flinching. "Then I will know why he did it. As it is, he's assumed to be guilty anyway."

"I don't think I want this job."

"Why?"

"If, some way, your husband found out about my investigation, then I may have contributed to his death."

"If you won't do it, I can get someone else. But they'll have to start all over at the beginning. Mr. Kirk—Devlin—Austin did not steal those proposals. But even if it were possible, I know he wouldn't have shot himself for something like that. He was a strong man, very strong. That's why Owen hired him and promoted him so rapidly."

Which circled back to the familiar question: Why did he do it?

And she seemed to read my mind. "Perhaps that's what I'm really after, Devlin: to know."

"Sometimes there is no explanation. Sometimes there's only the question, and we never do find the answer."

"Then I haven't lost anything, have I?"

It took only a few minutes to explain the terms. I quoted fees and probable expenses, and explained that costs could easily go higher—hoping, of course, that she'd reconsider and back out. But she agreed without a pause and quickly signed the contract. Then she shook my hand and smiled at me with those wide, green eyes. "This means very much to me; I'm very grateful."

I wasn't so pleased. "I can't guarantee either results or that you'll like what I find. Are you certain you want to do this?"

"Yes. I want—I need—to know something definitive."

I stared at the door as it closed behind her, aware of the faint scent that lingered, and then went over to the tall window and the white glare outside. I tried not to feel like it was a mistake to take the case. True, I was emotionally close to it—even after five months I still felt the worry that Haas had somehow learned he was being investigated. But Margaret was right: she could easily find another agency to do the work. And not only would they have to start all over, but, I told myself, they wouldn't look after her interests as well as I would. Logically, despite the unease I felt about it,

Kirk and Associates was the right choice.

"Dev—pull your head out, boy! Bang-bang! I could have been a whole Shiite terrorist team and you'd be worm shit by now." The door slammed and Bunch set a paper sack on the desk and came quickly to the window to search the street below. "Man, there was one nice-looking broad downstairs when I came in. There she is: eyeball that."

Below, Margaret picked her way across the ruts of wet snow to a Mercedes sedan and urged it gently through the snarl of trucks and out of sight.

"Why don't we get clients like that, Dev? You know, 'She came into the office with a walk that would have been banned in Boston.'"

"She doesn't walk that way. And they don't ban anything in Boston now. And she is our new client."

"Oh?"

"And Susan would break your kneecaps if she read your mind right now."

"Nah—she knows she doesn't have to worry. Not that much, anyway. But what's your problem? Your new house falling down? We get a client like that and you look like the Good Humor man with a flat tire."

"She's Austin Haas's widow. She wants us to find out if he did or didn't steal the proposals. If he didn't, she wants to know why he committed suicide."

"Jesus. We're back on that again? That guy won't stay buried!"

CHAPTER 5

My first step was to call Owen McAllister and explain it and ask to see all the company records on both projects, the ones the man had been reluctant to give me unlimited access to earlier. There was, as McAllister agreed, no reason now to worry about alarming a dead man.

"She's certain she wants to do this?"

"I asked her that, Mr. McAllister. She said yes. Definitely."

"Sarah and I haven't seen much of her and the children lately—time goes by faster and faster, as you young people seem shocked to discover. But she's borne up remarkably well. She's a strong woman."

"I would appreciate your authority to look at any documents that might be left—any at all."

"Oh, certainly. Of course. Just tell Bartlett I said it was all right. You remember him, don't you?"

The company's chief of security, a man whose smile never quite reached his eyes, and who earlier had resented Kirk and Associates coming in to evaluate his work. "Yes, sir."

McAllister's corporate headquarters was located downtown on Fourteenth Street, not far from our own office. But where Kirk and Associates had a large single room, McAllister had a large single building. I could have driven, but parking was always a problem all over downtown, and the walk felt good anyway. By the time I reached the lobby, my feet were damp from the melting snow, and I paused at the airlock to knock the remaining slush off my shoes.

Initial security was the familiar brightly lit information desk and a uniformed attendant strategically placed to survey the single street entry and the banks of elevators that formed the building's core. Out of sight below the counter, I knew, a newly added series of TV monitors surveyed the building's other accesses: the garage doors, the loading dock, the fire doors along the alley. The rest of the lobby was open space with no seats or potted plants to impede surveillance. It wasn't a very warm and comfortable lobby, but visitors who entered were supposed to have business and to waste no time getting where they wanted to go.

"Is Mr. Bartlett in, please?"

"I think so." The man studied me as he picked up a telephone that required no dialing. "Mr. Bartlett? A gentleman to see you." He hung up. "He'll be right out. You looking for work?"

"I probably will some day."

"You look like the kind of guy he likes to hire. He likes them big and clean cut."

Which pretty much fit his description. "Are you short of people?"

"We're always looking. There's a lot of turnover in this business, but the money can be good if you get into management. I'm planning on setting up my own business when I get some more experience. You might keep it in mind—I'll be looking for people, too."

"Thanks."

Behind the attendant, Bartlett opened his door and nodded shortly, his blue eyes unwarmed by recognition or anything else. "Hello, Kirk. What can I do for you?"

"Mr. McAllister authorized me to look at some records."

Bartlett hesitated a moment. "Come into the office." He shut the door and walked deliberately around to sit behind his desk. I chose one of the two leatherette chairs placed carefully to face strong lights that shone down from a corner behind Bartlett. On the wall in back of me, a second set of TV monitors flickered, and, half-hidden by a recess, another wall showed a battery of switches and indicators that connected to alarm systems all over the building. It was a standard security layout using the latest electronics, and Bunch and I had done a good job for McAllister when we designed it. But fundamentally it was similar to systems in use since some unknown caveman put up the first pile of branches as a defensive perimeter: deterrence devices, monitors, and response techniques.

Bunch had recommended most of the changes in physical security, and I had gone over the defenses against industrial espionage. Bartlett had seen each recommendation as an accusation against his abilities, and, McAllister once told me, he had to do some hard talking backed by a substantial raise to get the man to stay. Nonetheless, no security system was stronger than the individuals who made it up, and the clearance of personnel was one of the weakest spots in any defense. The use of an inside man—a patsy—was the least fallible and most favored technique for espionage, and since there was no foolproof protection against human nature, there was no foolproof protection, period. In a large corporation such as this one, the patsy could be anyone from a low-grade secretary or word processor to a vice president in charge of development.

"What kind of records?"

"Everything on the Columbine and Lake Center projects. And anything left on Austin Haas."

Bartlett's flat blue eyes blinked once; then he picked up a telephone and pressed a series of buttons. "This is Bartlett. Would you ask Mr. McAllister if he authorized a Mr. Kirk access to certain records?" His eyes never left my face as he waited. "Okay—thanks." He hung up. "I wondered how long the old man would wait."

"Wait for what?"

"To investigate Haas. I've heard the rumors." Bartlett's smile said there wasn't much that got past his ears.

I smiled back and nodded; what Bartlett didn't know, he couldn't gossip about. Although I doubted that the man gossiped with anyone, including his wife. There was a sense of prickly isolation that must have stayed with him in the bedroom as well as in his office.

"All right." Bartlett stood and holstered his radio-pack. "What Mr. McAllister wants, he gets. Come on."

I followed the lean man, who was only an inch or two shorter than I, to the elevator. Bartlett pressed the down button—"We moved the records office to the basement"—and when the elevator opened again under the fixed eye of a remote TV monitor, turned right down a softly lit hall to a door marked RECORDS.

The move had been one of my recommendations. Computer transmissions can be easily intercepted, and the old records office—on the building's top floor—was akin to a broadcast tower. At least down here the windowless walls and the surrounding earth helped to block random radiation of the signals.

The door opened to a small reception room walled off from the rows of desks and computers—another recommendation. A supervisor wearing a clip-on photo identity card hurried to the service window to smile hello.

"This is Mr. Kirk. Mr. McAllister's authorized him

access to the complete file on this ex-employee. He also wants the tapes and disks for the Columbine and Lake Center projects." Bartlett filled out a request slip and initialed it before turning to me. "It'll be a few minutes. You know your way back, right?"

I smiled. "I should by now."

"Yeah."

I sat on one of the padded benches and leafed through an old copy of *U.S. News*. Finally the woman came back with a sheaf of printouts and a pair of floppy disks in their square, white envelopes. "This is everything we have, Mr. Kirk. I remember reading about his death. I didn't know him that well—we said hello a few times—but it still came as a shock."

"Did he visit Records very often?"

"Oh, no. Someone from his office would usually come by to pick up what he wanted. That was when we were up on the top floor, you know. But he seemed like a very pleasant man when we spoke on the telephone. If you'll sign here, please."

The form gave the document codes and page numbers; I verified them and signed.

"All of our personnel records are confidential information."

"I understand. Can you tell me who cleaned out his desk?"

"Cleaned out . . . ? Oh, you mean after his death. That would have been Mr. Bartlett. He does that personally."

Once again, I had to get past the attendant on desk duty before being admitted to Bartlett's electronic fortress.

"You get everything you need?"

I showed him the printouts and disks. "Almost everything. Did you clean out Haas's desk after his death?"

"That's right. I pull all proprietary documents. We do it for all forms of termination and severance."

I could picture the expression on an employee's face when he found Bartlett waiting for him at the door and then was escorted to his desk and watched by those cold eyes as the employee—pink slip a bright mark of humiliation on the desk's blank surface—went through each drawer to take only his personal effects: a coffee cup, perhaps, or a photograph, a few personal letters (read first by Bartlett), perhaps a few books or pamphlets of his own—all placed in the envelope thoughtfully provided by the director of security. In case of a death, the rest of the contents would be locked in the desk and later sifted for information sensitive to the company. It was cruel, but necessary. The employee who wanted to get even was a prime candidate for sabotage and theft, and a dead man's desk could hold a lot of sensitive details about company business.

"What happened to the other stuff—the memos, notes, appointment books, and so on?" The detritus that every desk accumulated.

"Personal effects are sent to the survivors, in this case Mrs. Haas."

Bartlett would help because McAllister said to. But anything I didn't specifically ask for he wasn't going to give. "Do you have a record of what you found?"

Without answering, Bartlett reached for a logbook and began turning pages. He stopped and slid a finger down the sheet, "Seven classified documents all properly checked out." He read their call numbers. "Five incoming letters, one drafted response, fourteen in-house memos, one desk calendar with notations, one daily appointment book with notations." He looked up. "That was the proprietary material. The rest is listed as personal effects. They were sent on eighteen October by registered mail."

"Do you still have the calendar and appointment book?"

"We keep them on file for one year."

"May I have them?" I reminded the man, "Mr. McAllister said 'everything.' "

"Sign this form."

As I filled in the "Received by" line and dated it, Bartlett went to a large metal filing cabinet and pulled out one of the lower drawers. It moved heavy and silent like a morgue slab and the man, deliberate as ever, thumbed through the labeled brown envelopes until he came to Haas's.

"Here they are."

On my way out I resisted the impulse to smile at the TV camera mounted high in a dim corner which, I knew, led to one of the small screens in front of Bartlett's cold eyes. Instead, I returned the desk man's friendly nod and picked my way back through the fast-melting remnants of snow.

The printouts were only a little more complete than the ones I had searched earlier, but I didn't expect too much new. Their main purpose was to refresh my memory about the details of the man and the case, and to complete the financial records up to the date of final payment. They also detailed the death benefits to his survivors. I jotted down the amounts and the methods of payment. Haas had arranged distribution so that Margaret's life would be comfortable if not extravagant, provided she managed the money well; and the children had separate reserve funds for college or their maturity. It wasn't the document of a reckless man or one who was counting on a sudden and large windfall from some outside source. But of course it may have been drawn up long before the proposals were stolen —if Haas was the one to steal them.

The appointment book held an hour-by-hour list of the meetings, calls, cryptic names, and memory cues that a busy man used to organize his time. His secretary would have kept the more formal log of those who made their appointments in advance, and that's what all those slanted lines must have been that blocked out time by fifteen-minute units. If it wasn't an office visit, a name was written in and presumably Haas went there. Gradually, as I studied the pages, the routine of the man's office life took hazy shape: the first hour, from eight thirty to nine thirty, was always blank—time for assimilating the previous night's work or for organizing the day to come. Then the office visits, appointments with whoever the secretary introduced over the intercom. On Tuesdays and Fridays, regularly scheduled meetings were held at eleven; these were marked out with a line and initialed "Mac." The afternoons were much less organized, and here were the more personal notes of meetings outside the office, trips to sites or to manufacturers' showrooms, of an occasional afternoon marked "Tee-off: 2:10" or "dentist."

I began entering the names and initials of the visited and the visitors into my computer, coding each one with a recall number and programming the machine to seek first the sequence and then the frequency of the visits. Here, too, a vague pattern began to emerge. The in-office lists showed an increasing number of meetings with "Don" which started with one in February and then became nine in the two weeks before Haas's death. A number of random singles filled in a lot of space, and several short names or initials had consistent meetings, usually one every week or two. The afternoon list, those where Haas apparently left the office, were less indicative of a pattern. Even the golf times were scattered, and I was left with a long list of single meetings, a shorter one of a lot of meetings, and the shortest list of all—those names and initials he met with only three or four times at the most.

I ran the display one more time, then ordered a printout and, while the machine chattered rapidly to itself, telephoned McAllister's assistant once more.

"Mr. Haas's secretary? Carrie Busey. Yes, she's still with us."

I dialed the number given and identified myself.

"Miss Busey, you were Mr. Haas's secretary?"

The voice came back without nervousness or surprise. "I was."

"I have some questions about a few items that have come up concerning his daily office routines, and I wondered if I could take you to lunch and pick your brain."

"We're not supposed to discuss company business, Mr. Kirk."

"I understand. But as I said, I have ciearance—you may verify that with Mr. McAllister's office. And what I'm interested in is not so much the company's business as his. Who the meetings were with, what some of the rather cryptic entries in his appointment book might be, what you might remember about some of the people he saw."

"I suppose that's harmless enough." The cool voice added, "Though I will, of course, ask for written approval from Mr. McAllister's office."

"Of course." Written approval. She knew how to protect herself in the corporate jungle. "How about tomorrow at Gianelli's?"

The voice warmed a bit. "That sounds very nice."

"Is eleven thirty too early? We can get a quiet table then."

"I can manage."

Bunch, closing the door on the last of the conversation, raised his eyebrows. "Gianelli's? What's this one look like?"

I hung up. "I don't know."

"You don't know? You're taking her to a place like that and you don't know?"

"It's Haas's secretary. I wanted to impress her a little."

"That's more than a little. How come you get to take broads to Gianelli's and the best I get is Wendy's?"

"Oh, now, Bunch—you wouldn't enjoy it. You'd have to wear shoes, and you know what that does to the hair between your toes."

"Right. Silly me to forget. Here." He tossed a thick envelope on the desk and set a small stack of tape boxes beside it. "This envelope's the printout on the AeroLabs bid; I think we got a good chance with it. The tapes are everything you wanted on Haas—all the conversations, pickups, whatever we had on file. You name it, I put it all in chronological order on these."

I showed him the printout from my computer. "This is a list of his official contacts for six months prior to his death."

"And you want correlations with what we already have?"

"If it can be done. And if you think it's worth the time."

Bunch got that little frown which always came when he puzzled out a new twist for his machines to struggle with. For all that he liked to act the hairy and unwashed cowboy, he had a magical skill with electronic devices, and he always enjoyed a new challenge. "Let me think about it a little. Maybe I can rig something up."

Dialing again, I waited five or six rings before the telephone was answered by a child's voice. "The Haas residence."

"May I speak to Mrs. Haas?"

"Who's calling, please?" It sounded like the boy's thin voice—Austin, Jr.

"Devlin Kirk."

"Just a minute, please."

The phone went blank, then was picked up and the woman said "Hello." I heard the click of the extension as it hung up. "This is Devlin, Margaret. I'd like to know if you still have the envelope of personal effects from your husband's desk. I understand it was mailed to you last October."

"I think so—I'm sure I do."

"Can I come over and pick it up?"

"The children and I were just leaving. I promised them the afternoon at the zoo." She offered, "We should be back around six or seven. After dinner at McDonald's."

"I'll be by about seven. I may have to ask you a few things about some of the items. A lot of the abbreviations and phrases don't make much sense to a stranger reading them."

"All right. But perhaps you should come a bit later then. After the children are in bed. Say around eight thirty?"

"Better yet, if you can arrange for a sitter, I can arrange for a quiet place to have a drink and something to eat. You'll need it after a day at the zoo."

When she finally replied, I could hear the surprise lingering in her voice. "That does sound good."

"At seven, then."

I hung up and Bunch, shaking his head, caught my eye. "So it's 'Margaret' now? Lunch with Haas's secretary, dinner with his widow. Devlin, you're moving right into the man's life."

"It's a client, Bunch. Business."

"And I know what kind of business. Devlin Kirk, the widow's comforter. You have absolutely no shame, my lad. It's the only redeeming virtue I've ever found in you."

"Well I try not to pay my debts and I'm never on time."

"True, there may be hope for you yet." He gathered up the printout of Haas's lists of appointments. "Run yourself another one of these. I'll take this home and see what I can come up with. Susan sends her regards. Though if she heard you lining up all those women, she wouldn't bother."

"She'd start analyzing it."

"She analyzes everyone but me, Devlin. She just can't help herself."

"And you can't be analyzed?"

"That's what she says—I'm too integrated. An indivisible mass."

"In other words, a blockhead."

"No, an elemental force of irreducible masculinity." The elemental force quivered the landing as it went downstairs, and I began listening to the old tapes relate their fragmented account of a life whose end I already knew.

CHAPTER 6

Margaret met me at the door. She wore a skirt and jacket of muted plaid and a cashmere sweater that set off her eyes and emphasized the softness underneath. She seemed more girlish than when I saw her in the office, and certainly far less strained and tense, and as I stared, a tinge of color came to her cheeks, an echo of that vulnerability I had seen so nakedly the night her husband shot himself. "Is this all right? I wasn't certain what to wear."

"You look very nice."

"Thank you." The color deepened. "It's the first time I've been out since the funeral. But it's all right, isn't it? This is a business meeting, after all."

"Of course it's all right." I asked about the visit to the zoo and listened while I drove as she detailed what the children saw and did and said. It interested her, certainly, and it was good to hear the animation in her voice and to see her gradually lean back against the seat, tired from the effort but now relaxing and satisfied with the knowledge that she had given her children a day they would remember with pleasure.

"I'm boring you. Nothing's so boring as hearing a mother talk about her children."

"I'm not bored—I like kids." Which was true, and in fact I've occasionally wondered lately what kind of society we have when a statement like that has to be offered as an apology. It should be a given: an adult likes kids because they're the future, the continuity of life. But maybe that was the problem: kids did represent human life, a thing that so many adults were increasingly careless about—their own as well as others'. "I remember the elephants from when I was a kid. How they loomed up there against the sky and yet moved so smoothly and big and carefully as if they were afraid of stepping on me. It was always kind of surprising to look up that big gray hairy side and see an eye stare back at me."

We told other things that we remembered from childhood in the way that one memory will lead to another, and by the time I pulled into the parking lot of the restaurant, she was laughing. It was a very nice laugh, one that didn't get used enough, and one I enjoyed watching as well as hearing.

I'd chosen a restaurant close to the Belcaro compound, and we arrived just before the evening's rush. After ordering a glass of wine, we took our time with the menu.

She sipped and glanced around the tables slowly filling with diners. "Austin and I used to come here often."

I have to admit to a little twinge way down deep, very like something Bunch would laugh at as jealousy. But there was no reason for it, and I told myself it was only the normal distaste any man feels at being a surrogate for another. "So what do you recommend?"

We talked a bit about the menu and favorite dishes

and other restaurants we'd enjoyed, and by the time
the waiter, breezy and familiar, took our orders and the
request from the wine list, the conversation had drifted
over to likes and dislikes in books and theater.

"Before I forget—" She handed me a brown mailing
envelope that bulged at one end with a wad of loose
contents. It had been opened and resealed with tape.
"I'm not sure what's in it. I looked inside when it came,
and when I saw what it was I didn't feel like going
through it. And then I just forgot about it."

"Thanks. I'll get it back to you in a few days."

"Do you think it might help?"

"I don't know. It's more information than I had earlier. But even if he was guilty, I doubt that he would
have made any contacts with Aegis from his office. Let
alone put anything in writing. Still, it's best to look at
all of it."

"I hope. . . . Well, we'll see what you come up with."

I had a good idea what she hoped, and I hoped so too.
"Maybe you can help me unravel his appointment
book. I brought a list of initials and first names that I
don't recognize. Do any of them mean anything to
you?"

She studied the sheet of paper and I studied her: the
clean, delicate lines of her profile, her unconscious
grace of movement, the classical delicacy of her slender
neck, her shiny, black hair swinging loosely against her
cheeks as she bent over the paper. "This one—Bob—
that's probably Bob Schwartz." She looked up to meet
my eyes gazing at her and the dark of her pupils wid-
ened suddenly. "What's the matter?"

"Not a thing. I was just admiring you."

"Oh." She quickly turned back to the list and said,
"Thank you." Then, in a different voice, "Ron Stewart.
He's a land-use planner. I remember Austin had to
meet with him a lot."

"Working for the city?"

"No. The company. They were laying out the Columbine project and I remember that Austin was worried about the size of the lots. Ron wanted them smaller so there would be more to market and the cost of service units could be cut. Austin was pushing for larger sections that would offer a little more for the money and make a more attractive overall design."

"That decision would come pretty early in the project, wouldn't it?"

"Yes, but it's the only issue I remember them arguing over. The later meetings were on more routine things: the layout of services, drainage, commons areas." A crispness came into her tone when she spoke of her husband's business.

"You know a lot about it."

"Austin and I often talked about the job. Sometimes I was able to make a helpful suggestion." Her fork absently pushed against the fish. "I miss that. A lot of things I expected to feel—and I have. But I'm surprised at how much I miss sharing Austin's work, even only what he brought home." She smiled quietly. "God knows, I love my children, and I know how much they need me. Especially now. But I think I've just discovered that I've been increasingly bored." Those green eyes met mine again. "I don't know whether to thank you for that or not."

"Margaret, darling, you look simply wonderful!"

A fashionably thin blonde leaned over the table to peck at Margaret's cheek.

"Elaine—good to see you. How's Jerry?"

"Oh, same as ever—you know Jerry." She gestured behind her. "He's over there now. We weren't sure it was you." She smiled at me, and Margaret made the introductions. "Please don't stand up—oh my! Maybe you should; you're a big one, aren't you?" She glanced knowingly at Margaret. "Well, I just wanted to apologize for not having dropped by since—ah—the funeral.

But it seems like only yesterday—I mean time goes by so quickly, doesn't it, darling? It's so nice to see you out and enjoying yourself, dear."

"Mr. Kirk is—"

"In securities. I'm trying to convince Mrs. Haas to make some safe investments with her settlement."

"That's a wonderful idea. One can't be too safe, can one? We simply must get together for lunch, Margaret." She smiled widely once more at both of us before picking her way back to a table where, through the dimness, a man's vague face smiled our way and a hand lifted briefly.

"He works for McAllister, too?"

"Jerry Ewald. He's an architect in the design section. He was on the Lake Center project. We used to see a lot of them before Austin died."

"And nothing since."

She sipped her wine. "That's one of the things I expected. I read somewhere that a widow becomes an outcast. At least they don't practice suttee."

"Maybe not physically. But I suspect I've provided an item for the gossip mill. I apologize—I didn't think of that when I chose this restaurant."

"Nor should you have. And there's no reason to feel guilty, is there?"

"Of course not."

She identified a few more names and several sets of initials, among them the J.E. of Jerry Ewald sitting across the room, and I made notes beside the entries. Although, by the time the meal ended, most of the references still remained blank, there was at least something to get started with.

The ride back through the evening streets was a quick one and for the most part silent, though not uncomfortable. At the door, Margaret sounded sincere when she said she'd had a very nice time. "It was good to talk to an adult for a change. And to laugh at something besides the children's jokes."

"I'd like to do it again."

Something like a wince shadowed her face and she gazed out past the glare of the lamp beside the entry toward the cluster of lights that marked the distant neighboring house. "That would be nice. But . . . this sounds presumptuous . . . I really don't want to rush anything. There's still so much turmoil. And Austin— young Austin—still hurts so much. . . ."

"I understand. But we have to get together for business meetings occasionally. They might as well be pleasant."

We both smiled at that.

I spread the contents of Haas's desk across the top of my own, placing items in loosely organized rows. Tacked behind me on the cork board that formed one wall was a list of Haas's known and anonymous contacts as noted by calendar and appointment book. Now the job was to spot linkages between the dead man's activities, to build a network that would fill in the man's life for the six months or so preceding his death. There were holes in the method; as I told Margaret, if her husband had been trying to hide something, he wouldn't be likely to record it where it could be found. But so far it was all we had to go on, and a lot of men with a lot of experience in espionage had made the types of mistakes that could be turned up with this kind of sifting.

In time, the correlations sketched by the computer began to emerge and I could picture Haas's role in the company, as well as the people—a number still only initials or first names—he had met with. As expected, one group centered around the Columbine project, and the other around the Lake Center one. At several key points, Haas was the liaison between the two. And, like a handful of others in the company, he was one of the few whose overview put him in touch with all of the major components making up the team for each project. There was, of course, the possibility that one of these handful was the real thief—one of those that McAllister had put off-limits to my initial investigation: Dana Prescott, head of the Budget Office; Mark Trilling of Legal; Allan Fallico, construction supervisor; Bob Schwartz of Land Use; Howard Eberlein, Purchasing. Add each man's secretarial staff, those who would have handled the top-echelon correspondence and documents, and you had a platoon of possible suspects. But only one had committed suicide, and the idea was to find out if that one was guilty or not.

There were gaps in the network, but general patterns surfaced, and it was with some satisfaction that I began to figure out a few of the cryptic notations: "C IV w/ J on D"—"Columbine, phase IV, part D with J(erry) Ewald or J(ohnson)." It was probably Johnson in Accounting because, according to McAllister, the fourth phase of the development was the final cost-analysis stage where the various architectural plans would be submitted to Purchasing and Accounting for a last check on estimated costs. This would have been Section D of the project, which could have been a major building, or roads and drainage, or sewage and conduits. Whatever it was, Haas began to meet with "J" often in the final two weeks.

A third group of names and initials remained, a list of unattributed references that I had gone over once and set aside to look at after tracing out the known details. If any of the material held real promise, this did; and I was just turning to it when a familiar thunder rang on the iron stairs. A moment later Bunch came in to glance over the papers spread across the desk.

"Ah, for the exciting life of a detective—glamour, travel, romance!"

"System, detail, and luck." I explained my findings.

"You're doing better than I am."

"No correlations on the tapes?"

"Sure. Lots. What I don't have is any kind of pattern yet. I'll program it a few different ways and see what comes up. Anything here you want me to start feeding in?"

"I suppose we should start listing the identified references." Computers had taken the place of file drawers, contact cards, and—in many ways—notebooks. They were great for the retrieval and collation of information, but somebody still had to punch each item into the system. "Here's the list I have so far. What's the best way of programming it?"

Bunch glanced at the sheet. "No sweat. I'll code it so we can move it around wherever we want to. What'd you find out last night?"

"A few more names. And this is the stuff Bartlett cleaned out of Haas's desk. Most of it's junk."

"Most? What's not?"

I showed him a small slip of paper whose rough edge said it had been torn from a memo book. "These initials, 'D.N.' I haven't found any other reference to them anywhere yet." The page was sharply creased as if it had been folded and pressed in a book or wallet.

"There's a phone number beside the initials."

"I know."

Bunch sucked a squeak of air between his teeth. "All right, smartass. Whose number is it?"

I pressed the Play button on the tape recorder that routinely monitored our calls. A bell rattled once and a male voice, unhurried and authoritative, said "Hello." My voice asked, "Is Mr. Bunchcroft there?" The voice said "Who?" Then, "No. You've got the wrong number," and hung up.

"Why the hell'd you ask for me?"

"I knew you wouldn't be there. Besides, nobody knows who you are."

"That's only because I seek neither fame nor glory. Humble worker in the vineyard, that's me."

I slid the paper toward him. "Can the humble worker stomp this grape?"

The paper folded and almost disappeared between Bunch's thick fingers. "It shouldn't cost too much."

"Or take much time, right?" I glanced at my watch and grabbed my coat off the rack. "Gotta run—tight social schedule."

Bunch's voice followed me out the door, "I don't want to eat at Gianelli's anyway!"

The restaurant was another of those that had moved into a refurbished building in lower downtown, marking the tentative return of life to that corner of the city between Larimer and the railroad yards. After almost fifty years of neglect, the old brick façades with their cast-iron and plaster decorations had been rediscovered, and here and there along the narrow sidewalk wooden construction fences and pedestrian tunnels marked additional remodeling. The restaurant was in an ugly, square building of narrow frontage, and its only advertisement was the green awning that reached the street and bore GIANELLI'S RESTAURANT in white block letters on the side. On each side were buildings equally stark and still used for commerce. Gianelli—Bob Hirschorn to his friends—had told me with a straight face that the plain exterior wasn't just an economy measure but a deliberate contrast to the Victorian interior and its atmosphere of muted opulence. It was. A wide stairway led between gleaming brass rails up from the tiled entry to the reception desk, and a new maître d' with a thin mustache made me wait while he concentrated on his appointment book and seating chart. Finally he looked up. "Yes, sir—do you have a reservation?"

"Kirk. For two."

"Oh, yes." The mustache stiffened in a smile. "The lady has already arrived. This way, please."

"I'm sorry I'm late—let me apologize with a drink." Carrie Busey had dark blond hair that tumbled to her shoulders in stiffly sprayed curls, and cool gray eyes made larger by the wide glasses balanced on a small nose. Sculpted was the word that came to mind. She had the symmetrical evenness of a model and a smoothness of skin that hesitated to show either smile or frown. While we waited for the drinks, I thanked her for coming and she said it was all right, and that's about all she did say until after the bar waiter had set the cold glasses in front of us. Then at last she looked up at me.

"I only came because I do not believe that Austin killed himself, Mr. Kirk."

"Oh?"

She stirred the tiny straw that disappeared into a frosty gin and tonic. "He wasn't the type to do that."

I pooled the martini's sharp flavor on my tongue for a moment. Tanqueray gin, dry and up, and the smooth blend said Leila was at the bar. "People often do things that surprise us. Even people we think we know well."

"I was his secretary for five years." She looked at me without blinking and added, "And his lover for four."

"I see."

"I knew him better than anyone else. Even his wife. He would not kill himself."

"Are you ready to order, Mr. Kirk?"

The tuxedo at my shoulder was a welcome interruption. I had come believing I knew what to ask Miss Busey, but she had come with something entirely different to say. And her coolness in doing it was unsettling. I asked George what he recommended from today's menu but only half-listened to his answer. When he'd gathered the ornate cards and headed for the kitchen, I turned to Carrie Busey.

"Did Mrs. Haas know of your relationship?"

"I don't think Austin told her. But she knew. She went out of her way to be generous to me every Christmas."

There were ironies in that which I would have to ponder later. "Was Haas planning to divorce her?"

"No. Nor did I expect it. The children . . . the job . . . No."

"He told you that?"

"He didn't have to. I was happy with things the way they were, Mr. Kirk. Austin and I could be together periodically, and I had plenty of time for myself." Her head tilted as if she just realized something, and a glint of thin humor came into her eyes. "I'm not one of those women who can define herself only with a man. I do have a life of my own. And if I wanted to go to bed with anyone—you, for instance, Mr. Kirk—I would choose you. Not vice versa."

I believed her. "You chose Haas?"

"We chose each other."

"Still, there must have been pressures on him, especially if his wife suspected something."

"He could handle pressure. It's one of the things I admired most about him."

"Suppose there were other pressures?"

"What do you mean?"

Behind the round lenses, her eyes had gone flat and I guessed she knew what I meant. "Suppose he thought someone suspected him of selling corporate secrets?"

"You mean to the Aegis Group?"

"Yes."

"I've heard those rumors." The blond hair stiffly wagged no. "Austin would have fought. He was a very strong man—he could not have gotten where he was without being strong and aggressive and capable. He thrived under pressure, Mr. Kirk. That's what I'm trying to make you see. I worked with him, side by side, in some very chaotic and demanding crises, and not once was his will shaken. Not once did he lose his nerve."

"And in those moments he relied on you?"

Her chin lifted. "Yes!"

And so to bed. I finished my martini and lifted a finger. Across the narrow room, George nodded and headed quickly for the bar. "But suppose he had a secret crisis he couldn't share with you?"

"After the Columbine and Lake Center projects, we were all under suspicion, Mr. Kirk. As we should have been."

Two more drinks silently arrived, followed by the salads, small and carefully arranged on large, chilled metal plates, and beside them forks wrapped in icy cloths.

"Suppose, Miss Busey, there was good reason to suspect the man and he knew it? Suppose he believed he was about to be exposed?"

Her face hardened into porcelain. "He would have told me. I shared that part of his life, Mr. Kirk—the vital, the most alive part of his life: I shared it. Not his wife, not anyone else. If he made a deal with Aegis, he would have told me!"

"Would you have approved?"

She hesitated, then shrugged. "It happens all the time in business, and Austin had ambition. He knew I would support whatever he did."

The serving cart coasted across the carpet to the table and George presented each dish with a little flourish of introduction. I waited until the ceremony was over and the waiter had dropped out of earshot.

"Do you know if Haas had enemies?"

"Of course he did. Strong men make enemies."

"Anyone who hated him enough to want to frame him for the theft of the projects?"

"What do you mean?"

I told her about the anonymous call to McAllister's office, the one that said Haas had been approached by the Aegis Group.

She idly tugged at a curl of blond hair that sprang back into ranks when her fingers opened. "That only makes me more certain that he didn't kill himself."

"But do you have any idea who might have made that call?"

"No."

"You had access to the same information as Haas, didn't you?"

"Of course. We worked together." Her fork stopped in midair. "But don't draw the conclusion that I sold the information to Aegis."

"If it wasn't wrong for Haas, why should it be wrong for you?"

"It would have been a betrayal of Austin."

"But not of McAllister?"

"Austin came first." She leaned over the white table-cloth. "Mr. Kirk, Austin did not sell those trade secrets to those people. And he did not kill himself."

"He's dead."

"He was murdered. She killed him."

I studied the face that, for all its immobility, was even more intense. "You mean his wife?"

"Yes!"

The tines of my fork pushed my scallopini across the large, richly patterned dish. "That's a very serious accusation, Miss Busey. You shouldn't say something like that based only on your dislike for her."

"She was the only one in the house with him, wasn't she? He did not kill himself—he did not! And she's the only other one who could have!"

"But why should she?"

A note of satisfaction tinged her voice. "Jealousy."

Her gray eyes finally thawed with an emotion: hatred. I watched it surge up like blazing straw and then slowly ebb as she stared at me. "Why now, Miss Busey? Why didn't you bring this up when it happened?"

"Because I've had time to think, time to put things together so they make sense."

"The police were satisfied that it was a suicide, and for very good reasons. The wound was a close-range head wound, only one round had been fired from the weapon that killed him, and residue was found on Haas's hand."

"Residue?"

"Burned gunpowder. Anyone firing a pistol will have gunpowder residue on his hand."

"I don't care what they found. I know what I know." She reached down for her purse and took out a checkbook. "I want to hire you to prove that Austin did not kill himself, Mr. Kirk."

"I can't do that, Miss Busey. In the first place, I'm already working for someone on this case. Secondly, my search is for facts which lead to a conclusion, not vice versa."

"You're working for McAllister, aren't you? He wants the same thing I do—the truth."

"Which is what I'm after. If something turns up to show that Haas didn't kill himself, then you'll get what you want without having to pay for it."

She closed her purse and held it on her lap, gazing for a moment at the plate of cooling food. Then she looked up. "I see. Perhaps I should find someone else."

"You would be wasting your money."

"It's my money, isn't it?" She pushed her chair back.

"Miss Busey, may I ask a couple of questions?" I went on before she could say no. "When you learned of Haas's death, did you go through his desk? Did you remove anything?"

The gray eyes stared beyond me before she answered, and perhaps she was gazing again at that morning when she had come eagerly in to work expecting her lover and found only a brief message. "A few things, yes."

"What were they?"

"Personal things. Some notes I wrote him. A card we laughed over." She drew a deep breath. "Nothing that would tie him to the Aegis Group, because there was nothing like that in his desk." She stood abruptly, saying a quick good-bye and was gone before I could rise. Across the room, George followed her long-legged stride with a worried glance, then came to the table.

"Is the food satisfactory, Mr. Kirk?"

"It wasn't the food; it was the company."

"Ah." Quickly, he cleared the dish and silverware so it looked as if I were dining alone. "At least your meal should not go to waste, sir."

It was almost four when Bunch came into the office, wearing that tight little half smile of satisfaction he had whenever something fell into place. I remembered it from the first case we worked together when he was still in the police and I was still a Secret Service agent. A series of telephoned threats to the president had come from the Denver area, and—with more hindrance than help from the FBI—Bunch had managed to narrow down the source to a single corner of the city. That had been the first step in a long but ultimately successful siege of stake-outs and patient surveillance.

"How was Gianelli's?"

"The food was good. And we almost had another client for the same case."

"How's that?"

"Carrie Busey wanted to hire me to prove that Haas was murdered by his wife."

"Oh yeah? Don't tell me, let me guess: the secretary's jealous of the wife. Is it with reason?"

"With reason."

"And you told her you were already hired by the wife?"

"I managed to avoid that; she thinks we're working for McAllister. This is one very tough and vengeful lady. And she's absolutely certain that Haas had nothing to do with the Aegis Group."

"She is, is she?"

I eyed that little smile. "What'd you find out that's different?"

"That phone number you gave me—the one that came from Haas's desk."

"The one with the man's voice?"

"The same. It's a direct line to one of the executive offices for the Aegis Group. My contact wouldn't tell me who, because he didn't have a directory for all the internal numbers on that prefix. But it's definitely an Aegis number."

CHAPTER 7

Bunch eyed my expression. "You don't seem very happy about it, my man. This is what you literate types call a break in the case."

"Yeah, it is. But it still doesn't prove anything."

"Come on, Dev—this is an unlisted number. It's a private pipeline to the opposition. And it was in that envelope full of crap that came out of his damned desk." The big man peered at me. "Or do you mean you don't want it to prove anything?"

That was it. I had been thinking of Haas and Carrie Busey and the effect of their affair—if she did not already know of it—on Margaret. And now that little scrap of paper that had been buried in Haas's personal effects threatened to rake all that garbage and more to the surface again.

"She asked for it, Dev. She asked for the information because she wanted to be sure. And the reason she wanted to be sure was because she had her doubts. We both know that."

True enough. People often hired p.i.'s to find the evidence that would deny what, in their hearts, they suspected. And then were disappointed when the evidence confirmed their suspicions. I sighed and agreed that the telephone number meant a lot, and most of it bad. "But it's still not conclusive. And we don't know whose office number it is, do we?"

"No, we don't. And it could have been planted, too. By his secretary, who swears he didn't do it. Or by Bartlett, who can't find his ass with both hands. Or by Mrs. Haas, who's spending all that money so we can prove hubby innocent."

"Or by the same man who called McAllister about Haas. Spare me the sarcasm, Bunch. The fact is, it isn't enough."

He grunted. "Yeah—that phone call. But damn it, Dev, Haas committed suicide. And that phone call, this number, they all explain why he did. As far as I'm concerned, this is proof. And I think it's up to Mrs. Haas to decide if she wants something more. You've got this thing for damsels in distress and now you've found one. But remember, it's her money."

Bunch was right about that. This might be all the evidence that Margaret needed, and it wouldn't do to stretch out the case—and its expenses—without her approval. I sighed again and reached for the telephone.

Margaret answered this time, and she seemed genuinely pleased to hear my voice. And I was glad to talk about something else for a few moments. But after the how-are-yous and the what-have-you-been-doings, there was no easy way. "We found some evidence that Austin was in close touch with the Aegis Group, Margaret."

"What evidence?"

"An unlisted telephone number. It's a direct line to one of the office telephones at Aegis. It was in Austin's desk—in the envelope you gave me."

"My God . . ."

"It's not conclusive, and there's no indication that he ever used the number. But it was there."

"I see. I think I see. . . . It's just so hard to comprehend —I've tried to consider the possibility, of course. But it never seemed real before." The telephone line stayed open and silent. "I don't know what I'm going to tell our son."

"There's no need to tell him anything. Not until he asks, and not until he can understand."

"How can he understand? Even I can't understand." In the background, a distant squawk of children's voices rose to an excited squabble and then died away as a door slammed. "Do you know anything about this person? The one whose telephone it is?"

"No. It's an office at Aegis. I didn't know if you wanted to go any further with this."

"I want to know why he did it."

"Does that make any difference?"

"It might."

"He probably did it for the money. I'm sure there was a tremendous amount of money promised him."

"But we had enough money—he made a good salary."

Everybody always wants more, especially an ambitious man, especially if he had a mistress or two. "Why not just let it go, Margaret? He made a mistake, and paid a far greater price than he should have. Get on with your life and let the rest stay buried."

"I want to know, Devlin. If it was for so much money, then what happened to it? If it wasn't, then why?"

"You want us to keep digging?"

"Yes. Please. You will, won't you?"

"Of course. I'll be in touch."

Bunch raised his eyebrows.

"She wants to know why he did it."

"Like you told her—for the money."

"And she asked what happened to it."

"Yeah." He ran a large bulging knuckle along his jaw where his whiskers made a rasping sound. "That's a good question. If she don't know, then there's a hell of a big account somewhere that's going to be drawing interest for a long time."

"You figure he got the payoff when he delivered the plans?"

"Half up front and half on delivery. He'd be a fool if he didn't. And he didn't seem like a fool—except for shooting himself." Bunch nudged the slip of paper with the telephone number and sent it spinning across the waxed corner of the desk. "Where do you want to start?"

"Maybe Aegis paid by check. We'd have a trace on the money if they did."

"Yeah. And so would anybody else. My bet is cash only, and a lot of it. But any way you slice it, Aegis is the place to start. Want to flip for it?"

It came up tails—my job. Bunch patted my shoulder. "It's about time you did some real work."

The telephone book's white pages had the address of the Aegis Group, and a stint in the Chamber of Commerce reference works gave me a little more than that, but only a little. Listed as a development corporation, it had the necessary state licenses to "undertake any manner of lawful business" granted two years ago, and what few references to it in business and financial publications said cryptically that the group was involved in "business enterprises." That meant, I supposed, that they didn't want to be excluded from anything that might make a profit. The only other information about them came from McAllister, whose view was biased.

The president and chairman was one W. S. Merrick, and its executive secretary was Leonard Kaffey, neither of whose initials fit the "D.N." on that slip of paper. Those were the only officers listed, which wasn't all that unusual. I dialed the public number, which was the corporation's switchboard, and asked for Mr. Kaffey's office. A few moments later, the representative of Devlin Securities and Investments had an appointment for the following morning.

Seventeenth Street—Denver's financial district— seemed to grow longer and deeper as new buildings kept rising, and by the time I reached its southern end, within beckoning distance of the state capitol's shiny gold dome, the high walls had pinched the sky into a narrow slit of blue. The lobby of the Action West building, one of the newest, offered no relief from the canyon outside. Entering it was like walking under a poised boulder—the heavy design and massive cubes of lobby services emphasized the tower's weight hovering over the tiny humans crawling beneath it. The Aegis offices, however, were entirely different. Small separate rooms surrounded the large general work and reception area, and light fell through banks of windows that stretched up to a second level of private offices surrounding the atrium and reached by an open and gently raked staircase. The hominess was reinforced by a scattering of comfortable chairs for waiting, by a color scheme emphasizing wooden beams and sand-colored plaster, and by a receptionist whose secretarial skills might be unknown but whose ornamental qualities were flagrant.

"My name's Kirk. I have an appointment with Mr. Kaffey."

"Just a moment, please."

No sterile intercom system here; she walked on long, slender legs to one of the corner offices and knocked briefly before opening the door. A moment later she came back and nodded at the tan leather chairs. "It'll be just a couple of minutes. Won't you sit down?"

I chose the one nearest her desk. "It looks like a nice office to work in."

At the other desks, men and women dealt with papers and telephones, and one area was spotted by half a dozen computer terminals busily beeping and clicking to each other.

"I like it. And we've certainly been busy lately!"

"The company's new, isn't it? I understand it was chartered only a couple of years ago."

"I don't know. I've only been here about a year—about the time they rented these offices. But they're very nice people to work for." She looked toward a doorway and a lean, balding man wearing a gray suit. "Here's Mr. Kaffey."

He offered a bony hand and an equally fleshless smile. "Come in. You're with the . . . ?"

"Devlin Securities and Investments." I handed Kaffey one of my collection of business cards. "We're a Canadian group interested in the possibilities of investment in this area."

"I see. Yeah—that's a volatile currency, right?" His corner office had windows and space and everything else an important man's office should have. All of it slightly oversized so that Kaffey seemed to shrink when he settled behind the expanse of wooden desk. He aimed a couple of fingers toward a heavy couch that half faced the vista beyond the tinted glass: other office towers rising as high as this one, and, in the distance, the wall of mountains forming the western horizon where the thin vapor trail of a jet streaked toward San Francisco. "Drink?"

"It's a bit early for me, thanks."

He put the bottle back unopened. "What brought you to us, Mr. . . . ?"

"Kirk. We learned that you're developing two major projects, a shopping center and an industrial park. They seem very promising, and we're looking to invest in that kind of enterprise."

"Yeah. Right. They're good projects. But we haven't

made any announcements. What makes you think we need . . . ?"

"Capital? Well, they're both big projects. Probably two of the biggest in the last ten years in this region. I also hear that you received funding from First Western. They're quite conservative, and we trust their judgment."

Kaffey leaned back in his chair and crossed his hands behind his head and said nothing.

"I also happen to know that the amount you borrowed isn't sufficient to cover the full cost of developing both projects, Mr. Kaffey. In fact, it's surprisingly small. We suspect—we hope—that you need further financing. I want to convince you that our money is just as good as anyone's—and perhaps less expensive."

Under their sleepy lids, Kaffey's dark eyes studied me as if to memorize my face. "That information's not generally known. Do you have someone over there who . . . ?"

I smiled modestly and decided not to mention Owen McAllister as my source. "We try to be alert to trends and to move quickly when opportunities arise. That's just good business, right?"

"Right. Good business."

"Our principals are quite excited by this possibility. But of course we'd like to know a little more before we invest. The usual questions about the cost and income projections, growth potential, that sort of thing. Is there someone you could put me in touch with who might answer that type of question?"

"Well, I might. But you see, Mr. Kirk, we aren't looking for any more backers. We have what we need. Things may come up in the future—we're always looking ahead, you understand. But for these two, we don't need any more. . . ."

"That's quite disappointing. We heard sometime back from Mr. Haas that you would be taking over the projects. But we weren't in a position to move on it at that time."

"Haas?"

"He worked for the McAllister Corporation before his untimely death."

"I read something about that."

"He said we should get in touch with you."

"He said that?"

"I had the impression that he'd be leaving McAllister to work for you."

"I hadn't heard that."

"And in fact he told me he was instrumental in your getting the contracts."

The sleepy eyes did not blink, and the mind behind them wasn't drowsy at all. Kaffey rested his forearms on the desk. "Just who are you working for? McAllister?"

"Me? No—I represent D.S.I." I pointed to the calling card. "From Canada. Why do you think I work for McAllister?"

"Because he's been making noises about some kind of lawsuit. He thinks Aegis stole his ideas. But he's lying. We underbid him, that's all."

"Litigation? The projects might be tied up in the courts? That would certainly worry our principals."

"You can stop acting, Kirk. Or whatever your name is. McAllister doesn't have a case." Kaffey picked up the calling card and ran his thumb over the engraved surface before he crumpled the pasteboard into a small wad. "So if you're here trying to link the Aegis Group to Haas, you can forget it. Nobody here knew him." He flipped the wad toward the oversized trash can where it rattled against the empty tin. "Tell McAllister he doesn't have a prayer. And you—don't you ever come into this building again. You understand?"

The secretary smiled brightly at me and said, "Have a nice day."

. . .

"He made you?"

"As soon as I mentioned Haas. I think they've been waiting for someone to try to link them together."

"That would help make the case, wouldn't it? To show they had access to McAllister's trade secrets."

I nodded. "It would at least be a threat."

"So Haas being dead means they don't have to worry about him testifying."

"It was a suicide, Bunch. Convenient, but still a suicide."

"Convenient is right. And a hell of a good motive as well. If McAllister could prove damages, he could end up owning those projects after all."

"You have to add 'means' and 'opportunity,' neither of which fits his suicide."

"Maybe they drove him to it. Maybe they threatened him with McAllister."

"Why should they? He was already under their thumb."

"But damn it, it fits so well: with Haas out of the way, there's no link to Aegis, no basis for a suit against them."

"There's also no reason to believe Haas committed suicide just to be a nice guy." I wandered to the window and gazed out over the familiar flat roofs while above, equally familiar and as flat, the piano began a series of scales. "Is there anyone you can ask about Aegis?"

Bunch looked up. "Sure—White Collar division. You want a run-down?"

"Anything you can get."

He telephoned a number and asked for Sergeant Lewellen. "Lew? This is Bunch. . . . Yeah, fine. How about you?"

I half listened as Bunch traded jokes with his friend and finally asked if the White Collar Crimes section had any information on the Aegis Group. When he hung up, he shook his head. "They never ran across them. Lew says he'll keep his eyes open, but there's nothing on them now."

The telephone rang and Bunch, his hand still on the receiver, picked it up. "Kirk and Associates—just a minute." He held it out to me.

"This is Devlin Kirk."

"And this is Vincent Landrum. You going to be there for a while, right?"

"For what?"

"For business, Kirk. You and me." The line clicked into a buzz.

"That was Vinny Landrum. He's coming over."

"That low-life?" Bunch snorted something from his nose and went over to the window to spit it out. "What the hell's he want?"

"He said it was business."

"His kind of business gives the profession a bad name. You should have told him we don't do divorces."

The Vincent Landrum Detective Agency advertised itself for investigations of all kinds but the man's specialty was divorce. Bunch guessed there wasn't a motel owner within fifty miles who didn't have Landrum's business card tacked up by his telephone and a standing offer of a hundred dollars for cooperation. In Colorado, anybody could hang out his shingle and call himself a p.i., and Vinny was one of the anybodies. When he came into the office, it was with the rolling gait that some short people use to take up more space, and his glance around the room was as friendly as a tax form.

"The chairs—that's real leather? And a new desk—real wood? You guys must be doing all right."

"What are you after, Vinny?"

"Hey, Bunchcroft, I'm just trying to be friendly. We're all in the same racket, right?"

"Don't rub it in."

"You said something about business, Vinny."

He sat on the couch and tapped a cigarette out of its package, taking his time with the lighter and the first draw or two. His lank, sandy hair, blow dried into layers, was long enough to cover the tips of his ears, and his restless eyes touched on each item in the office. "I got a new client, name of Busey. Carrie Busey. Know her?"

"Of course."

"Yeah—she told me she talked with you. She don't think her boss blew his own brains out. She thinks somebody did it for him."

"I know."

"Yeah. Well, she wants me to prove it."

"Jesus," muttered Bunch.

Landrum glanced at him. "The lady's got a right to her suspicions, Bunchcroft. And this is a democracy—as long as she's got the money, she has a right to find out if they're true."

"The police think it was a suicide," I said.

"Yeah. I read the reports. But Miss Busey don't believe it, and she's paying." He squirted a long thread of smoke into the air. "A real ice maiden, that one. But I bet she's something else when she thaws out. That kind always are—they want it so much they're afraid to admit it. But when they do get it, man, they go crazy!"

"She's crazy already to hire you."

Landrum glanced at Bunch and stifled what he was going to say. Instead he hunched around to face me alone. "She tells me you're working on this, too. For McAllister."

"We're on it."

"Well if we're both on it, we'd be fools not to pool our information. There's no sense going over the same ground twice, is there?"

"What the hell ground have you gone over once, Vinny? What have you got to pool that we don't already know?"

"I can find out things, Bunchcroft, by God as good as you and maybe better! Look, I come over here with a business proposition. Save both of us a little time and overhead. You don't want to work together, that's fine with me! Probably do better on my own anyway."

"All the information we have points to suicide," I said.

"Like what? What do you have?"

"Pretty much what you do: the police report."

"And what about this phone call—the one that said Haas was selling out to Aegis? You were on him for that before he died, right?"

"Maybe."

"Yeah, maybe! So what'd you find out? Was he in bed with Aegis or not?"

"What do you have to trade?"

"Trade? Nothing right now. But anything I do get, you'll get."

Bunch snorted, "We don't need AIDS."

"We do our own work, Landrum. If you come up with something to trade, maybe we'll cut a deal. But Vinny—I know that Carrie Busey thinks Haas's wife killed him and that's what she wants you to prove, whether it's true or not. Anything you do come up with had better be squeaky clean."

Landrum was on his feet, grinding out his cigarette under his toe. "Yeah, what I figured: you people think your shit don't stink. You don't want to work together, fine. But I get something, you can kiss my ass for it."

"That'd be no worse than kissing your rosy sweet lips." Bunch smiled at the door as it closed loudly behind Landrum. "I think he's unhappy with us, Dev."

"I think he wanted us to do his work for him."

"What else is new? That broad—what's her name? Busey? She didn't waste much time."

"She's wasting her money."

"Sure. But who did finger Haas?"

I shrugged. "If we ever find out, we'll probably get our proof whether or not he was guilty."

"As far as I'm concerned, we got our proof: that pipeline to Aegis. And if he wasn't, why'd he commit suicide?"

We were back at the fundamental conflict: the strongest indication that Haas was the thief was his suicide. Yet the evidence to so conveniently explain his suicide was weak.

"I don't know, Bunch. That's what we're supposed to find out, and right now I don't have a single idea that leads anywhere. Come on—we're late for our workout."

CHAPTER 8

We met Susan at the health club, the three of us joining the scattering of other joggers running around the green strip of padded track that circled the rows of exercise machines. Susan's trim leotard gradually dampened with perspiration as we clicked off each quarter-mile, and Bunch simply sweated, soaking the heavy cotton of his sleeveless shirt.

"I don't like running inside," he said. "It's too damn hot and boring."

That was true; the steady thump of feet and the constantly repeated series of walls and machines created a mind-numbing monotony.

But Susan's thoughts weren't on the running. "One of our clients committed suicide last night."

"There's that word again," said Bunch.

I listened to the muffled thud of my heels.

"He was fourteen. They found him this morning in his room when he didn't come down to breakfast."

"This was at the Refuge Home?"

She nodded, the blond ponytail jerking from side to side with her pace. "We thought we were making progress with him. He was an abused child with minor learning disabilities. He kept slipping through the cracks in school because he wasn't sufficiently handicapped to get help there, but we finally got a placement for him."

Bunch said, "Another one of God's little jokes. I think that's where half the people come from that we lock up."

"I really thought we were making progress."

We ran another half lap, the steady slap of shoes pacing my thoughts. "Do you feel like it's your fault?"

"I wonder what more I could have done. I wonder where I screwed up."

I knew the feeling.

"You don't want to start that," said Bunch. "There's too many variables. You start blaming yourself for that, pretty soon you're blaming yourself for everything. Ask Dev."

We finished the twentieth lap and slowed to a walk, stretching our muscles as they cooled down. "I thought of that," she said. "You and Mrs. Haas—and how much worse it must be for you two."

It wasn't something I wanted to talk about, but the tone of her voice told me how much she hurt. "You just have to figure there were reasons you could never know or anticipate—that it would have happened no matter what you did."

"You've been able to convince yourself of that?"

"Some of the time."

"And the rest of the time you're angry? At yourself? At your father?"

"Don't forget God," said Bunch. "He's the one who claims He made all this."

"Don't start that again, Susan."

"Well I admit to feeling anger. Toward myself, and

toward Tim for wasting himself like that. And I'm trying to understand how to cope with such anger. How can you keep it so tightly bottled up?"

"Because there's no sense pissing all over my shoe tops about it. It's just something I live with."

"And you're afraid someone might think you're looking for pity?"

"I don't need pity."

"Come on, you two. Cut it out, now."

"It's not asking for pity," she said. "It's trying to understand your own feelings about it. Granted there's no clear answer to why they did it, but for our own sakes we ought to explore how we feel about it."

"I know damned well how I feel about it: lousy. I know how you feel about it, too. But you've got your way of handling it, and I've got mine. Let's just leave it at that."

"Did you ever stop to think why you accepted the Haas case?"

"Because a client asked me to."

"Yeah—and we like money."

"You don't think you might be trying to answer questions about your own father's suicide by investigating his?"

I wondered if she seriously believed that or if it was just something else out of another textbook. "You're letting theory take the place of fact, Susan. It's a case I'm paid to investigate, and one we're not having much luck on."

"It's also a case you're more personally involved with than you'll admit."

Bunch was no help. All he did was grin. "Naw, Suze, he admits it. In fact he wants to serve and protect the widow Haas. I've tried to warn him. I told him only divorce lawyers sleep with their customers. But will he listen to me? No way."

She ignored Bunch. "There are surface facts and

there are subsurface facts, Dev. And you don't seem to be aware of the latter."

"I'm aware of hypothetical crock when I hear it. What I'm not aware of is what difference it makes to you."

"Because now I have a clearer idea of how you feel about your father's death. I'm aware of how much Tim's suicide has colored my attitude toward other clients, and how easily my guilt feelings tempt me to treat them as if they were another Tim. Maybe I'll even begin to feel anger toward them for still being alive. Just like you felt anger toward that man at the Chute. But if I know what to expect—if we know what to expect—we can control it."

"I don't think Haas is my father, if that worries you. And I don't accept your analysis of what you know damned little about. Now, if it doesn't disturb you too much, I'd like to lead my own life without you continually trying to assess it. If you want to pick on somebody, pick on Bunch."

"She tries. It doesn't work. That's why she goes after you."

Susan sighed and headed for one of the stomach-tightening machines. "I think that's why I love you, Bunch. With you, there's no possible worry about analysis."

Bunch grinned at me. "She's got a piece of the rock."

Susan's words stung enough to linger in my thoughts as I reached my new home, half of a remodeled town-house near Washington Park. The affluence of Kirk and Associates had lifted me out of the small set of rooms I'd rented, and the tax break on home mortgage interest made it better to own than to lease. So I found a corner of Denver which was one of those quiet residential enclaves that had old homes and large trees and a scattering of corner businesses—mom-and-pop grocery stores, laundries, liquor stores, an occasional neighborhood tavern or restaurant—that gave it a sense of community. A number of the homes were being bought by people moving back into the city, and I felt lucky to find a nineteenth-century duplex that an architect had lived in and remodeled. He had planned to keep it for himself, but finally decided to sell. And when he did, I was there with the bank's cash. As I pulled the 3000 up to the high stone curbing and walked to my side of the building, Mrs. Ottoboni's stereo quavered an operatic tenor that filled the two quiet porches with an aching, yearning note. The sound did not carry through the walls, though. The original builders, generous with cheap brick, had put a thickness between the two townhouses that not even a hammer could violate, and the architect had added extra soundproofing to keep out the street noises. The result was a sanctuary of silence that, after the abrasion of the city's constant bustle, felt like cool shade on a hot day. But through the peaceful quiet of the living room with its high, old-fashioned ceiling, the red alert light of the telephone answering machine gleamed a hot summons. I listened to the messages replay as I trimmed the shades and windows to the late afternoon sun: someone else's machine offering my machine a fantastic and rare opportunity to invest in mountain property, a notice that the Disabled Veterans truck would be in the neighborhood next Saturday, and a voice that said, "This is Michael Loomis, Devlin. Could you telephone me at your earliest convenience?" followed by his number. I poured a mug of thick Belhaven ale before dialing, and my mouth was full of the first long swallow when Loomis answered.

"This is Devlin. I'm returning your call, Professor."

"Your voice sounds a bit odd."

"Curing a dry throat. How have you been?"

"The flesh is undeniably weak, Devlin. One would

think that a sedentary occupation such as mine wouldn't make demands on one's physique, but I seem to have a touch of sciatica lately. However, I didn't call to complain about my health. I understand from Owen McAllister that you're once more looking into the Austin Haas thing."

"Yes."

"I knew Margaret before she married the man—she was one of my graduate students. A very bright girl and certainly undeserving of all that's happened to her. She is the one initiating the inquiry, is she not?"

"She hired me, yes."

"So Owen told me. He also told me that he's worried her curiosity might stem from morbid causes. He thinks she may still be overwrought, and that any further trauma—whatever you might turn up—could induce some sort of irrational behavior."

"She seems very stable to me. And very determined to know the truth."

"Yes. The truth. Well, certainly it's no business of mine or Owen's and you're well within your rights to tell us so. However, since I know the both of you rather well, Owen asked me as a favor if I wouldn't inquire about her welfare. Not to inhibit your investigation, understand, but to ensure that her health, physically and especially mentally, would not be prejudiced by adverse findings concerning her husband. Owen hoped, in light of your past association with him— which I may say has been very fortuitous for you—that you wouldn't mind his asking about her. He would have done it himself, but he's off on another trip. You must know that he still feels some responsibility for the unfortunate results of the earlier investigation, though he doesn't want to seem in any way presumptuous. I, on the other hand, have never suffered feelings of guilt for any of my various presumptions, ha ha."

A touch of professorial humor there. "She's been able

to handle what I've turned up so far."

"Oh? Then you did find a connection between Austin and the Aegis Group?"

"Nothing that would stand up in court, Professor. And nothing I feel free to discuss without Mrs. Haas's permission."

"Quite right, Devlin. And wrong of me to ask. Purely a spontaneous reaction on my part. Nonetheless, and strictly between us two, I do think Owen would feel a little less guilty if there were evidence that Austin Haas did, indeed, sell the trade secrets to Aegis. Right now, of course, he believes he may have pushed a possibly innocent man to his death."

"I have no conclusive evidence of that. But if some does turn up, I'll explain to Mrs. Haas how Mr. McAllister feels, and maybe she'll tell him about anything we've found out."

"That's very thoughtful of you, Devlin. And very diplomatic as well. I'll explain your stand to Owen. Thank you for returning my call, and please do come over and visit sometime—I've seen so little of you since Douglas passed away."

He hadn't seen much of me before my father's death, either. He and my father were business partners rather than close friends, and I remembered my father telling me once, shortly before he shot himself, that he wished he had not teamed up with Loomis—that he was afraid he had gotten into a deal that was over his head. But their business investment, a small plant that manufactured a new chemical used in video display screens, had become highly profitable soon after my father killed himself—and after the tangle of claims from the death had caused the stock to revert to the surviving partner. It had all been legal; I studied every line of each document word by word. But there was a lingering flavor of unfairness about it, intensified by the grief and resentment I felt at the time, so I made no effort to stay in touch with my father's ex-partner. In fact, I was surprised when Loomis asked me to visit Owen McAllister with him. But the results of that request had been very profitable for Kirk and Associates—as Loomis just reminded me.

Wandering across the living room with its dim ceiling brightened by plaster rosettes that caught and reflected the lingering daylight, I stood at one of the bay windows that reached out to the long light of late afternoon sun to bring it inside. As Bunch once told me, I tended to stare out windows whenever I turned something over in my mind. He was right, and the thing that drew me now to stare sightless over the outside strip of garden that separated my side of the duplex from the house next door, was the whole tangle of Loomis, McAllister, and Margaret.

I did not owe McAllister anything. I had been hired to do a couple of jobs for the man and had given fair work for the money received. Yet—and this was the itch that kept recurring—Loomis kept implying a debt. The recent good fortune of Kirk and Associates was due to the luck of working for someone like Owen McAllister. And that, in turn, was because Loomis had introduced me to the man. Now McAllister wanted information about a case that no longer concerned him. Except on humanitarian grounds. What objection could I have to that except a little nip of jealousy. Was that it? Did I resent someone else trying to look after Margaret? Was I covering that feeling by calling McAllister's interest nosiness? The irony was, the woman had not asked anyone to look after her, not McAllister and certainly not Devlin Kirk.

The small tiled fireplace was laid and I wandered over to light the kindling and shavings that I preferred to use instead of newspaper with its acrid smoke and thick ash. The remnant of winter's chill would return with the shadows, and the fire, yellow and dancing through the glass doors, could hold it off for a few more hours. The temptation to call Renee crossed my mind, but it was faint and fleeting and better that way. The break had been made and for both of us there was more relief than regret. Besides, the eyes that hovered in my imagination weren't dark but a sea green that verged on blue, and the voice playing over in memory was not Renee's.

Irritably, I began mixing the vegetable sauce for to-night's halibut steak and covered the fish to steam in its juices. Then I poured the rest of the Belhaven into a mug and turned on the television to catch the last half of the news. It was easier on the mind to listen to the long litany of other people's problems than to poke around the ill-defined boundaries of my own.

The worry lay in the back of my mind like a dog sleeping in a corner and was roused a couple of days later when Bunch came into the office with several rolls of blueprints tucked under his arm. "What the hell's the matter with you, Dev? You've been looking out that window since I left. Here—look at these AeroLabs designs for a change." He spread one of the blueprints across the desk and smoothed it with the side of a wide hand. We had landed the AeroLabs contract to evaluate and update the electronic surveillance and detection systems in a plant that had just received a Department of Defense contract. The job was another of those that had turned up as a result of the initial work with McAllister.

"We got the go-ahead to put sensors in these corridors here. Government specs leave it open to what kind should be installed. I say pressure sensors. What do you think?"

We discussed the merits and shortcomings of heat sensors versus pressure sensors versus motion sensors that would help form a barrier around the wing that housed classified operations. As usual, Bunch made his argument and then waited for me to pick holes in it. Then we would trade positions, me offering alternative defenses, while Bunch would invent ways to defeat them. But this morning the process went slowly and finally Bunch said, "Why do I get this feeling that I don't have your undivided attention, partner?"

"I was thinking about Vinny Landrum."

"You were thinking about the widow Haas, you mean. And what Landrum might spill about her hubby and his secretary."

That was a big part of it. The rest was what other harm Landrum might do to Margaret and her children while he scurried around trying to prove that she murdered her husband.

"Have you talked to her? Told her about Vinny?"

"No. He's not going to find a damn thing, and there's no sense worrying her over nothing. I hope he'll just blow away like the rest of the trash."

"Good luck."

"What's that mean?"

Bunch took a deep breath and held it a second or two while he tried to frame the words. "He won't find anything on Mrs. Haas. But he might come up with something on hubby."

"Something like what?"

"I—we—got an appointment with a guy this afternoon. It's something I've been working on with those tapes from the Haas surveillance."

"What kind of guy?"

"This guy I know over at Tramway Tech."

A few blocks away, that was the downtown campus of one of the state universities. "Want to tell me what it's about?"

Bunch tapped the blueprints. "After we go over this. These people are paying us and paying us good, so first things first, partner. And remember: if we do the work right, people tell other people. And so far we've been doing good. Let's keep it that way."

"And it all started with McAllister. And Loomis."

"It sure did."

"Do you ever feel that we owe them anything?"

"Hell, yeah—they gave us our start. Why?"

"I don't know. I get the feeling McAllister's looking over my shoulder." I told Bunch about the call from Loomis. "He has reason to ask, I guess—he's concerned about Margaret. But the way Loomis put it made it seem as if we owed McAllister."

"We owe him thanks, but that's about it. You told him the right thing. Even if the McAllister job was our big break, the rest has been up to us. And right now we've got this one to worry about if we want to keep the string going."

Bunch was right about priorities, anyway. I pushed everything back into that corner of my mind where the dog stirred uneasily, and forced my attention to the sets of blueprints and the various options and their advantages. When, after a quick lunch of sandwiches that left a few grease spots on the diagrams, we had finally agreed on the system of warning and detection devices to recommend to AeroLabs, Bunch rolled the blueprints into a bundle and grunted, "What time is it?"

He never wore a watch. Those with the leather bands were tight enough to cut circulation, and the stretch kind tended to spring into fragments when he flexed his forearm.

"A little after two."

"Crap—we're late. Come on."

The old red-brick building that housed this corner of the university had once been the headquarters and maintenance buildings of the Tramway Corporation when Denver had street cars. But the office tower had become administration offices for the school and the car barn behind had been cut up and converted into cramped and windowless classrooms. A swarm of people, not all of them young but most wearing Levi's and carrying books, stirred around the entrance to the office tower, and Bunch led me up a creaky elevator and through a warren of musty hallways into some adjoining new addition.

"Is this another gadget freak you've found?"

"Yeah, kinda. But, Dev, it's a whole new world. Wait'll you see what he's got. I met the guy once when he was testifying for the DA on voice identification."

"An expert witness? What's this going to cost us?"

"Well if he had to testify, it would be expensive, yeah. But right now, it's only a couple bottles of Scotch." Bunch shook his head. "Talk about your heavy drinkers, these college teachers are pros."

We turned into a pair of doors marked PHONETIC SCIENCE LABORATORIES. The room reminded me of every science lab I'd been in from high school through college. But instead of glass beakers and retorts and mazes of hoses and clamps, the long benches in the room held a bewildering variety of electronic equipment and enough dials and gauges to keep Bunch fascinated for a year. I understood the big man's enthusiasm.

"Dev, this is Harry Goodman. Devlin Kirk."

Goodman, about my age and a head shorter, had a mustache and goatee that framed pink, fleshy lips. "Hi. You want to see the tapes?"

Bunch answered for both of us, "Yeah, Doc."

"Certainly. This made a fine project for a couple of my graduate students, by the way. We've all learned a lot from it."

We followed the white lab coat down one aisle between a series of dusty black consoles faced by needle gauges and past a large steel-and-glass rectangle labeled SOUND BOOTH. On one end of a cleared bench, a series of paper strips was laid flat and anchored at each curling corner by pieces of stray electronic equipment. "The first set of readouts is voice number one, the second is number two, and—no great surprise—the third voice is three, the control voice. The voice whose identity we know," he added for my benefit.

"I understand."

"Fine. The top sheet is the sonograph record; that longer tape on the bottom is the oscillograph. Now you have to remember, all three of these voices were taken over the telephone, so they're not a hundred percent accurate. The telephone transmitter screens out certain frequencies at both ends of the scale."

"This sonograph"—Bunch had to show off a little—"it makes a graph of how sound is made in the mouth, right, Doc?"

"Sound production in the entire vocal tract including the larynx, that's right."

I looked at the first sheet that was slightly larger than a page of typing paper. Its color was a gray white, and an irregular pattern of dark smudges seemed to be burned into it.

"The relative light and dark etching corresponds to the pitch and intensity of the sound production. Where the sound is weak, we get a light burn. Where it's strong, the burn is heavy. Now here's the phrase whose sound production we've looked at." Goodman pointed to lightly penciled letters spread along the lower edge of the sheet. They spelled "Yeah? Who? No. You got the wrong number."

"That's the voice from the number I called—the Aegis number."

"Right," said Bunch. "And we're only just beginning."

"This, you see, is the lingual-velar plosive—the *g* sound in 'got.'" He pointed to a smudge. "It's quite hard, an intensity of production that's much stronger than many people make, and most likely generated with more force. This pale mark here is another diagnostic mark, the final *r* in 'number.' Or at least it should be. The speaker almost drops it off. My guess is that he substitutes a schwa sound for the retracted *r* in final position. Instead of making the sound with his tongue lifted like this—'*r*'—he just does it with his lips: '*uh.*'"

I found my own mouth following Goodman's demonstrations.

"Show him the oscillograph, Doc."

"That's the tape down here." An ink line traced down the strip of paper in a variety of flowing and spiky patterns. "Any sound production raises the line. This graph doesn't indicate the locus of production, but it does measure the sound after it's produced: the volume, duration, aspirations, and any kind of stutter or quirk in the sound itself."

On the tape a sharp spike of ink marked the *g* sound and corroborated the explosive quality indicated by the sonograph. Goodman also pointed out the slightly longer duration of the final *r* sounds, a duration that partially compensated, he said, for the loss of the retracted *r*. Other critical diagnostic marks were found in the duration of the vowel production in relation to a consonant in the word "wrong," and in something he called a "slight integrated schwa" that he pointed out on the graph but which I hadn't heard following the final *t* in "got."

"These are the kinds of idiosyncratic things we look for, especially since the voices don't repeat exactly the same sentences. As I said, my students had a real challenge. So did I."

"A sound gets changed if the sounds around it change, right, Doc?"

"Usually, yes. Ideally you want the same environment for the sounds you're comparing. We came pretty close, though."

"Show him the other tapes. Here, Dev—here's voice two."

Another set of papers showed the same kinds of marking, and along their bottom margins, I made out "Hello, Austin, it's me. I got a tee-off at four on Thursday." I looked at the graphs that analyzed the sounds but they didn't tell me much. "Is it the same voice?"

Goodman shook his head. "I can't be certain from just that. The 'hello' is the same. But more indicative is that almost silent schwa behind 'got' and the characteristic final *r* in 'four.' If he'd repeated the same phrasing as in voice one, I could be more definite."

"This here's voice three, Dev. It ties these two together."

This set of tapes measured the known control voice saying "Hello? A what? A tee-off? Who is this? Yeah, you got the wrong number!"

"I tried to make him repeat as many key words as possible," said Bunch proudly. "Doc says I did all right."

"It wouldn't stand up in court, but I think it's adequate to establish a highly probable similarity," said Goodman.

"So all three voices are probably the same?"

"And all three," smiled Bunch, "belong to that Aegis number you called. That's who I called for voice three."

I remembered the scattered notations in Haas's appointment book calling for tee-offs and stating various times. "So it wasn't just golf that Haas was playing."

Bunch shook his head. "It was footsie."

CHAPTER 9

At this time of night, Seventeenth Street was more canyonlike than ever. The orange glare of sodium lights pooled on sidewalks and curbs and empty asphalt, and drained color from the silent store fronts and sharply etched clusters of garbage cans waiting for the morning pickup. A drying streak of wet marked the passage of the street sweeper; from the distance and faint through the narrow slits of side canyons, we heard the occasional moan of a train blowing crossings along the west side of the city. Above, banks of unlit windows rose into darkness and the black pinched together over our heads. Bunch glanced at my watch. "It's about that time."

Time for the routine coffee break of the police patrols on a quiet midweek night. Time for the building's single night watchman to sleep behind his desk or be somewhere on his rounds. Time for me to follow Bunch from the dim recess of the stark patio at the base of the Action West building. During the day—at lunch hour in warm weather, anyway—the concrete walls and benches were softened by people. Empty at night, they loomed unnatural and sterile and emphasized the lifelessness of an area that devoted everything to the pocketbook and nothing to the soul.

Bunch strode quickly to the brightly lit glass doors and probed a thin sensor into the joint between the two panels of glass. A few seconds later I heard him grunt with satisfaction and the man's large finger began to work with surprising delicacy at the tumblers in the lock.

"Okay, Dev. It's open. Watch the treadplate."

We sidled past the heavy door and stepped gingerly around the edges of a large rubber mat that during the day caught the street dirt, and during the night concealed an alarm plate. As Bunch had said earlier when we strolled through the lobby with the workday crowd, "Hell, if we can't outsmart an alarm system like this, we shouldn't be in the business."

The empty observation desk glowed whitely. We darted across the stark space of the lobby before the watchman wandered back to his post, our tennis shoes making occasional squeaks on the fresh wax of the floor. Beyond the rows of elevator doors, we found the fire stairs and started the long, spiraling climb up to the thirty-fifth floor. We reached the last landing and paused in the dull glow of the emergency bulb to catch our breath and let our quivering legs rest a moment. Then I glanced at Bunch who nodded and gently opened the thick metal door. Its latch echoed loudly into the blackness of the corridor and we followed the probe of the flashlight beam to the shiny wooden doors of the Aegis Group offices. I held the light while Bunch tested for any additional electronics.

"I don't think they have any sensors, but it only takes a minute to check it out. Be damned embarrassing if the president and vice president of Kirk and Associates got busted for breaking and entering."

When he stepped back, I slid the rippled metal blade of the pick into the lock's cylinder, my hands pale in the pair of thin, disposable rubber gloves. Carefully, the tumblers nudged into place and a moment later the door swung silently in.

The thin glow of the city filtered through the atrium, showing desks and chairs as shadowy smudges. I led Bunch to the receptionist's desk, shielding the flashlight lens with my fingers. The drawers were locked, but taped on the retractable writing board under the desktop I found what we came for: the directory of in-house telephone numbers, information that Bunch's contact in the telephone company had not been able to provide. I began copying down the extensions and the names preceding them from the worn sheet while Bunch prowled silently through the lifeless rooms.

"Is the number there?"

"Yeah. It belongs to a David Neeley." Good old D.N. from my list of Haas's contacts. "I'll be through in a minute."

Bending close over the sheet that smelled faintly of the secretary's perfume, I was almost down to the bottom of the column when Bunch said "Uh-oh."

"What do you mean, 'uh-oh'?"

"Uh-oh, I just screwed the goose. You about through over there?"

"What's wrong?"

"I found a door with a silent alarm on it. I just tripped the son-of-a-bitch."

"A couple seconds—just a few more names."

Bunch trotted to the hallway doors and peered into the blackness. "Better make it now, Dev—the elevator's already halfway up."

I shoved the writing board back and hurried after Bunch. We quickly locked the door behind us and ran past the flicker of numbers above the elevators, our tennis shoes squeaking loudly now. Tumbling into the stairwell, we used the slick steel rails to glide down the flights three and four steps at a time. My pace fell into an urgent rhythm—step, slide, step, thump, turn, step —that made the series of landings a spinning blur in the dim glow of bulbs. At the door marked GROUND FLOOR, Bunch slowed to catch his breath and I pulled ahead and motioned him to wait. Carefully I went down a step at a time into the stale air of the basement and un-screwed the light behind the last fire door. Then, easing it open, I felt my way along the concrete wall toward the red glow of the exit sign.

A white light speared me like a moth to the wall and an excited voice yelled "All right—I see you—hold it right there! I'm the watchman and I got a gun—you hold it right there."

I froze, slowly lifting both hands empty and spread, and blinked into the glare. "No gun—you just take it easy. I'll stand right here."

"You better, goddamn it! You better!"

"Take it easy, now. You can see me. No gun. You got me."

The light and the voice came closer. "Damn right I have. I knew you'd be coming down the fire stairs soon's I sent that elevator up. How'd you get in here? Put your hands up—higher—higher!"

The flashlight wobbled briefly and canted at an angle. A hand came into the light to pat the front of my dark jacket and from the blackness behind the flashlight an odor of cigarette breath said, "Stand still, now. Don't you try nothing!"

"You're supposed to face me to the wall for that."

"Don't you tell me what to do! By God, I know what I'm doing—I—"

The voice shifted into a startled yelp and I dropped down as the flashlight spun and caught a massive hand clasped around the guard's fingers and pistol. Then the light shattered on the floor and, blinking against the lingering red glare in my eyes, I heard Bunch. "Now I got the pistol, old timer. All we want is out. You just sit still and everything will be all right."

"Don't hurt me! I got a wife—a sick one—and grandkids. I wouldn't have this damn job if my wife wasn't sick!"

"Hell, we don't want to hurt you. We just don't want to get caught."

The tangled shadows of Bunch and the guard disappeared, leaving me to grope blindly toward the fire door. A moment later Bunch was back, his shape a thicker darkness beside me.

"Is the guard okay?"

"Yeah. I tied him up with his pants. He'll be loose in a couple minutes."

The push bar had the usual warning: ALARM SOUNDS IF DOOR OPENED. Bunch swung his penlight around the margins of the doorframe to locate the wiring. Quickly, he clipped a small copper bridge across the leads. Then pressing the door open, we escaped into the cold air of the dark alley.

"Sorry about that alarm, Dev. They didn't have one on the hallway doors, so I didn't figure one for an inside door."

I drove while Bunch rustled around in a paper bag for a couple of beers and popped the lids. "I didn't think that guard would come after us. He sent the elevator up empty and then went down to wait for us. Smart old bugger."

"It took guts, all right." Bunch, his mouth full, handed me a can. "I always get thirsty after a gig like that." He swallowed again deeply. "Why do you think they had an alarm door inside?"

"It's probably their security room for the proprietary stuff. They'll think someone was after their planning documents."

"Someone like McAllister." He ran the flashlight down the list I'd copied. "Does Neeley's name mean anything to you?"

"Not the name. The initials. There was a D.N. that showed up in Haas's appointment books. My guess is it's the same."

"I'll give Lewellen a call and see if he's got anything."

A small item deep inside the *Rocky Mountain News* headlined "Guard Assaulted in Action West Building": and quoted Anthony Crinelli, 62, saying that he had been jumped by three assailants while checking out a silent alarm triggered in the Aegis Group offices on the thirty-fifth floor. One was described as a tall white male in his late twenties or early thirties, medium-length brown hair and blue eyes, and a small vertical scar above the left side of his mouth. There was no description of the other two who had moved up behind Crinelli and overpowered him while he was attempting to arrest the first suspect. A spokesman for the Aegis Group said nothing appeared to be missing and declined further comment. The development company is currently involved in two extensive real-estate ventures in Aurora and unincorporated Jefferson County.

I ran a finger down the hairline scar that led to my upper lip. The guard had a clear look at me in the shadowless glare of that flashlight, and it was a good thing there wasn't a mug shot somewhere in Denver police files or I'd be standing in a line-up right now. The next time, we'd have to go formal—a stocking over the face.

I tossed the newspaper aside and once more spread the Haas folder across my desk to search out all the "tee-off" times and days. The computer had come up with no correlations for any of the names on the Aegis directory, and the D.N. initials that I remembered simply sat on a blank square for a day in September and told me nothing. That left the golf games, real and supposed. I had located a couple and was entering their dates and times into the computer when the telephone rang and Margaret asked if she was interrupting anything.

"Not at all. I've been thinking of you."

She paused as if to interpret that, then said, "That's nice to know."

The voice had a soft note that did something warm in my chest, and I heard myself ask if she would like to see a play that I happened to have a pair of tickets for. Or at least I would as soon as we hung up. "It's a comedy—it'll help brighten a dull week."

"I could use a little comedy."

"What's wrong?"

"Elaine Ewald—remember her? You met her at Ricci's."

The restaurant where the blond woman came over to the table to snoop. "I remember."

"She called me last night. Apparently someone's going around the neighborhood asking things about me."

"What things?"

Margaret hesitated. "Questions. About the night Austin shot himself. What did anyone see or hear. Did they ever hear Austin and me quarreling. Would there be any reason I might want Austin dead."

I watched a wisp of steam lift out of the dark shimmer of my coffee cup. "It's nothing you should get upset over, Margaret."

She said quietly, "That sounds as if you know something about it."

"I think I do. Please don't let it worry you."

"Don't let it worry me! Devlin, Elaine said it sounded as if someone were almost accusing me of killing Austin. If you do know something, I want you to tell me."

"I think I know who it is."

"Well, who? And why is he doing this?"

"Take it easy, Margaret. I want to find out a few things first. Why don't I pick you up about seven and maybe I'll have something definite then."

"I . . . I suppose so. Yes, all right. I'm sorry I sounded shrill—it's just such a horrible accusation."

"And we both know it's a damned lie. I'll see you this evening."

The Vincent Landrum Detective Agency was over on Pennsylvania in an old mansion that had been remodeled for offices. The two floors at the front of the building were occupied by lawyers who gave Vinny some work now and then; visitors who wanted the detective were directed along a narrow sidewalk to the back and then up a flight of worn stairs to a small alcove tucked under the slope of the shingled roof. From the ground floor came the steady clatter of a quick-print shop, and the office facing Landrum's bore the sign TRIPLE A ANSWERING SERVICE.

"Busy, Vinny?"

"Well, well. My day is complete. And so early, too."

I closed the scarred door behind me. The room was small; a desk and two wooden chairs facing it took up most of the space. Dusty metal filing cabinets stood here and there, and in one corner was a coat rack dangling a wrinkled trench coat and topped by a brown fedora. A half-open door showed a tiny washroom with toilet and sink. Landrum lowered his feet from the desk and rocked forward in the creaking swivel chair. On the desk stood a tape recorder with a wire that ran to the headset clamped against one of Vinny's ears; scattered across a stained blotter were strips of negatives and color Polaroid shots of a man and woman busy with each other and unaware of the camera. "Something you're selling, Kirk? Or are you just trying to be Mr. Sunshine?"

I leaned an elbow on the tall filing cabinet that crowded the doorway. "I'm not selling. And I'm not smiling. I understand you're working over in the Belcaro area."

"I heard a rumor you liked to play detective."

"Some of the questions you're asking come close to slander, Vinny."

"Up yours, Kirk. I can ask what I want, where I want. It's called First Amendment freedoms."

I moved toward the desk and Landrum looked up, suddenly wary. "Not true, Vinny. It may be legal, but it won't be safe."

"Don't pull any shit, Kirk. I'm warning you."

"You didn't find out anything, did you?"

"Never mind what I found out. You don't want to work with me, I'm not working with you."

"You didn't find out anything because there's nothing to find out." I grabbed the front of his jacket and lifted him out of the chair. "And now you're going to stop harassing."

"Let go, goddamn it—you're wrinkling my skin!"

"Mrs. Haas doesn't know anything about her husband and Carrie Busey. You don't want to be the one to tell her, Vinny."

He grinned up at me. "Yeah? You worried about that?"

"Vinny . . ."

"Goddamn quit it! That hurts!"

"Hear me, Vinny: she's a nice lady with two nice kids and nice memories of her husband. Don't bring them any pain."

"I hear you—let go!"

I sat him back in the creaking chair and smoothed his jacket and gave him a tap of manly playfulness under the chin. It was a corny act but I really believe he expected it; it matched the trenchcoat in the corner. "I'll be watching, Vinny."

. . .

The rest of the day was spent with Bunch at AeroLabs on a final walk-through to compare the security system diagrams to the actual site. There were always changes that had to be made on the diagrams, and it was a little after seven before I pulled up at the Belcaro gatehouse to tell the guard who I was visiting.

"All right, sir. That's really a nice car. What kind is it?" This guard was a new one, in his late teens or early twenties, probably a college kid, and sure enough I caught sight of a book propped open on a shelf just inside the door.

"An Austin-Healy 3000. I only use it for special occasions."

"It's a classic, all right. Have a good evening."

Margaret was reading to the children when the babysitter let me in. They looked up briefly and then back to the brightly colored pages of the book. She smiled without breaking the quiet rhythm of the lines and nodded me to a chair. When she finished, she asked the children if they remembered Mr. Kirk.

Austin, Jr., slid off the couch from his mother's side and held out a small hand. "How do you do." Shauna, the toes of her pajamas flopping loosely, said "Hello" and settled more firmly on her mother's lap.

"All right, now," she said. "Story's over and up we go."

The girl clutched more tightly as the babysitter, a teenage girl who had been studying me from the corner of her eyes, came forward to lift her from Margaret's lap. "Come on, Shauna. I'll read to you upstairs."

"I want Mama!"

"I'll come up with you. But I'll only stay a minute," Margaret said.

"Hey, we'll all come up. We'll make a parade—Austin, you hop in front and be the leader."

A few minutes later as we came back downstairs, Margaret smiled. "You're very good with children. I'll bet you were the oldest."

"I was the only. But I have a lot of cousins—I used to visit my Uncle Wyn and stay over with his kids." I held her wrap and she slipped it over her shoulders in a faint breath of familiar perfume.

"Do you know where we're going? I'd like to leave a telephone number for Tammy."

I told her and gave her the seat numbers and she jotted it down on the pad beside the telephone. Once we were clear of street traffic and on the freeway leading downtown, she apologized again for being so nervous this morning. "It was just such an ugly, ugly thing to hear."

"I don't think you have to worry about it anymore."

"Did you find out who it was?"

"Yes, but let's talk about it at dinner. It's not worth talking about now."

The theater was inside the hulking concrete walls of the performing arts center, and we mingled with the crowds that filled the long, echoing galleria leading from the parking garage to the brightly lit foyer. Occasionally a man's eyes lingered with admiration on Margaret and followed her through the crowd, and I felt good about the light touch of her hand on my arm as I guided her toward the entry. We settled into the plush seats and Margaret glanced at the rows of faces banking up each side of the auditorium. "These are very good seats."

"My uncle's. He always buys season tickets to support the theater, but he doesn't use them much. His children have moved away."

That led to questions about my family and I asked about hers. Her mother and father lived in Chicago and although he was officially retired, he was still very active as a consultant. Haas's parents had recently been transferred to San Francisco where he was manager for the Pacific Coast region of a retail chain. "They've asked me to move out there. They want to be near their grandchildren. That's all they have left of Austin."

"Are you going?"

"I don't know. I like this area, but that's the only thing that keeps us here now. If we're going to move, I suppose it should be fairly soon, before the children start settling into school and friendships. It's so hard for them to leave those things behind and start again when they're older."

"It's not something you're going to decide right away, is it?"

"No. There's no real rush."

"That's good."

She didn't follow up and I didn't press. The lights over the open thrust of the stage began to dim and, as the audience noise ebbed, an actor entered from the wings.

Later at intermission, as we stood in a quiet eddy at the edge of the crowd and sipped a glass of wine, Margaret asked more about my family.

"I see now," she said, "why you're so kind toward Austin and Shauna."

"That may be part of it."

"Was your father a good friend of Professor Loomis?"

"They were business partners more than friends. And not too long at that."

"Still, it seems a bit callous of him not to at least offer you some of your father's stock."

"In the kind of partnership they had, all stock from a deceased partner reverted automatically to the company to be purchased by the surviving partners. Technically, it wasn't his to offer. Besides, it wasn't worth all that much when Dad died. The real jump came a little later."

"But you still see a lot of the professor?"

"No—as a matter of fact, I hadn't seen him since the funeral until he called me a few months ago."

"He had a job for you?"

"Not him. An acquaintance." Someone, the words crossed my mind, who wanted me to investigate your husband. An act that probably contributed to his suicide. "You know Loomis, don't you? He told me you were a graduate student of his."

"Oh, yes—at Columbia. I was working on my MBA, but that was years ago, and I was just one of dozens of his students."

"It couldn't have been too many years ago—you don't have that many."

"My, aren't you gallant, sir!"

"It depends on my inspiration, ma'am." The bell signaled the end of intermission and I stuffed our thin plastic wine glasses into the rapidly filling trash can and joined the eddy back into the auditorium. "You decided not to get your MBA?"

"I met Austin. After that, graduate school didn't seem so important. Nothing did, except . . . Well, as things turned out, I would have been wise to complete my degree, wouldn't I?"

"You still can."

"I've thought about it. I'm going to have to do something. But the children are so young. And you saw how Shauna acted when I was getting ready to leave; they're still quite insecure—I think they're afraid they might lose me, too." She added, "Fortunately the insurance settlement has been enough so that I don't have to think about working for awhile."

And Haas had elected the option that paid off the house in the event of his death, so she didn't have that large bill to meet every month. I knew the details of the settlement as well as she did; and although the amount was comfortable for now, it would gradually be eaten away by inflation and by growing children. But not for awhile—not before she could decide on some career of her own. Or someone married her. And given the quick laughter that chased away the lingering pain in those deep green eyes, given the supple womanliness beside me and the tiny fragrance from her black and gleaming hair, she would not lack for suitors. Nor did the idea of marriage seem so foreign a thought.

It wasn't until after the theater when we had settled behind the quiet table at the restaurant and scanned the menu with its handwritten list of the evening's few entrees that she asked about Vinny Landrum.

"You did find out something about the person who has been intimating those things, didn't you?"

I had been trying all evening to frame words that would tell the truth but leave out the worst. And still did not have them. "A little bit. Enough to know that you don't have to worry about him."

"Please tell me, Devlin."

I sipped my wine. "It's a private detective—one Vinny Landrum. He told me he was hired by someone who doesn't think your husband committed suicide."

"But he did!"

"Everyone knows that—almost everyone. Landrum's the kind of p.i. who'll make as much as he can off a person's delusions. It was a suicide and he knows it."

Margaret leaned back to let the waiter top off her glass and settle the wine back into its ice bucket. "Do you know who hired him?"

"What difference does that make? There's no truth in it."

"I want to know."

I flicked a bread crumb from the linen near the butter dish. "His secretary. Miss Busey."

"Carrie? Carrie hired this man?"

"Yes."

"But why?"

"Because she doesn't think he killed himself. She doesn't think he was the kind to do something like that."

Margaret in turn studied the bleached tablecloth in the glow of the candle and her long fingers stroked one of its dim wrinkles.

"Landrum asked those questions because he figured you were the only one in the house with your husband. You were the only alternative."

"I see."

"Now he knows it was a suicide, and that's what he's going to tell Carrie Busey."

"But why is she so convinced that Austin didn't do it?"

I could have lied, but I didn't. Not quite, anyway. "She was in love with him."

"Oh."

"It's not that unusual. You know that. A lot of secretaries fall in love with their bosses. Especially someone who's dynamic and in the middle of exciting events. And after all, you loved him. Is it so strange that someone else would, too?"

"I . . . I suppose not. But it seems rather strange to learn of all this . . . this passion that I knew nothing about." The wide, green eyes lifted to mine. "She must have been terribly jealous all that time. She must still feel that way to hire a private detective."

"Probably. But it's not something you have to worry about now."

Her glossy black hair swung gently as she gazed at some vision trapped in the icy crystal of her water glass. "That poor woman."

When the waiter had cleared the plates and brought coffee and the small, bright glasses of after-dinner liqueurs, she asked me if I had discovered anything more about why her husband had sold out to Aegis.

"Nothing about why—other than the possibility of the money. Probably quite a lot of it. We did learn who his contact was."

"Who?"

"A David Neeley. Did your husband ever mention him?"

She searched her memory. "Not that I remember. Have you talked to him?"

"No. And that might be pretty difficult to do. Aegis doesn't want any connection at all established between your husband and their company."

"Why?"

"Because it might give McAllister grounds for a suit. Even if he lost it, the projects could be tied up for a long time in litigation. The Aegis Group could lose a lot of money."

"So suddenly Austin's a curse to them. They used him, they got what they needed, and now they don't even want to admit that he was alive!"

It didn't matter anymore who used whom or who got what. I sipped at the golden dollop of Drambuie.

"That's all right." The bitterness was gone from her voice.

I looked up to see her smiling at me. "What is?"

"I'm more resigned to the possibility now—that Austin was leading a kind of double life. I suppose we can never know someone else entirely, even a husband and the father of one's children."

Her lips may have said she was resigned to it, but her eyes told me something else. "I think it would be best to stop the investigation, Margaret. If he didn't do it for the money, he may have done it for the challenge. Who knows? Our chances of finding out anything more are pretty slim. It looks like he did it. Let's just leave it at that."

I could see only the top of her bowed head and half expected a tear to stain the tablecloth. But it didn't.

Instead, she took a deep breath and raised a pallid face.
"I think you're right."

We paused at the door of her home; west, across the
gently rising blackness sprinkled with the shimmering
lights of streets and homes, a dim horizon glow silhouetted the ragged peaks and ridges of the mountains. Just
above them, sharply painted, a quarter moon tilted
large and white and low against a sky that seemed dark
blue in its velvety clearness.

"It's supposed to rain soon," I said.

"Why's that?"

"The moon—it spills water when it's tilted like that."

"That's silly!"

"But true. It has to be true—my sainted mother told
me."

"And you believe what women tell you?"

"No reason not to."

"I think, Mr. Kirk, you're in for some heartache."

"Possibly. But until it happens, I'd rather believe
than disbelieve. I see too much of suspicion and decep-
tion, anyway."

"Well, you won't be burdened with any more of my
suspicions."

"Some are less burdensome than others. I hope I can
keep seeing you, Margaret. I really enjoyed this evening. I enjoy being with you."

Her hand rested lightly on my arm. "I've enjoyed it
too, Dev. I really have."

I studied the pale light that touched her profile and
made even darker the shadow of her hair and eyes and
the full lips that parted over glistening teeth. "And that
means I can see more of you."

"Are you so certain what it means?"

"I'm certain I don't want you to say no."

"Then I won't say no."

I leaned toward her but she drew back slightly and there was a moment of awkwardness before she laughed with a nervous, breathless sound. "It's been years since I've been on a date. I feel a bit silly and now I've gone and spoiled the moment, haven't I?"

"No." Holding her gently to me, I caressed the silk of her hair and did not try again to kiss her. "You've made the moment more comfortable . . . more honest." The rigidness went out of her body and for an instant I felt her curving softness warm against the angles and planes of my own flesh as she held me in return.

Then she pulled away and fumbled her key into the latch. "I'd better get in; I told Tammy's mother I'd be home early, and now it's not so early." She paused, the low light of the entry behind her. "I've truly enjoyed myself tonight." She kissed me quickly and lightly on the cheek. "Do call."

The Healy seemed to drive itself back to the house; at least my hands and feet worked automatically because my mind lingered back at Margaret's doorway, replaying what she said and how she looked and how, with delightful unfamiliarity, her body had been warm and soft against my own. It wasn't until I had driven past my front door toward the narrow alley leading to the garage that my mind registered the car parked in the deeper shadows of a low-hanging tree down the street from my duplex. It was one of a line of cars that always filled the curbs in a neighborhood where there was little off-street parking and a lot of rented rooms in basements and upper floors. But unlike the other automobiles, this one had two shadowy figures lounging low against the seatbacks in the familiar slouch of surveillance.

In the Healy's rearview mirrors, I caught the dim stir of the figures; and as I slowly turned the corner, I saw the car's door swing open. Then the scene glided out of the mirrors as I swung into the alley toward the pale glimmer of the garage.

I heard them before I saw them, the crackle of grit between shoe leather and the concrete of the narrow walk that led beside the house to the street in front. Two men pushed through the tattered blackness of a lilac bush into the pale moonlight and saw me. Wordless, they rushed forward, one coming in low for the legs, the other a blurred fist aimed at my face.

I kicked at one and parried the other, rolling the heavy body high over my shoulders and yanking down hard to spill the man solidly against the earth. But the second drove in, his fists thudding solidly into my stomach and punching the air out in a muffled grunt. I chopped down at the silent figure's neck, the side of my hand jarring against hairy flesh, and an arm tangled around my face and jaw and another set of fists began swinging wildly against my head and kidneys. An instant later we were tangled on the ground, rolling and gouging with fingers and knees and I felt the weight of the two of them begin to press me against the earth. I freed an arm to drive the blade of my hand solidly across a nose, but missed the follow-up, the heel of my hand landing on the bristly cheek instead of the shattered nasal bone. A solid, numbing thud sprayed red sparks across my vision and another cracked down on my collarbone to numb my arm and flop it useless at my side. I twisted hard and heard the sap thwack into the lawn beside my ear and kicked my heel at the knee hovering on the edge of vision. It caught a corner of bone and a man's choked voice gargled "Goddamn!" Rolling to my feet, my arm beginning to tingle with the needles of returning feeling, I backed against the cold brick of the house and waited as the two separated and began to close in from each side.

The glare of a yard light suddenly flicked on, followed by the frightened, angry voice of Mrs. Ottoboni.

"What's going on out there? I've called the police and I can see you men and I have a shotgun here!"

The two men, one with a long ponytail tangled and twisted wildly around his head, the other with a smear of glistening red wiped through his mustache, glanced up at the blinding glare and the voice behind it. Ponytail sprinted back into the darkness beside the house, and bloody face, starting after him, paused. "You were told, Kirk, but you wouldn't listen. We're going to get your ass, man!"

The numbness of my head was turning into a stabbing pain that winced my right eye shut, and I gingerly probed into the ache of my shoulder for the telltale spur of a broken collarbone.

"Mr. Kirk? Are you all right?"

"I'm a lot better than before you came out, Mrs. Ottoboni." The break wasn't there, but the bruised flesh and bone had begun to throb deeply. "Thanks."

"Oh, my goodness, you're hurt. Come up here—come on, let me see what they've done to you."

"I'll be all right. Really."

"Nonsense. You get over here right now." She opened the gate between our yards and steered me into the light, a broom clutched in one hand.

"Where's your shotgun?"

"This is it. That's the only thing I could think to say." Staring at my head, she said, "My goodness, you've been hit!"

She reached toward the side of my head and I instinctively jerked back and sent another blade of pain through my skull.

"Come in and sit down." She led me into the kitchen and hurried to the refrigerator where I heard her rattling ice cubes.

"That was a dangerous trick, Mrs. Ottoboni."

"Well, I did call the police, though." She tilted her head back to look through the lower half of her glasses.

"Hold still now." She pressed a cloth full of ice against the hot flesh. "This'll help. When Mario was alive he used to get into some real fights at the foundry—the Italians and the bohunks, always fighting." She lifted the cloth and then pressed it down again, the cold, knotty bundle easing the pain. "That was when he was young, of course. He settled down after we got married. My, listen to me run on! I guess it's the muggers in my own back yard—I really can't believe it. It makes me so nervous all I can do is talk. Are you hurt anywhere else? How many of them were there?"

The ice had begun to trickle into water by the time we heard the heavy tread of official shoes on the porch, followed by the solid rap of large knuckles on the door.

"That must be the law—I'll answer. You just sit right there and don't try to stand up. Whatever they hit you with cut your scalp and you don't want to start it bleeding again. Sit still, now."

She hurried through the house and I gently rotated my shoulder to work out the remaining tingle and numbness. I heard the creak and jingle of pistol belts and equipment, and a moment later looked up at the bulky blue uniforms crowding into the kitchen and looking back at me with professional interest.

CHAPTER 10

"So you filed a complaint. So what'd you tell them?" Bunch, too, looked with professional interest at the red lump that swelled under the hair on the side of my head.

"Don't touch it, Bunch!"

"It doesn't feel sore to me."

"It's going to if you don't leave it alone." I sipped my coffee and let the hot liquid ease slowly across my tongue so it wouldn't jar my head. It was sorer this morning than it had been last night when the police finally left and Mrs. Ottoboni stopped fussing with the ice bag and I could at last sink into bed. "I gave them a description, that's all. They listed it as a mugging."

"One of them said your name?"

"They knew who they were after. But the cops don't need to know that."

Bunch heaved off the corner of the desk. "The only toes we've stepped on lately have been Aegis's."

"That watchman got a good look at me and gave my

description to the police. I suppose Leonard Kaffey recognized me."

"So why didn't Kaffey tell the cops who to look for?"

"That's a good question. Why didn't I tell the cops everything?"

"Because you've got something to hide."

"And that sounds like a good answer."

He thought a minute. "The connection with Haas?"

I made the mistake of nodding. "It could be. It seems a little overreactive, but that's probably it."

"Yeah. I don't know about 'overreactive,' though—you figure both those projects together come close to a billion dollars, that's a lot to protect." The man's weight made the floorboards squeak as he went to the window. "Still, I think that scumbag was just blowing smoke. I don't think they've got the guts to try it again." He came back to the desk and used the tip of his little finger to punch numbers into the telephone. "Lew? This is Bunch. Did you ever come up with anything on the corporation name I gave you—the Aegis Group?" He waited. "Yeah, that's the names we got, too. They're clean?" Bunch pulled the list of Aegis telephone numbers closer. "Here's some more names from the same place; see if they connect with anything." He read the list to Detective Lewellen who asked him to repeat a couple. "Yeah. I appreciate it, Lew."

Hanging up the receiver, he told me, "All he had were the listed officers—Merrick and Kaffey—and nothing on them. He's going to check out the others and get back to me."

"What do you expect?"

"Probably not a damn thing. But it does cross my mind that an outfit that whistles up two-bit muscle like that might have some reason for needing it." The man's heavy shoulders rose and fell. "If your skull hadn't got rattled, you might have thought of that yourself. Then again, probably not."

"Whose skull got rattled?" Uncle Wyn let himself in without knocking. "Good morning, boys."

"Hello, Mr. Kirk. Devlin here—your ever-loving nephew. He tried to beat up a couple of muggers last night."

"Yeah? You all right? You hurt?"

"A couple of bumps and bruises, that's all, Uncle."

"So what happened?"

"Nothing much—a little scuffle."

"I hope you got your licks in. Two of them, you say?"

"Yes, sir," answered Bunch. "But they got away, so our hero here doesn't get any medals."

"Not too much sympathy, either, it sounds like. That's a pretty bad bump. Have you seen a doctor?"

"No need to, Uncle. It's not a concussion."

"Now you're talking like the man who catches beanballs."

"That was the safest place, Mr. Kirk. He'll be all right."

"I hope you boys know what you're up to. I don't want anything to happen to you, Dev."

"That makes two of us, Uncle. I'm being careful."

Uncle Wyn didn't seem convinced, but he wouldn't push it. He'd done his best to talk me out of this kind of work when Bunch and I first went to him for backing, and he hadn't been successful then. "Well, I didn't stop by to nag you about your health, though that might not be such a bad idea. It's that Loomis guy. He gave me a call yesterday."

"He wanted to invest a little? Get rich in the market?"

"Not likely. He asked if I knew anything about you working for a Mrs. Margaret Haas. I don't. And if I did, I wouldn't tell that bastard."

"Why didn't he ask you, Dev?" Bunch wanted to know.

"He already did. I told him as much as I wanted to."

"I guess he thought I'd be glad to hear from him," said Uncle Wyn. "I just thought you should know."

For all that the man worried about my line of work, he got a vicarious thrill out of it, perhaps a faint echo of the competition and teamwork and excitement of his baseball days. Now he had brought information that might bear on a real case, and his voice held a note of pleased excitement.

"Thanks for telling us, Uncle Wyn. You want some coffee?"

"I'll get it, son. You don't look too full of piss and vinegar."

"I'm okay." And I really did feel better. Well enough, anyway, to be interested in the whys of Loomis's round-about way of finding out what I was up to. But I waited until Uncle Wyn had left before talking it over with Bunch.

"It doesn't make any sense to me, either, Dev. And I don't see why McAllister's so worried about the widow Haas. And why he doesn't ask you himself instead of getting Loomis to do it."

"McAllister feels guilty about Haas. And he's probably out of town; he spends half his life on airplanes. Besides, she was one of the professor's graduate students a few years ago, so he's interested too. What I really can't understand is the urgency that would make him go to my uncle. I don't think they've spoken since my father's funeral. Uncle Wyn doesn't like the man and hasn't kept it a secret. For Loomis to ask a favor of him . . ."

"Maybe he didn't have a choice. Maybe McAllister told him to do it. Loomis is always sucking up to the guy." Bunch began unrolling the blueprints for the AeroLabs layout and anchored the corners of the stiff paper. "How about Mrs. Ottoboni? She settled down yet?"

"She brought me tea this morning. At six-thirty. She

woke me up to tell me she was still too excited to sleep."

"Oh, yeah? What is this thing you've got for widows, Dev?"

Loomis may have been worried about Margaret, but as far as I was concerned, the Haas case was dropped, and a good thing for a couple of reasons. The AeroLabs job had moved into the bidding phase and took up most of our time now, and there were inquiries from prospective clients that were serious enough to call for detailed cost estimates. I also had to rough out a contract for one prospect who wanted us to look into employee pilfering. But I did manage to see Margaret and each time was better; it was nice to discover the nuances to her beauty, moments when she thought she was unobserved and the light angled across the planes of her face to emphasize its symmetry and repose. And we always found more to talk about, the pleasure of discovering the world from each other's perspective and of bringing our pasts together to enrich a present moment. I couldn't list the topics we touched on—though they usually had something to do with people—and afterward I would find myself gazing into space and remembering a witty, precise observation she had made about someone. And being grateful that Bunch hadn't seen that half-assed grin on my face. By now, both Austin and Shauna were calling me Dev and I'd taken them all to the Natural History Museum to crane up at the dinosaur bones and to make ugh noises over the mummies, to the opening of the Zephyrs' season where we huddled under a plastic wrap and tried to pretend we were warm, on blissfully quiet picnics in the foothills where Austin and Shauna chased the bright flicker of spring butterflies or floated sticks down the foaming torrents that drained the melting snows of the high peaks. Once, as Austin and I tossed bread crumbs toward the swirl of small fish in the shallows of Clear Creek, he tried to tell me about the terrible night when he woke to the icy turmoil of his father's death. It was confused, of course, but he remembered hearing the shot, though he did not know what it was at the time. He dreamed he woke up—something in the dream woke him up—and he heard a muffled thud and then he called for his mother and she came running up the stairs and in his dream his mother—the thing he thought was his mother—stood in the doorway and her shadow peeled the skin off her hands and arms and then reached for him and he really woke up, and he knew something bad had happened and he was afraid and screamed for his mother. It was something he hadn't been able to tell even her—how afraid he had been and, even now, still was. I let him tell it all, spilling it out like bile from the depths of his body, a lingering illness finally spewed out, and we felt closer for having spoken of it. Maybe for all her theorizing, Susan knew something about release.

Margaret said nothing more about Haas or Aegis, and mentioned nothing about Carrie Busey or Vinny Landrum. Nor did she say anything about love, but then I didn't ask. Without stating anything, Margaret made it clear that she did not want to commit herself; it was still too soon after her husband's death, and there were still too many unsettled areas of her own life for her to make any major decisions. And I didn't press her; my father could have married after my mother's death, but he didn't. Not for my sake, but because—as he told me once—he had married for life. His own as well as my mother's. That was the kind of love I wanted too, and it was worth nurturing, worth approaching slowly, worth the enjoyment of verifying.

Yet our kisses had moved from cheek to lips and on our last date had become long and deep and yearning for both of us.

Susan seemed to think it was a good idea. "You need

a family, Dev. You need that kind of love to help take the place of your father."

"I'm glad you think so, Susan. Do you want to read my palm, too?"

"Come on, guys, cut it out—let's just enjoy the run."

Bunch stretched the pace and left us no breath for arguing. We followed the dirt path beside the strip of asphalt road undulating across the prairie and toward the line of snow-glimmered peaks. To our right, the broad sheet of water penned into the reservoir was dotted with the white flicker of sails, and beyond that was etched the level horizon of the dam and then the distant clusters of office towers that marked the several centers of the sprawling, hazy city. Here, where the trail dipped and rose in rhythmic waves across the channels of Cherry Creek, cottonwoods and hackberry bushes closed over the sun-glared earth to offer momentary relief.

"I'm glad it's not crowded." It was too pretty a day for bickering, and Susan was willing to change the subject.

So was I. "When it cools off a little—they'll be out then."

A pair of laboring bicyclists zipped past, the bright colors of their jerseys bobbing with the thrust of their legs as they strained to race each other up the gentle incline. Behind, I heard the whine of a distant automobile engine, and across the rolling green of unmown prairie, the sharp buzz of a model airplane swooping in circles against the cloudless blue.

"A mile to go." The span of Bunch's shirt was dark with sweat and he ran with the short steps of a heavy man. Susan's lean stride lengthened to keep up, and, following her, I felt myself slip into the hypnotic rhythm of pace and breath. Behind, the engine's sound shifted into a louder snarl and a prickle of warning stirred at the back of my neck, and I glanced over my shoulder. A car swerved across the lanes toward us.

"Look out!" I shoved at Susan with both hands and dove headfirst away from the path of the hooking fender. Rolling across the stony ground, I yelled again at Bunch and from the corner of my eye saw his surprised face look back and then the big man jumped too. The swoop of metal blocked my view and I had a flash of a mustached face glaring down in angry triumph, its teeth showing in a curse, and then the car was past, careening back onto the pavement with a roar of engine and the stinging spray of dirt kicked up behind.

"Susan—Suze—are you all right?" Bunch, rolling up to his knees, peered wide-eyed at the figure lying on the ground.

I reached her first, my fingers groping for a pulse in the coolness of her tanned wrist. Her neck had an awkward twist to it, and, gently, I probed a finger into her mouth to be certain her tongue was clear of her throat.

"Jesus, Devlin, is she all right?"

"Her heart's beating, she's breathing. Don't move her neck, Bunch. Can you see where she was hit?"

"Her head—there's blood in her hair."

"Hey—you folks need some help?" A helmeted bicyclist squealed to a halt at the road's edge. "Man, I saw what that asshole did! You need an ambulance?"

"Yeah," called Bunch. "Quick!"

The cyclist turned and sprinted back toward the park entry and the gatehouse with its attendant.

"She's out. That's a bad head wound."

"What about her neck?" asked Bunch.

"I think it's just twisted, but we'd better not move her." Beneath her head, rising out of the hard packed earth like the dome of a mushroom, a pale stone glistened with the wet of fresh blood.

By the time the ambulance arrived, coasting forward among the small crowd of runners and cyclists who had stopped, Susan was half-conscious and moaning. Bunch talked to her steadily, trying to keep her awake, trying to keep her from lifting her head. The crew, carefully bracing her shoulders and neck, slipped a board under her torso and strapped her to it; then, with our help, they lifted her to the stretcher and carried her toward the white-and-orange ambulance.

"It was those two, wasn't it? The ones who hit on you a few weeks ago?"

I saw again the flicker of the blurred face at the window of the car looming over me. "The one with the mustache was driving."

Bunch rolled one fist inside the other to crack his knuckles with a muffled crunch. "I should have thought. I should have been watching."

"We both should have been watching."

The medical technicians strapped Susan in place and the driver ran to the cab; Bunch clambered in behind the other, the heavy machine lurching under his weight.

"Did you get a license?"

"No. It happened too fast."

The door swung shut and the ambulance, siren a rising wail, ground away.

A motorist offered me a ride to our car, and a few minutes later I sped up the long incline that led over the dam and toward Swedish Hospital.

As I drove, I went over in memory each instant of the attack and the things that I should have done differently. I should have looked sooner, a split second sooner, when I first heard the car's motor rev higher as the driver shifted into a lower gear. I should have swung Susan clear instead of lunging with all my frightened weight to sling her stumbling and out of control. I should have moved away from the two running in front so they would have been clear. I should have known from the beginning that they would try again. Looking back, there were a lot of things I could have done that would have left Susan frightened but safe instead of moaning unconscious in the back of an ambulance.

"They knew where to find us," Bunch had said while he crouched over the twisted form. "They tailed us until they had a chance."

Margaret. The children. If they had been following me, they knew about them, too. I pressed the gas pedal and weaved through the heavier traffic that began feeding into the highway.

The hospital, surrounded by large trees that sheltered the neighboring streets, sat at the top of a low hill, and the emergency entrance led away from the traffic at the front of the building into its lower levels. I followed the signs for visitors to a reception shelf where I found Bunch filling out personal data and finance sheets. Then we were guided into a room where a cluster of figures hovered around Susan. An x-ray hung damp against the opaque white of a viewing glass and showed the ghostly pale of bones, the fragile blot of a skull, the black of flesh.

"What's it look like, Doc?"

The man studying the sheet with a magnifying glass turned, slightly startled to see the figure towering at his shoulder. "The neck doesn't seem to be broken."

"That's good. What's the damage?"

He pointed to a shadowy area near the middle of the skull's glow. "Here's the fracture—a pretty severe depression with some bleeding. What happened?"

A nurse began making notes on a clipboard as Bunch and I explained the injury. Why she bothered was unclear, because over the next few hours as Susan was moved from emergency to x-ray and then to intensive care, every new doctor asked the same questions and more nurses copied the same answers onto more clipboards. Finally she rested behind the drawn curtain in one of a row of beds, electrodes monitoring her pulse on a softly pinging screen, and tubes and bottles dangling from hangers at the corners of the bed. She had passed out again in the ambulance and as yet had not made another sound.

"I'm going to stay for awhile, Dev." Bunch's voice rumbled in the muffled, constant murmur of the intensive care unit. "They're talking about doing a CAT scan. Can you handle the AeroLabs people?"

"No problem." Installation was supposed to start tomorrow and as always there were last-minute preparations to go over with the subcontractors. "I'll call in a couple of hours."

"Okay, Dev. Thanks. And look over your shoulder."

I took Bunch's advice as I drove the company's Ford home to change clothes. I approached the house from a different direction; I cruised each street to check out the parked cars before pulling to the curb. In short, I did those things that I ought to have done before I brought harm to Susan. Mrs. Ottoboni peeked over the low fence that guarded the back yards from the street and waved a handful of lilac blossoms at me. "Mr. Kirk —why don't you take some of these? They have to be trimmed and it's a shame just to throw them in the trash."

"Thanks, Mrs. O." I cradled the fragrant mass in my hands. "You haven't noticed either of those two men hanging around, have you?"

"No, and it's a good thing for them I haven't. How's your head?"

"It's fine now, no little thanks to you. I don't want to alarm you, but it's possible those people may come back. They'd be after me, but I wouldn't like you to be taken by surprise."

"Oh? I thought you told me detectives led pretty quiet lives."

That's what I told her when I moved in. "Yes, ma'am. Generally, we do. But these two men seem to have some kind of vendetta against me. I don't think they'll try anything here—not with you around. But you might keep an eye out for strangers in the neighborhood."

"You bet I will! And I'm glad your life is getting a little more exciting. Strapping young man like you needs that. And don't you worry about me. I got a good sharp pair of eyes, and I'm a little old lady in tennis shoes who doesn't intend to surrender my way of living to any bunch of hoodlums."

"Yes, ma'am."

I placed the lilac stems in a vase of water and telephoned Margaret.

"Hi—good to hear from you!"

I didn't merely imagine the warmth in her voice and it honed my worry for her. "Margaret, I won't be able to make dinner tonight."

"Oh—I'm disappointed. The children will be too. But thanks for calling. Can you come by later?"

"It might not be a good idea for me to see you too soon."

The line was silent and then she said quietly, "That's up to you, Devlin, of course."

"Hey, whoa—it's not what you think!"

"Then what is it?"

"Some people are following me. I don't want to give them a chance to try anything when I'm with you or the kids."

"What do you mean, 'try anything'?"

I told her about Susan.

"Oh, Devlin, I'm so sorry! Is there some way I can help?"

"No. She's in good hands and Bunch is with her. I'll be checking with him soon. She was hurt because she was near me, Margaret. I don't want to take any chances with you."

"I understand, Devlin. And I appreciate it. Are you certain that it's safe? For Austin and Shauna, I mean. One reads so many horrible things. . . ."

"I'm sure they'll be all right, and so will you. But if you do notice anyone or if you have any fears at all, call me. You have my numbers."

"All right." She asked, "Devlin, will we be able to see each other at all?"

"Sure. We'll just have to be careful, that's all. And this won't last long—I promise you that."

The meeting with the subs took the rest of the afternoon and part of the evening; at the office in the morning I was on the telephone chasing down the inevitable loose threads that turned up in last night's meetings. I had a session with Martin, the construction manager, and spent a long time on the series of calls that always had to be made when the pace of a project sped up and the installation dates came due. But all the activity couldn't keep my thoughts from returning to Susan and to what her injuries meant for Margaret. The fence, the guard at the entrance to the compound, these were slender protection, but it was better than nothing. Still, I'd feel better if I could arrange some kind of surveillance—something that she didn't have to know about and worry over. There were a couple of p.i.'s who were good enough to trust—people I'd worked with before. But the best protection would be a bodyguard. Though that wasn't too likely. Before we'd hung up, I mentioned the possibility to Margaret, but she did not want one. Definitely. After all, she said, I'd told her they were after me, not anyone else; she would be careful; she felt safe in her home with its own security devices. It was me she was worried about, and she wanted me to be very careful. "We've just discovered each other, Dev. I don't want to lose that."

"What are you smiling at?" Uncle Wyn tossed his wool cap on the desk and eyed me. "A young man staring out the window with a goofy smile like that—it must be springtime."

"Just something personal, Uncle. There's not much to smile at, anyway."

"I heard about Susan on the car radio. A hit and run?"

"Yeah. But she was just unlucky. It was me they wanted."

"Oh, Christ, Devlin." He stifled whatever he was going to say, the lips under the long, crooked nose pinching shut. Then he shook his head. "Just be careful, my boy."

"Don't worry, Uncle."

"Easier said than done, but I'll give it a shot. How's Susan?"

"She's still in intensive care and still unconscious. I talked to Bunch this morning and he'll call when he knows something."

"If there's anything I can do . . ."

"There's not much anyone can do right now. We just wait and see."

"That poor girl. And damn anyone who would do that."

That was something else that had been buzzing around in my thoughts.

"How are you and Mrs. Haas getting along?"

I looked up. "Fine. I was thinking of her when you came in."

"Yeah. That's what I figured." He stood, a pending figure in a light gray topcoat considering carefully his next words. "I try not to stick my nose in your life, Devlin. You know that. But since Douglas died, I've sort of adopted you whether you like it or not. It's because I do care. You understand what I'm trying to say?"

"Maybe. Why don't you just say it?"

"Right. Okay, I will. Mrs. Haas is a wonderful woman. You wouldn't care for her unless she was. And even if I don't know anything about the security business, I do know a little something about women. You know," he added with awkward formality, "affairs of the heart."

" 'Affairs of the heart'? That's an old-fashioned phrase, Uncle."

"Yeah, well, damn it, this is serious and I'm trying to be serious. A regular Dutch uncle. So believe me—I know a little something about women. I'm sure a woman like her isn't interested in a quick affair. Just like I know you wouldn't take advantage of . . . of her bereavement for that."

I waited.

"So you of course are considering marriage."

I waited.

"Yeah . . . ah . . . of course. What I want to know is, how much you've thought about the responsibilities, Devlin. Marrying a woman with two children is not only expensive but a tremendous responsibility."

"I have thought about it, Uncle."

"Well then, have you thought about what it means for your line of work? Somebody tried to kill you yesterday, you tell me, and they're still out there."

I waited.

"Well, damn it, here's what I'm trying to say, and you're not making it easy: have you considered what your line of work would mean for Mrs. Haas and her children?"

"Yes, I have. I knew a number of Secret Service agents who were married, Uncle. And if it was a good marriage, it lasted. It will be a strain, but other people have managed in similar situations, and from what I know of Margaret, we would too."

He hesitated again. "This should be asked too: have you faced the idea that the kids are by another man?"

I considered that. "I like those kids, Uncle. Very much. I don't doubt that I could love them as my own. For one thing, they're a part of Margaret. For another, they're new souls just entering into a pretty harsh world. And I'd like to do what I can to guide and help and—yes—love them toward what they'll have to face."

Uncle Wyn heaved a deep breath, his face tilted down to study the waxed top of the desk. "I know a little bit about jealousy, too. But you just taught me something of magnanimity. And you put words on something I feel about you, Dev." He looked up, a slight smile lifting the corners of his mouth. "I think I worry more about you than about Ellen or Brenda or Allan. Well, maybe not Allan. But since he moved out to the Coast, you got to carry his share of my worry, too."

"I understand, Uncle. And I appreciate it."

"Yeah, well, let's not be too magnanimous. But think about this: in a lot of ways, you still got a lot to learn about this world, Dev. Hell, we all do. But you're in a dangerous line of work and now you're thinking about getting instant family."

"Uncle—"

"Let me finish—I just want you to hear this: there's room in my firm for you. And not make work, either. It's got responsibility and a lot of money in the future for some very hard work. It's something I know you can handle. Wait a minute—I'll be finished in a minute. I'm not leaning on you for an answer now; I just want you to know you got this alternative. If things go the way they seem and you find a problem between your present business and what you'll owe Mrs. Haas and her children, the offer's there. Always."

"Thanks, Uncle."

We talked about a few other things, but the man had said what he came to say. And when the door closed behind him, I sighed and got busy on the telephone.

When, late in the afternoon just before I closed the office, the telephone rang, I picked it up expecting a call from one of the electronics suppliers in California. But it was Bunch.

"She's still unconscious, Dev. But the doc says her reflex actions are improving. He expects her to come out of it soon." Bunch added, "I called her mother. She's coming in tonight from Des Moines."

"Want me to meet her at the airport?"

"I'd appreciate it."

"No problem. What about the CAT scan?"

"The doc decided to wait." Somewhere behind Bunch's voice a flat metallic quack paged doctor somebody. "Dev, we're not letting this one slide."

"I've been doing some thinking about that."

"And?"

"And I figure they still want me."

"Have you seen them? By Christ—"

"Not yet. But I want them to know I'm healthy. That they got the wrong one."

"I see." Bunch thought it over. "We want to be careful with this one. I don't want those bastards to get away."

Neither did I. Nor did I want to scare them off by going after them too quickly. That had been behind my earlier call to an acquaintance at a radio station that featured twenty-four-hour news: local woman jogger injured in hit-run accident; two people running with her escaped injury. The joggers were unable to give police a description of the vehicle. I thought that if one news source decided it was a story, others would follow; and, sure enough, the six o'clock local coverage on one of the television stations had a three-second item, while another station used it to lead into a thirty-second editorial against the growing animosity between joggers and drivers.

"You think that'll bring them back?" Restless, Bunch strode back and forth in front of the fireplace, his bulk shrinking my living room.

"It's all we have to go with right now. I can't see us walking up and down Colfax Avenue with pistols in hand and yelling for them to come out and fight."

"Yeah. Well. Maybe we should just go over to Neeley's office and wipe the goddamn place up."

"Evidence, Bunch. We want to know for certain he did hire them. Besides, I think it's a personal thing with those two scumbags now. That's why they'll take the bait—getting Susan wasn't enough. They're after me because they couldn't do it right the first time."

Susan regained consciousness, more or less, for a little while in the early evening, and when I turned up at her bedside with her mother, Mrs. Faulk, we all had the satisfaction of a groggy smile from her fever-cracked lips. Then the nurse shooed Bunch and me out of the ICU and I talked him into a drink at my house. There wasn't much he could do walking up and down the corridor except get in the way of the nurses.

"They're talking brain damage, Dev."

"What?"

"The concussion. It did a lot of damage, and they're not sure how she'll come out of it."

"Jesus, Bunch."

"Jesus doesn't have a damn thing to do with it. I learned that a long time ago when I saw what Jesus let people do to children." Bunch crossed the room again and slammed the heel of his hand against the wall, rattling the window in its frame.

"It's too early to tell how badly she's affected, Bunch."

"Yeah. Right. Except I've seen people, Dev: car accidents, bullet wounds, blunt instruments—all that crap that scrambles the brains. It does things—they can't remember words, they can't thread a needle or even hold a pencil. Sometimes they can't even wipe themselves."

Bunch's voice did not rise and he talked as if he were reading stock-market quotations, but the man's hand had a slight tremor as it balled into a large fist against the stuccoed wall.

"The docs don't know yet, Bunch. They can't know. It's too soon to tell how bad the damage is."

"Yeah. I know." The fist relaxed and Bunch dragged the hand across his sleepless face. "They told me I could come back at eight. I'm going to grab something to eat and go on over."

"I'll be by after I check the job."

He nodded. "How's AeroLabs? Anything you want me to do?"

"No. I went over it all with Martin this morning. He's set to go tonight." The idea was to do much of the wiring and remodeling at night when the company was closed, both so production wouldn't be disturbed and for security purposes. "I'll see how it's going and then come by the hospital."

Susan was asleep when, half-lost in the maze of softly lit corridors, I finally located room 522 where she had been moved since the afternoon. Mrs. Faulk, a slender woman in her fifties, looked up from a magazine and smiled welcome as I came in.

"Asleep?"

She nodded. "It's the best thing for her."

Susan's tanned and healthy face already had that yellowish cast that came from illness and hospitals. The swirl of blond hair over the pillow seemed limp and lifeless as well, and one of Bunch's large fingers stroked a tendril of it gently. I set a potted plant on a table already crowded with flowers. "Has she said anything? Any change?"

"She said hello to her mother," said Bunch. "Mostly she's been sleeping."

We watched the motionless form on the high, efficient-looking hospital bed.

"Why don't you two go on," said Mrs. Faulk. "I know you're working tonight, and there's not a thing to do while she's asleep like this."

But Bunch was reluctant to go and it was another half-hour before the two of us rode down the oversize elevator for the lobby and the parking lot across the street where the Ford sat in nondescript anonymity.

"She's scheduled for more x-rays and the CAT scan in the morning." Bunch looked out the window at the lights gliding past. "They'll have a better idea how bad it is then."

I swung the car toward the bustle and glare of Hampden and turned east toward the AeroLabs buildings. "Her mother's staying with her?" A cot had been made up in a dark corner of the room.

"Yeah. For tonight, anyway. I guess they let relatives do that if it's serious enough." He shrugged. "I'm not a relative, so I can't stay. They didn't even want to let me in the room with her after Mrs. Faulk got there."

I started to say something when the radiophone wheedled its electronic chirp. "Devlin Kirk."

"This is Vinny Landrum. We got to meet."

"What's your problem?"

"Not over this thing. Man, I mean it—we got to meet!"

"It's Vinny. He wants to talk about something." Then back to the radiophone. "I'm tied up for a couple hours. How about eleven at my office?"

"Not there. Remember where I saw you last time? Don't say it—just tell me if you remember."

That wasn't too hard; it was Landrum's office. "Yes."

"Outside there. Eleven." The voice clicked off.

"What's that lint ball want?"

"Whatever it is, he didn't want to broadcast it." That's what a radiophone traded for convenience—a transmission frequency that anyone with a shortwave receiver could pick up. And whatever was bothering Vinny, he was trying to keep it from someone.

CHAPTER 11 ◖▬

"**Y**ou got me into this, Kirk. Now you got to help me out."

Bunch and I stood in a shadowy recess near the stairway that led up to Landrum's office. A faint nightlight shone through the window of the quick copy center on the first floor and splashed a pale rectangle across a patch of worn yard toward the alley. On a corner glowed a serve-yourself gas station and beyond that was the steady flicker of automobile lights on a busy street. Here, in one of those neighborhoods that was still half-residential, Landrum's hoarse whisper seemed to echo against the rear of dark homes across the alley.

"Into what, Vinny? What did I get you into?"

"Keep it down, man!" His sweaty face glinted as he peeked along the side of the house toward the avenue in front. "That Haas thing—you know, that fucking broad Carrie Busey."

"Me? I got you into that?"

"Shh! Hell yes, you did. You didn't take the case did you? So she came to me, didn't she? And when I said we should work together you crapped on me, Kirk. You and meatball, here, you both crapped on me. So it's your fault! You and that goddamned broad who's causing all the trouble."

"What trouble, Vinny?"

"She's dead, that's what trouble!" From somewhere in the distance, an emergency vehicle made a tiny howl in the dark. Landrum listened to it and wiped his nape with his hand. "Dead. Shot."

"Who did it?"

"I don't know who did it!" He caught his voice rising and stifled it, looking again past the corner of the house. "I don't know who did it. She's upstairs. In my office."

"Somebody got shot in your office and you don't know who did it?" Bunch craned to stare up at the dark windows on the landing above. "You call the cops?"

"Not yet, man—I wanted to talk to you first. Once they get ahold of me, shit only knows when they'll let me go again."

"Well, Vinny, I'd say you got yourself a real problem. But I don't know what you want Dev and me to do about it."

"It's got something to do with that Haas case—that 'suicide.'"

"What do you mean?"

"Figure it out. What did Carrie Busey hire me for?"

"I told you to lay off Margaret Haas."

"Yeah? Well Carrie didn't want me to lay off her. And she was paying the freight, Kirk. Not you."

"She's not paying the freight now, Vinny. She's dead." I wrapped my hand tightly around Landrum's arm and felt the muscle squirm under my fingers. "Now I'm going to pay you some freight."

"Wait a minute—wait, goddamn it all! Somebody

killed her! It wasn't me so it was somebody who wanted her out of the way. Because we were on to something."

"What something?"

Landrum sucked in a deep breath. "I don't know."

I lifted the man's jaw with a knuckle. "What something?"

"I don't know, damn it! It's just what I figure. Why else would she get killed? And I figure somebody thinks I know, too. You got to help me—it's your fault!"

"He's got something there, Dev. She was killed for a reason. Let's take a look before worm-breath calls the cops."

We went up in the dark, the stairs creaking under our weight. Inside, Landrum lowered the blinds and then flicked on the lights. Carrie Busey sprawled back in one of the two wooden chairs facing Landrum's desk. One leg had jerked forward and stiffened; the other was still bent at the knee. Both hands were clutched tightly beside her purse which was on her lap and gaping open; and her head, with its stiffly piled blond hair, dangled face up over the back of the chair. Between her open eyes a purple hole had been punched and a small thread of blood had dried along one of the faint wrinkles of her forehead. Not much blood had spurted from the wound because most of it had gone out the back of her skull, spraying the wall behind the chair and then dropping in a gummy beard of sagging brains through her hair and onto the rug behind.

"See? Fucking dead!"

"We see, Vinny."

Bunch peered at the bullet hole with its corona of dark powder burn singeing the flesh. "Fired at close range. Less than a foot, I'd say."

The murderer probably stood just about where Bunch bent forward to study the wound. From the posture, Busey probably sat frightened and stiff in front of the pistol, straight up in the chair with her legs tucked under it and both hands clutching the purse for something to hold on to. Or to keep it from the killer. Then the shot. That close. That square to the target of forehead and between the terrified woman's open eyes. The killer did not want to miss, and he had wanted her to see it coming.

"How'd she get in here, Vinny?"

"I—ah—she had a key."

"You gave her a key to your office?"

"It's the key to my apartment, too. I set the locks the same. I don't like running around with a whole bunch of keys wearing holes in my pocket."

"That's real efficiency," Bunch said. "You're a real genius. Tell us, genius, what was she doing with the key to your apartment?"

Landrum glanced at me and then back at Bunch. "We had this thing going."

"You what?"

"It's no big deal, Kirk. You and that Haas broad got your thing going. A little smoochy-smoochy on the front porch—I seen you. Well, me and Carrie had something going too." He added, "She didn't have all the money in the world, you know, and I was putting in a lot of time on this case. So I sort of did her a favor."

"How do you pay your rent?"

"Come on, she wanted it as much as I did. I told you about the ice-maiden type. It was a business deal and she didn't mind at all. Hell, she liked it—it's not the size of the tool, you know."

"You're all tool, Vinny." Bunch stepped back and was surveying the small office. "Are you missing anything?"

Landrum looked around too. "I don't know. I just came in here and saw her and got the hell out again."

"Where'd you call us from?"

"The White Spot, over on Speer. I drove around for a while trying to think what the hell was going on. And to make sure nobody was tailing me."

"When did you find her?" I asked.

"Seven, seven thirty. I figure she was shot maybe an hour before. After working hours, anyway, or somebody around here would have heard it."

That made sense. I kept my distance from the victim and walked slowly around the chair looking for anything that might be meaningful. Landrum began rifling through the drawers of his desk. Bunch, a handkerchief wrapped around his fingers, gingerly lifted the purse from Busey's lap and brought it over to the light. Carefully, he used a pencil eraser to move the objects inside. "Her wallet's here. It doesn't look like it's been opened."

"I don't think this was a robbery. Not for money, anyway."

"Yeah." But that didn't tell either of us what else might have been taken from the open purse. "Dev, look here."

I peered into the purse where Bunch used the pencil to unfold a slip of paper. In the glare of the desk lamp, I made out the word "Loomis" followed by a telephone number.

"What'd you guys find?" Landrum tried to look around Bunch's arm, which kept moving in front of his eyes. "What'd you come up with?"

The rest of the purse's contents were the things that should have been there: the wallet, a key case, some loose change and bills wadded up and dropped in, cosmetics, a small packet of Kleenex, a comb, a bottle of Midol, a Tampax.

"What do you know about Loomis?" I asked.

"Who?"

"Professor Michael Loomis."

"I don't know any professor."

Bunch set the purse back in the corpse's lap as it had been found. "Did Carrie Busey ever mention him?"

Landrum shook his head. "Not that I remember. What's he got to do with this?"

That was a good question and neither Bunch nor I had an answer.

"What about your files for Busey?" I asked. "Did anyone go through those?"

"No. They were in the file drawer and it's still locked. Hey—where're you guys going?"

"Get a beer. Home for a good night's sleep. The usual."

"Hey—hey, wait a minute. I'm going with you."

"You're going to be busy talking to the cops, Vinny. We have things to do."

"Don't leave me here, Kirk!"

"Why not? It's your office. Your client, too."

"I told you, goddamn it—whoever did this might be after me!"

"Why?"

"I don't know why! Why was she offed?"

"You tell us, Vinny."

"I don't know!"

"Then we can't help you, can we?"

"But I don't! I honest to God don't know!"

Bunch followed me down the steps, and behind him Landrum hurried to turn off the lights and fumble with the door's lock. He caught up with us at the bottom of the stairs, his whisper sharp in the dark. "Will you bastards wait up?"

"Got something to tell us?"

"If I knew something, I'd tell you. I swear it! But I don't and that's what's got me scared. I don't even know what they're after!"

"Who's they?"

"Whoever did this!" His thumb jerked toward the floor above. "I don't know who they is. But she sure as hell didn't do it herself."

Our shadows loomed over the shorter man and finally I said, "Come on, then. We'll get a cup of coffee and you'll go over it with us. Everything you've been doing."

"Okay—it's a deal." He stepped between the two shadows. "Let's take your car."

Landrum had left his car parked on the avenue in front of his office because he still wasn't sure whether or not he was being tailed. "I figure if somebody's on me, they're out there watching my car, you know?" His baggy eyes looked hopefully up at us through the haze of steam rising from his cup. Working back from his meeting with Bunch and me in the alley, he detailed what he had been doing for Carrie Busey. Most of his time had been spent on periodic surveillance of Margaret—"I already interviewed all the neighbors before you tried to strong-arm me, Kirk"—and he had followed her when she and the children went out with me, a fact that robbed those times of some of their pleasure. "You never even knew you had a tail, did you?"

"What did you expect to find out?"

"Something that said she killed her husband. That's all Carrie could think about. Talk about your one-track minds."

"And?"

"And nothing. Total blank. It was driving Carrie nuts. I told her to let it alone for awhile—that Mrs. Haas was still looking over her shoulder. But Carrie kept saying that she would have to make a move for the money sooner or later."

"What money?"

"From the Aegis payoff her husband got. You thought I couldn't figure that out, right? Carrie told me a little, the rest of it I put together. My guess is Margaret Haas popped hubby for the money, then she stashed it somewhere. Bank account, whatever. And she's waiting for all the noise to die down before she goes after it. So far, she hasn't spent a dime more than she can cover legitimately, so she's still figuring how to account for the payoff money when she gets it."

"You're full of crap, Landrum."

"Hey, I'm not playing kissy-face with her. I can look at the possibilities; you can't."

"Then why'd she hire me to find out whether or not her husband had worked for Aegis?"

"She hired you? I thought McAllister hired you."

"Wrong, Landrum. She did."

The man's sandy eyebrows bunched together in puzzlement. "It don't make sense."

"It does if she didn't kill her husband."

"But Carrie was so sure the guy wouldn't commit suicide. . . ."

"You be sure of this, Landrum: if you ever have anything at all to do with Margaret Haas again, I'm going to unscrew your head from the waist up."

"I got no reason to, Kirk. Not anymore." He sipped his coffee. "I hope I got no reason to."

"You don't."

"So you say. But tell me, why was Carrie blown away? And in my office? And what happened to the payoff?"

The money question was the same one that Margaret had asked so many weeks ago, and the only answer I had come up with was that Haas had opened a bank account in some other name or had hidden the cash somewhere. In either event the money was now lost. As for the death of Carrie Busey, nothing that Landrum told us offered any reason. Nor was there any reason why she should have Loomis's name in her purse.

"Well," Bunch picked up the check and glanced at the figures. "All this has been fun, Vinny. But the hour is late and my youth is fleeting. You going to call the cops?"

He shook his head. "I figure I'll wait and find her in

the morning. Natural like, when I go in to work, you know?" Less hassle that way." He stood to leave when we did.

"Where are you going?"

"With you. I don't have any wheels."

"We're going home, Vinny. You're not going there."

"Just give me a lift, okay? There's this place I can stay tonight. It's not too far, for God's sake. You can at least do that much after all this crap you brought down on me."

Discovery of the body came too late for the morning papers, but a short notice made the radio news as I joined the pulse of crosstown traffic that filled the one-way streets. A woman, age twenty-eight, found shot to death in a private detective's office. Name withheld until next of kin notified. The story sounded like a good one, and the announcer's voice stressed the angle of a local private detective.

Bunch was over at the hospital for the nine thirty visiting hours, and I started the day with a quick check of the previous night's work at AeroLabs. Then I called Margaret. "I just wanted to know how you're doing."

"Aside from missing you, I'm doing fine."

That was two reasons for me to feel good. We talked a bit about Susan and what Austin and Shauna had done, and about whether or not it would be safe to take them shopping. That's when I told her about Carrie Busey's death. The line was silent for a long time before she asked if there was any connection between that and Susan's injury.

"Bunch and I have talked that over. I don't think so. Granted, the Aegis Group does keep coming up—first with your husband, then those two hoods. But I don't see any ties at all with Busey."

"Why would anyone do that? It's horrible."

"Do you know if she and Loomis knew each other?"

"Professor Loomis? No, I don't. Why?"

"His name and home telephone number were in her purse."

She thought back. "I suppose they might have met. He's a friend of Mr. McAllister and I'm sure he visited the offices."

"Can you think of any reason why she would be in touch with him?"

"You mean because she was Austin's secretary? I really don't know, Devlin. You know I haven't had much contact with the corporation since Austin's death. What's so important about it?"

"Nothing that I know of."

"Then maybe you should ask Professor Loomis. There's probably a commonplace explanation." A note of quiet humor, "You're so used to dealing with underhanded motives and devious plots, Dev, that I think you overlook the obvious sometimes."

That was probably true, and it was as good a course of action as any. My next call was to the good professor —his home number, the one that matched the number found in Busey's purse.

"It's Devlin Kirk, Professor. I wondered if I might ask you something."

The voice sounded slightly terse and strained. "Of course, Devlin. Certainly."

"Austin Haas's secretary, Carrie Busey, was found—"

"Shot. Yes, I know. I just finished talking with a policeman, and I'll tell you the same thing I told him: as far as I know I never met the woman or talked with her."

"Do you have any idea why she might have your name and number?"

"Absolutely none. She could easily have gotten it from someone at the McAllister Corporation. Perhaps she wanted my advice about an investment; perhaps she wanted information about one of my classes. It's not uncommon for a prospective student to call and ask about my courses."

Listening to the voice, I suddenly wished I could see the man's eyes. "Do you know if she ever had any contact with the Aegis Group?"

"I have just told you, I did not know her at all."

"But she was Haas's secretary. If anyone would have known that he was dealing with Aegis, she would."

"That may be true, Devlin. But it is beyond my ken. I repeat: I do not know the woman and I have no idea why she was murdered. I don't wish to sound abrupt, but I'm late for an appointment already."

"Thanks for your time, Professor."

I was running the brief conversation through my mind and trying to trace out any threads and hints that the words generated when Bunch came into the office. "She woke up, Dev. She recognized me."

"Great!"

"Not all that great—she's having problems talking, but at least she's awake and she knows where she is and who she's talking to."

"When can I see her?"

"Probably tonight at visiting hours. The nurse said she'd be busy today with more x-rays and tests and crap. And a lot of rest. They want her system to get over the shock so they can find out how bad the damage is." Bunch poured himself a cup of coffee and settled into the groan of one of the leather chairs. "Mrs. Faulk says they've even started therapy already. Movement exercises, that kind of thing. The sooner the better, she says."

Bunch told me a little more about Susan's condition and the extent of possible brain damage. "A lot of times the undamaged part of the brain can take over some of the functions of the damaged part." Bunch liked the thought of the injury being only temporary and I hoped it was true, too. "But they say it'll take time. It's all a lot of maybes except that it'll take time." We talked, too, about Susan's mother and what we could do for her. Finally, as we settled on taking her to dinner before visiting hours, the telephone rang and an unfamiliar voice asked for Bunch. "It's yours."

"Hey, Lew!" Bunch covered the mouthpiece and gestured. "Sergeant Lewellen—White Collar Crimes."

I flipped on the telephone speaker in time to hear the voice say ". . . of those names are pretty interesting."

"How's that, Lew?"

"Nothing definite. But they've turned up in a couple of operations down in Vegas. Always on the fringes, you understand—fellow travelers, like."

"Mob? You're telling me the Aegis Group has mob connections?"

"I can't tell you anything that definite. It's pretty hazy. The names have turned up, that's all. As far as I know, they're legitimate businessmen. What I guess is they run the straight operations; the start-up money comes from the mob, and they set up businesses to put the money to work."

"Fronts?"

"No. Not at first, anyway. Straight businesses—clean. It's just that they get their bankroll cheap. They might do a little laundering; it depends on the kind of business that's set up. But the wrinkle is to use the crooked money to diversify into legitimate areas: transportation, restaurants, brokerage firms, even diaper services."

"Real-estate development?"

"Sure. That's a favorite. It's got close ties with construction and the Teamsters, and it can juggle a lot of money."

"What names paid off?"

"Three: Brewer, Jacetti, and Neeley. Neeley's a known associate of Spilotro down in Vegas. We think he's probably one of Spilotro's main money-movers, but that's just a guess. The other two we don't know much about at all. So far they're just names that turned up a few times in the computer."

"Jesus, Lew, I thought Denver was pretty clean of that stuff."

"It is. From what I can find out, the Aegis Group is clean. That's the angle: find a location that's away from the main operations and in an investment area with good potential, then quietly set up a legitimate business that you can run your money through and make a profit on. The only thing is, the business gets its start with a hefty loan from the mob. And who knows what happens down the road when the mob gets hungry."

That explained a lot about Kaffey and why he had no interest in taking money from Devlin Investments. It explained their paranoia about the break-in at their office—and their type of response. And it made the late spring sunlight dim a bit with the remnants of winter's chill when I thought about all the new implications.

"And if things get sticky, they might call in a little muscle from the godfather, is that it?"

"Yeah, that too. But the idea is not to need it. Keep a low profile, you know?" The detective added, "If you hadn't come to me, I wouldn't have known about this company or the people in it. There's no reason to. How'd you get on it?"

Bunch glanced my way and I mouthed, "Not over the phone."

"Let's meet and talk about that," said Bunch.

The site was a park of reclaimed river bottom where Cherry Creek joined the South Platte river. It was the original site of Denver, where gold was first discovered, and now concrete terraces made broad steps down the banks to the plunge of dark water over boulders and retaining walls. Here and there, benches offered a little rest and, in the summer, time to watch kids splash in the pools of slack water or inner tube down the chutes from one level to the next. This early in spring, the water was too cold and swift for swimming, but half a dozen kayakers were testing their strength among the bamboo poles of a slalom course marked in a near channel of the river.

"You ever do that, Bunch?" Lewellen was in his forties and wore a brown, three-piece suit that wrinkled comfortably as he lounged back in the sun.

"No. Devlin has. He likes to row boats."

"I'd be afraid the thing would turn over and I couldn't get up again." The man's heavy shoulders gave a convulsive twitch. "Christ, what a way to die." He shifted on the bench and shoved the butt of his pistol to a more comfortable spot in his back. "Okay, so what led you to Aegis?"

I told him a little of our work for McAllister.

"I remember that Haas shooting. No question about it, a suicide. The only problem was motive, and now you've turned that up."

"We checked out a telephone number and it tied Haas directly to Neeley."

Lewellen used his thumb to push a corner of his brown mustache toward his teeth to chew on the hairs for a minute. "Did Aegis find out about you?"

"What's that mean?" asked Bunch.

Lewellen's wide hand swept past the park and the river. "Meeting here instead of talking over the phone. There's got to be some reason."

"Well, Lew, yeah." Bunch cleared his throat and told him about the two men attacking me, and about the hit-and-run that injured Susan.

"Was that you? I saw it on the eye. How's the girl doing?"

"She got hurt," said Bunch. "But she's going to make

it. It's going to take a long time, but she'll make it."

"Good to hear that, anyway." He chewed again. "How'd they get onto you?"

"I went to see Leonard Kaffey," I said. "He thought I was pulling some deal for McAllister—trying to link Aegis with Haas so McAllister would have grounds for a suit."

"Hell, you wouldn't have grounds for a suit if you had pictures of them kissing each other's ass. You got to show an unbroken chain of possession."

"Nobody else had reason to send somebody after Dev."

Lewellen nodded slowly. "Those people are really paranoid, that's true. It's not worth it. They got all the money in the world, and most of it tax free. But it's not worth living like that. What do these two look like?"

I gave him a description.

"Can't place either one. Probably imports. Greenies, probably, just getting started. Which"—he smiled at me—"means you've got a good chance of seeing them again."

"They have something to prove?"

"You better believe it. Their first, maybe second solo job for the big boys. They do good with you, they move up in the organization, get a promotion, maybe some territory of their own for sharking or shake-downs. My guess is right now they're waiting to see what you do. You back off, they go home and have a party. You don't, they'll hit on you again."

"We're not backing off," said Bunch.

The detective's eyes slanted toward the heavy figure sitting beside him. "Now I'm supposed to say to you, 'No vigilante stuff.' Bullshit. If you get rid of those scumbags, I'll buy you dinner." He held up a finger. "As long as it at least looks legal."

"How about self-defense?"

"That's legal. What do you want me to do?"

"Can you dig up something on the Aegis Group?"

"I've looked. It's a legit business. Member of the Chamber of Commerce and everything. No complaints. Can't hassle them without a reason."

"You can't screen their calls a little? Check out those Vegas connections?"

He laced his fingers together and bent the knuckles back to crack them. "The unit has to be careful about that. If we have one lawsuit that proves damages to somebody's tender reputation, there's no more unit— that's a promise from the legislature. But"—he heaved himself to his feet and shook hands—"maybe a snoop here, a peek there. Who knows what probable cause might turn up?"

The first call when we got back to the office was Bunch asking the hospital for an update on Susan's condition. "They say she's resting comfortably." He hung up and stared off across the roofs toward the wall of mountains where the hot sun had begun to bring out dark lines of rock through the winter snows. "Any ideas?"

I dialed McAllister's direct number. "Just a long shot." The man's private secretary answered and I identified myself. "Is Mr. McAllister available?"

"One moment and I'll see."

Which is about all it took. "Kirk! I was just thinking of you. Carrie Busey's murder—have you heard about that?"

"Yes, sir."

"I can't get a damned thing out of the police. I've put my lawyers on it, but all they do is tell me what the police's rights are. Damn their rights—I want to know what's going on. Have you heard anything?"

"I know a little about it."

"Well?"

"I know she was shot once from a close distance and

that she was found in the office of Vincent Landrum, a private detective who was working for her. I don't think the police have any idea why she was shot or who did it."

"That's more than my lawyers have been able to find out. But not very damned much."

"She'd hired Landrum to look into Austin Haas's death."

"She what? What the hell for?"

I could see his pale red eyebrows pop up into the age spots that freckled his forehead. "She didn't think it was a suicide."

"That's nonsense! You know what the police report said. And you know why he did it."

"Apparently she was convinced that Haas wasn't the type to kill himself. That someone else must have done it."

"Sheer nonsense!"

"Yes, sir. But that's what she thought."

"For God's sake." The voice pulled away from the telephone to say something to someone and then came back. "Was she killed because of that, Kirk?"

"I don't think so. I talked to Landrum and he said he found nothing to contradict the police report on Haas."

"Damned right he didn't."

"And Landrum's still alive. If he had found anything, they'd have tried for both of them. Whoever killed her knew where to find him."

"I follow. What about this detective—Landrum? Could he have killed her?"

"As far as I know, he had no reason to. But the police will check him out for an alibi."

"I see. I think I see. No, damn it, I don't see at all. Why was the girl killed?"

That led us to the reason for my call. "Mr. McAllister, I don't know why she was killed. It could have been an aborted robbery or even a thrill killing. Or it might have been something else." ·

"What something else?"

"I'm not sure—it's just a feeling. The reason I called is to ask a favor from you. Would you let it be known that you've hired Kirk and Associates to try to prove that the Aegis Group stole your plans for the Columbine and Lakeside projects?"

The line was quiet for a breath or two. "Do you think that has anything to do with that girl's murder?"

"There's no reason to think so at all. But their name keeps coming up. And Haas was working for them."

"You're certain of that?"

"Yes, sir."

"Are you telling me everything you know about this, Kirk?"

"No, sir."

"Ha! All right, Devlin. I'll tell some people around town and the word will get back to Aegis, don't worry. And in fact, I'll do it right—you are hired, by God, to look into any relationship between Aegis and Carrie Busey's death."

CHAPTER 12

I hoped that was the right way to go; we were playing hunches instead of fact, and that always brought
a lot of risk. But there came those times when a
hunch was all one had.

"Connect the dots, and it makes some sense, Dev.
Aegis could lose a lot if Haas is tied to them."

"You heard what Lewellen told us. Somebody would
have to prove more than just a connection. They'd have
to show a chain of possession of the software, and even
then the laws governing copyright and trademark are
pretty vague when it comes to intangible property."

"Yeah, right. But try this on: what if Carrie Busey
didn't tell Landrum everything? I mean, who would?
What if she knew all along that Haas had been working
for Aegis—and what if she had been helping him? And
what if she even knew where that payoff money is?
Maybe that's what Aegis is after—they want that payoff
back. It's got to be a hell of a lot of money, and it would

be incriminating. And somebody went through her purse for something."

I leaned back and studied Bunch's face. The left ear had a ripple of broken cartilage along the rim; the wide, square jaw had a habit of sliding forward when he was angry; and the mashed nose went straight down to a bulb of flesh that looked like a small potato. It was not the face of a genius but of a linebacker, which he had been at Wyoming. But that scarred face held a good mind, I knew, and beneath the carelessness he showed toward so many things, Bunch was both quick and sensitive. "What if, indeed." And what if, for that reason, Aegis Group wanted her out of the way? They had already shown us some muscle, and shooting one unarmed woman was about as easy as hitting another with a car. But if so, why did they leave Landrum alone? How could they be certain Busey hadn't told Landrum all that she knew?

We picked up Mrs. Faulk at the hospital around six and took her to one of the new restaurants opening up in the Tivoli Building, a remodeled brewery that sprawled its wings and towers over a city block not far from our offices. Sporadically Bunch and I tried to steer conversation away from Susan and the hospital, but inevitably it came back to her.

"They did the CAT scan and found some hemorrhaging across from the injury. The radiologist did say it wasn't as severe as it might have been."

"Good—that's real good." Bunch had finished eating long before we had and he tried not to keep glancing at my watch. Instead, he read the little card held in a metal clip and set between the salt and pepper and a small rose vase. "This place was built in the 1880s and lasted as a brewery for about a hundred years."

Mrs. Faulk looked around the brickwork and period decorations—beer barrelheads anchored to the wall, and old-time advertisements for Hienbrau and Denver's Own. And, in fact, until the dessert came, we finally managed to talk about things other than the injury.

"This is very thoughtful of you. I'd forgotten there was a world outside the hospital." Mrs. Faulk smiled and I saw Susan's wide, slightly lopsided grin beneath that of the still attractive older woman. Her mother's face promised that Susan could age as gracefully and as beautifully—if she still had that chance. "But we'd better go before you get too anxious, Bunch."

"Hey, Mrs. Faulk, no rush. Enjoy the cake—I was just checking Dev's watch, that's all."

"I'm anxious too." She smiled. "Let's go."

Susan had been moved again, from a private to a double room. She lay propped up in bed, the curtain drawn between the two units and another clump of flowers on the stand beside the bed, this one from the staff of the clinic where she worked. In the corner above, her television set flickered. From the bed on the other side of the curtain came the tiny noise of another channel from a speaker beside the pillow, and in one of the chairs, a worn-looking woman glanced up to smile at us politely and then turn back to the figure lying still beneath the thin white blankets.

"Susan?" Mrs. Faulk's voice was soft against the tinny buzz of the television speaker.

Her dark eyelids lifted heavily and she slowly turned her eyes to her mother's face. A slight smile of welcome and a hand drawn from beneath the cover to weakly grip her mother's fingers.

"Hi, Suze. You're looking a lot better."

Her head turned to Bunch and she gropingly offered the other hand. "Liar."

I had to strain to hear her whisper. "He's right. You do."

The dull eyes searched me out. "Hi. You okay?"

"I'm fine. You're going to be fine, too."

The eyes closed on a long sigh, but the faintly smiling mouth said she was still awake. There was an awkward moment of wondering what to say next, and then Mrs. Faulk began telling family stories of Susan as a little girl. Occasionally, amid the muted laughter, Susan's head would shake gently and she'd whisper "Not true," and for a while the three of us standing around the still figure created an aura of warmth and protection that seemed to be a tangible barrier against any more hurt. Slowly, Susan's face relaxed into sleep and at some moment her fingers eased their grip on the hands of Bunch and her mother, and her breath came in steady, shallow draughts.

"She's asleep."

"Yeah." Bunch's heavy fingers softly replaced the blanket over her arms.

"I know you two have things to do. Why don't you go —she'll probably sleep through visiting hours."

Bunch glanced at the wall clock. "There's another forty-five minutes. She might wake up again."

"You're of course welcome to stay, Bunch—I'm not trying to get rid of you."

Bunch nodded and settled on one of the leatherette chairs; I lingered a few minutes before excusing myself. I'd promised to see Margaret before going to AeroLabs, and Bunch shooed me out with a wave of his hand.

Coming out of the hospital was like coming out of an afternoon movie; it was surprising to see that twilight still hung in the sky, and that the rest of the world was uninterrupted in its round of bustling traffic. The insular feel of the hospital lingered in my mind even as I drove through streets crowded with the cars and trucks of the fast-growing southern edge of the metropolitan area. But by the time I neared the Belcaro Estates gatehouse, I had managed to shake most of the depression that clung like a faintly unpleasant odor. I could not dismiss Susan's ill-looking, blank face lying in sleep against the metal bed. It was not an image I wanted to place Margaret in, and, with the caution that had become routine since Susan's injury, I made a few extra turns and kept a close eye on the rearview mirror.

"Devlin!" Margaret hugged me tightly at the door. "Come in—the children will be so happy to see you!"

They were. Shauna's earlier shyness had given way to a warming grin and the stiff-legged run of a child still learning how to work her legs. And now she lifted her arms for me to hoist her giggling into the air. Austin, too, was glad to see me, and if he was too much the young man to show such enthusiasm, he was still happy to be swung almost as high as the ceiling that he said looked so big when seen from this close.

"Shauna, Austin—for goodness' sakes settle down!"

It took them a few minutes, then Austin had to show me the latest addition to his track-car set and Shauna, wanting attention too, brought out a doll's dress that I had seen before but pretended I hadn't. When, after a firmer tone from Margaret, the children finally had their baths and were zipped into pajamas, I read them a story, one warm, small body close against each side and beginning to sag with weariness and that kind of comfort that comes from trust and caring and—yes— love. By nine thirty, they were in bed and asleep, the doors to their rooms slightly ajar to the light of the hallway.

"That calls for a glass of wine." Margaret's shoulders rose and fell with a relieved breath. "And some conversation about something other than grocery prices or Muppets."

"In a minute." My hands glided down to her waist and pressed her gently toward me; she yielded with a fluid, warm motion, leaning her body tightly against mine as we kissed, our lips slowly opening into a long mingling of newness and familiarity.

"I don't think I need any wine after that." She gazed up into my eyes, her own a shade of dark green that I would have dived into if I could.

"Well I'm thirsty. Among other things."

She took a deep breath and pulled away. "Other things. Yes. Biology is so unfair, isn't it?"

"It makes its own demands."

"And has no social conscience at all. Come on—you can open the bottle."

While she lifted a pair of glasses from a cabinet, I peeled the foil from around the cork. "My uncle had a paternal talk with me about you."

"Oh?"

I tilted a splash of wine into my glass, filled hers, and then filled my own. "He wanted to know if I was think-ing of marrying you. I told him I was."

"Devlin, please . . ."

"A man has the right to think. Besides, I haven't asked you, have I?"

She was silent for a long moment, studying the glint of dark red in her glass. "I hope you don't." She added quickly, "Not for a while, anyway."

"I understand that. But he did ask some questions that I should have been more concerned with myself."

"Such as?"

"How you and the children would fit in with my line of work." I followed her from the tile and wood of the kitchen back through the living room with its scattered tall greenery and into the alcove that faced the fire-place. "I went over to see Susan tonight. Bunch and I."

"How is she?"

"Mostly lucid. Very sleepy still. That could be the antiswelling medicine."

"Here's to her recovery. A speedy one."

"And complete." We sipped. "But seeing her injured made me think about you and the children."

"I'm not sure I understand."

"I wonder how fair it would be for you if we did get married. Even now, I'm worried about you."

"But you said that wouldn't last long. And the future's not something we have to plan right now, is it?" The shadow of the lamp made her smile slightly sad.

"Not right now, no."

"Then let's not. Besides, I never feel threatened when you're around."

I thought about that. "Not at all?"

"Not in any way that I'm going to admit." She sipped the wine. "Have you found out anything more about poor Carrie Busey? Do the police have anything?"

I told her what little had turned up, and about Bunch's idea of her possible knowledge of the theft.

"Why would she know about it?"

"She was his secretary. Assuming that your husband didn't tell her, she could have found out on her own. If so, she might have known something about the payoff, too." A stray thought crossed my mind. "Perhaps she was blackmailing your husband—that would explain his suicide."

"But that doesn't make sense. You said she hired that man to prove that Austin didn't kill himself."

"There are a lot of loose ends," I admitted. "A lot of things just don't make sense. But Aegis always seems to be in the background."

"It's so bizarre."

"If they thought she knew something, they had good motives to kill her: the threat that McAllister might be to them, the payoff money that's never been located. And they were behind the attacks on me and Susan."

"Are you sure?"

"The first time, they said something. The second time, I saw one of them."

"If you know who they are, what about the police? Why can't you have them arrested?"

"I know what they look like, not who they are. Or

where." And they knew I wouldn't be going to the police to explain about breaking into the Aegis offices.

Margaret pushed her long fingers back through the heavy fall of her black hair. "They sound so cruel."

"They are." I swirled the clear red liquid up the curving sides of my glass and watched its color drain back like fresh blood. "Margaret—"

"What?"

"Your husband. Did he make any trips to Las Vegas before he died?"

"Austin?" She blinked. "I can't think of any. He often made business trips for Owen, of course, but I can't recall any there. Why?"

"Apparently the Aegis people have connections to Vegas. Mob connections. I just wondered."

Her silence lengthened. Finally, she said, "I accept that Austin . . . stole the plans for the projects and sold them to Aegis. I have to accept that. But I can't believe that he was involved with organized crime. Not knowingly. Not willingly."

"I'm not saying that he knew. Aegis is a legitimate company and the Vegas connection isn't all that definite."

"Then what would it mean if he had gone to Las Vegas?"

"Probably nothing. Possibly that's where he met Neeley or whoever approved his deal with Aegis. Maybe that's where he got the payoff."

"If there were a payoff." A bitter note came into her voice. "That hasn't been proven, has it? If you could find the money, you'd have the final proof of Austin's complicity, wouldn't you?"

"You wanted me to look for that kind of evidence, Margaret."

"I know. I suppose it hurt me more than I can admit to learn things about the man I spent so much of my life with. A man I used to love. I suppose it still hurts."

I slowly finished my wine. "Of course it does." I set the glass hesitantly on its coaster. "I'd better go." A man she used to love. "I have to look over the work at AeroLabs. They're finishing the installations tonight."

She put her half-full glass on the end table and leaned her head back on the sofa. The soft light from the lamp seemed to gather in her eyes, which looked wide and large and yet sleepy. "It's still early." Her arm lay along the sofa back, the flesh touched by the lamplight and made warm in its glow. Slowly, her hand turned palm up and open toward me. "Please stay awhile."

The first indication of the success of the rumor about us working again for McAllister came in a telephone call from Leonard Kaffey.

"You're Kirk? The one who came by here with that cockamamie story about investing in our company?"

"That wasn't one of my brighter moments, Mr. Kaffey."

"From what I've seen, it might have been. I hear you're working for . . . ?"

"McAllister. You hear right."

"I hear you're supposed to be investigating . . . ?"

"You hear right about that, too."

"It's lies, Kirk. We never heard of that woman."

"We'll find out, won't we?"

The line's silence drew into a weighty length. "I was hoping what I heard was wrong."

"Why's that, Mr. Kaffey."

"Complications, Kirk. Life should not be so complicated. Much better for all concerned if things are kept simple, you know?"

The line clicked dead and I glanced at Bunch who had been listening to the monitor. "He wanted things kept simple."

"Sure he did, that bastard. A simple assault here, a

simple homicide there." Bunch turned off the monitor and replayed the tape of Kaffey's words. "So now what?"

"It's their move. Kaffey found out what he called for; now they'll try something."

Bunch's knuckles gave a muffled series of pops as he mashed one fist inside the other. "Something they didn't want to do unless they were sure?"

"That's my guess."

"I hope to hell they try soon."

I didn't think they would—it was too close to the call from Kaffey. If the thugs followed their usual pattern, they would wait until we had relaxed our guard and then come at us from some blind side. The answer was, of course, not to relax and not to offer a blind side. But I had been wrong before.

In the meantime, life went on. The AeroLabs project was into its last phase and we spent a lot of time there checking out the circuits in a final inspection before giving the subs our okay. There was the usual handful of problems, generally the result of a faulty relay or switch or an occasional wrong hook-up. That was Bunch's forte, and he sniffed them out with Martin hanging over his shoulder to give a deep sigh at every additional expense. That was one of the pleasures of working with Martin: he was a penny pincher who knew it saved money to do the job right the first time —provided there was a good chance of getting caught. And with Bunch the chances were very good indeed. My job was to familiarize the security people with the newly installed equipment, to show them the little they needed for operations, preventive maintenance, and test procedures, and to establish security routines and methods that would complement the equipment. It's surprising how many corporations will spend like a drunken computer freak on fancy new gear and think that's all there is to it. Then they either cut back on personnel to cover the cost of equipment, or they don't train their people to get the most out of their new toys and supplement those areas where the gadgets are weak. They forget that the primary line of defense is still people, and they forget that the foolproof system has never been invented—that the persistence of human greed and of time itself is against them. But then, as my father would have been quick to remind me, it's against all of us; and if one aspect of the proper life for man was to create a momentary stay against time's confusion, another might be a momentary stay against greed. Or perhaps confusion and greed were one. Waxing philosophical, I was; that usually happened at the end of a long day when I could at last prop my shoeless feet up at the edge of the flickering fireplace and take my time sipping a tall, heavy mug of Belhaven. That was also the time when the telephone usually rang.

"Kirk? It's me—Vinny. What's this shit I hear you're working on Carrie's murder, man?"

"Rumor has a thousand tongues."

"Does that mean it's true?"

"It's true."

"That's my case, Kirk! You're moving into my territory!"

"Your case? Who's paying to make it your case?"

"Nobody has to, man. She was a client. I been thinking—word gets around I let my clients get squelched and don't do anything about it, pretty soon I got no clients."

"Public relations! I hadn't thought of that angle. Is that what you're telling the cops?"

"What?"

"It's their case, too, Landrum. And you telling them to stay out of your territory?"

"Yeah, well, that's different, and you know it. Besides, they're goddamn happy to let somebody else do their work for them. The bastards."

"Do I detect bitterness?"

"You know it. They held me for seventy-one hours on nothing. Didn't even check out my alibi, the bastards, until the second day. Just put me in the can and sat on me. On suspicion."

"Frankly, Vinny, I can't blame them."

"Shit. Listen, Busey was my client, so I got a claim. You know that. Cut me in, Kirk—let me work with you on this one. There are things I know about her that you don't and you're going to have to come to me sooner or later. Besides, she was a friend, too. Like I told you, we had something going. I didn't want to admit this before, but all this has really got me broke up. I had a lot of time to think—seventy-one fucking hours—and Carrie wasn't so bad, you know? I owe her."

"What are you asking for, Vinny?"

"Nothing special—the usual fees and expenses."

"A hundred bucks a day for one week. No expenses. If you come up with anything, you get a bonus." And I would probably get lumps from Bunch for doing it. But for a change there was a little truth in what Vinny said: he knew Busey better than we did.

"A hundred—? How in shit's name can I live on that? What're you getting from McAllister? Two thousand a week? Three? And you tell me a lousy hundred a day?"

"You're doing it because Busey was a friend, remember? And that's the offer—take it or leave it."

"I got no choice, do I?"

"Start tracing out her day—who saw her last, if she was with anyone, if any of the people in the neighboring buildings saw her enter your office or saw anyone else go in."

"I know my fucking job, Kirk."

"And I don't want that information to come second-hand from police reports—do your own legwork."

He didn't hang up yet. "I want half up front or it's no deal."

"Come by the office tomorrow."

"I'll be there early."

He was, layered hair freshly blow dried and a heavy fragrance of some kind of perfumed male pheromone radiating from him. He read the check carefully before folding it away in his wallet. "I don't know how much I can find out in just a week. I got other clients with business to look after, too."

Bunch answered, "If you want social security, get old. The contract's for a week, and that's eight days longer than I'd give you."

"We'll talk about it at the end of the week," I said. "Don't forget our generous bonus plan: we pay for results."

"Hey, the Vincent Landrum Detective Agency gets results; it says so on my business card. I'll check in tonight. So long, Homer."

Bunch, his mouth a sour twist, eyed me.

"He knew her, Bunch. Better than we did. He can save us a lot of time tracing her movements. And he'll be all right for the scut work."

"Maybe. But he's still a living, breathing dog turd."

"Did you get anything from homicide?"

He snorted the last of Vinny's fragrance from his nostrils and tossed a manila folder on the desk. "Yeah, here. They don't have a thing. They really figured Landrum for the job, but his alibi held up."

I read over the shiny Xeroxed sheets. They included the pathologist's findings, which confirmed the cause of death to be the gunshot wound, and the diary of the investigation up to the present date: witnesses interviewed, evidence catalogued, and lab findings. Vinny's name rated a paragraph that, reluctantly, showed his alibi to be supported by several witnesses who neither knew him beforehand nor had any reason to lie for him. Right now, the file was resting undisturbed in the division's Open drawer and would stay there until something new turned up.

"Did you talk with Kiefer?"

"Yeah. He couldn't tell me anything more than what's in the file—which, of course, we're not supposed to have. So put it in the safe when you're through." Bunch added, "He wanted to know what our angle was."

"What'd you tell him?"

"That McAllister hired us to look into it and we were just getting started."

That was part of the truth, anyway, and all that was necessary right now. Perhaps this occupation was, as my father had worried, eroding my sense of morality. But that could happen anywhere and to anyone. The world wasn't the home of morality; that resided somewhere in the self and tried to work its way out into the world through what you did. You clung, as we had discussed it, to whatever you believed—to the idea that the ends don't justify the means, or to your sense of right and wrong—even if some occupations placed you in situations where more choices of that kind had to be made. But whatever the job, you had to work with the material the world gave you, no matter how corrupt or immoral it might be, because that was usually the only material there was. The main thing was to try to hang on to that narrow territory of right and wrong that you could defend against the world, and then you hoped to draw a balance between what you had to do and the justice and morality and virtue you felt in what you accomplished. That's how my father had concluded, anyway, as we talked on the telephone. The next evening he blew his brains out. It was a hell of a way to change his mind.

"Dev? You listening?"

"What?"

"I said I can't take that damned piano anymore. I'm going over to the hospital to see Susan. You want to come along?"

"Yeah—let's see how she's doing."

Mrs. Faulk was there as usual and was glad to see us. Susan had just finished a physical therapy session and was back in bed, sitting up with her hair freshly washed and dried. She looked scrubbed and pale and porcelain-like, the kind of lack of color that comes from missing the sun, and her eyes despite being brighter and quicker, had gained a kind of puzzled pleading as if she were trapped in a glass maze somewhere inside her skull and could see us out there but could not work her way past the silent barriers to reach us.

"Suze! Hi, Suze—you look great!"

The word struggled somewhere in her throat before it finally rose to her lips, "Bunch."

"She's having more trouble speaking," Mrs. Faulk murmured to me. "She's back to one-word responses."

"Regressing?"

"The doctor said it wasn't unusual. It's probably temporary."

Susan's eyes turned to me and she held still for a moment, groping to find the name lost somewhere at the edge of recall. Then the effort crumbled into tears and her voice gasped roughly, "Shit-shit-shit!" and her slender fist pounded against the white blanket.

"Hey, now, take it easy—you can't do it all at once." I held the fist and stroked it until it began to loosen and she managed to stifle the angry sobs. Bunch dabbed at her eyes and nose with a Kleenex. "You'll make it— you've got a lot of help. It'll just take time."

"She always was so eager for everything." Mrs. Faulk managed to keep her own eyes dry as she smiled at her daughter. "So athletic. So self-confident."

"She will be again."

"Yeah, she will," said Bunch. "Hell, she's getting there now—that's why she's fighting. Right, Suze?"

Her head, sunk back against the pillow, nodded faintly and she stared at the trapeze bar dangling over her head.

"I've heard of a therapist who has a clinic up in Boulder," said Mrs. Faulk. "She integrates occupational therapy and speech therapy in a new way. They say she's very good."

"Don't worry about the cost," said Bunch. "Anything the insurance doesn't cover, I'll help out with."

"That's not necessary, Bunch. But thank you."

"I want to, Mrs. Faulk. I want to be able to do something."

The woman's hand, as slender as her daughter's but showing the exercise of years, rested a moment on Bunch's shoulder in gentle benediction. "You are."

Mrs. Faulk and I moved away from the bed to leave Bunch and Susan alone. On the other side of the curtain, the patient in the second bed shifted and grunted with a twinge of pain and settled back into the chatty narcotic of daytime television.

"Have the police ever found out anything about the person who did this?"

I shook my head. "I don't expect them to. Not unless they're very lucky."

"It doesn't seem right that he could do this and then disappear completely." Absently, she straightened the fleece pad that softened Susan's wheelchair. "It isn't revenge I want but . . . some indication of responsibility. Something on that person's part that shows he cares about what he did to another human being."

She wasn't likely to get it. Their only regret was that they didn't hit the person they were after; and if there was any emotion at all for what they did to Susan, it was the satisfaction of having hurt someone Bunch and I cared for. But there was no sense telling that to Mrs.

Faulk; it would only deepen the shadows of a world that was unfair and make it tilt into malevolence for her. The world still held sunshine, even if it was only outside a hospital window, or caught in the petals of the flowers beside the bed. There was no need to darken those things for her, too.

"I suppose if he hadn't been so frightened, he wouldn't have driven off, would he? Perhaps he's suffering in ways we don't know."

"Perhaps." More likely gloating in ways that would be difficult for Mrs. Faulk to comprehend. But not impossible for me, because I knew that in all of us was the seed of that satisfaction in hurting someone. It seemed so long ago now that Susan had seen it surface in me, and it was still there when I thought about those two. The seed of willful destruction in all of us, my father had called it, whether the destruction of others or of ourselves. And, he'd added, the two were usually one. Words of wisdom from a man who was to destroy himself. Words, at least. And maybe words that only measured the limits of wisdom without leading us to the goal.

I gave Susan a final hug before we left and this time, with a silently mouthed hint from Bunch, she managed my name and we all clapped and smiled and she looked pleased with herself. In the car, Bunch broke the silence once to say, "She's going to make it." And I answered, "Yes."

We were swinging with the column of traffic through the stoplight leading onto University Boulevard when, in the rearview mirror, I glimpsed a car that seemed vaguely familiar—a nondescript sedan of modest, tan color. I'd seen it in the mirror recently, and now it seemed to hover at a fixed distance behind us.

"What's wrong?" Bunch didn't look back but watched my eyes study the mirror.

"Maybe we've picked up the scumbags. Let's find out."

"Don't rush it, Dev. Go on down to I-25."

We did, arcing through the cloverleaf that fed into the northbound lanes. Behind, the tan car blinked its turn and followed, two or three vehicles back. I held my speed steady on the freeway, just over the fifty-five limit, which meant that ninety percent of the cars zipped past in the fast lanes. But not the tan one. Sometimes dropping back, shifting occasionally from one lane to another, the car always managed to glide closer with the approach of every off-ramp and to fall away when the exit had been passed.

"I think we got us one, Dev. I think we got a nibble."

"Let's see if we can hook him."

Signaling the turn at the Sixth Avenue exit, I led the tan car south on Kalamath and into the tangle of over- and underpasses that made that area a bewildering snarl of sharp turns and dead-end streets. Other traffic sloughed off heading for the factory or warehouse or distributor's office that the roads serviced, but the tan vehicle, torn between coming too close or losing us on one of the sharp angles, hung at the edge of vision. Lumbering across an aged bridge over the South Platte, I led it through the Valverde neighborhood and finally to an almost empty stretch of pitted and forgotten highway that wound along the west bank of the river. There we stopped.

"What's it doing?"

"Sitting."

"How many?"

Where the road's curve pinched away in the rearview mirror, I could make out a pair of shadows against the glare of the car's windshield. "Two."

"You got a weapon?"

I'd started carrying it. "Yes."

"Let's get out and look at the river." Bunch glanced at the cylinder of his pistol and moved the hammer off the single empty chamber.

Unhurriedly, we opened the doors and strolled up the small berm and over it to the strip of asphalt that formed a bike path just above the highwater mark. A thick screen of trees curtained off the far bank and through the trunks I could see the flow of the river, muddy with spring runoff, spitting and boiling against shoals of boulders and then smoothing again where the bottom evened out in thick, black mud.

"They're coming."

Bunch stretched his shoulders and pretended not to watch the car move slowly toward us, its top glinting above the rise of ground. I tossed a rock or two toward a pair of mallards tipping their bottoms up in the shallows and waited.

But nothing happened. The car's roof slowed almost to a stop, hesitated, then gradually picked up speed and glided out of sight around the next bend, withdrawing like the nervous tentacle of something that waits hungrily in a crevice on the bed of the sea.

"Damn!"

CHAPTER 13

T he threat hovered on the fringe of consciousness like a dark, blurred shape that disappeared when you turned to look at it. But which always came back so that you almost got used to it. Almost, but not quite, and the corner of your mind that guarded the thing would wake up if it moved or grew or changed shape in any way. But it wasn't something you focused your whole life on; there were too many other things to do, and Carrie Busey's death was the thing of the moment. It was not only a cold trail but one scrambled by the heavy feet of police detectives who had gone over the evidence first. We didn't find much that the police had not already gathered, and Bunch had to use up a lot of good will and even go in debt here and there to get what he could out of official files and, equally important, unofficial gossip.

"What it boils down to, Dev, is a killing that should have a motive but nobody can come up with one."

"It's definitely not a stranger-to-stranger or a thrill killing?"

"Everybody I talked to said it doesn't feel that way." He shrugged. "No evidence, of course, but that's how they feel about it. They've still got their suspicions about Landrum."

That had shown up between the lines of the official investigation. Landrum and Busey had been seen together a number of times; and she frequented his apartment, even letting herself in with her own key, neighbors had reported. As cynical as it sounded, homicide detectives always looked closely at the friends and relatives of a victim as the most likely to have a motive. And half the time they were right.

"They even think he might have hired somebody to do it," said Bunch. "Hired somebody, set up his alibi, and then called her over there."

"He could have. But why? What the hell would he gain from killing her? And paying someone a lot of money to do it?"

Bunch thought a minute. "Maybe he found out where the Aegis payoff is and didn't want to split it?"

I didn't trust Landrum all that much either, but seeing him as the killer made no sense. "Then why did he panic and call us when he found her? Why not just wait until morning as he finally did, and leave us out of it altogether?"

Bunch had no answer for that one, and it didn't help his disposition. "Yeah. And the only reason he'd have done it—the only reason he ever does a damn thing— is for money. And if he got that much money out of it, he wouldn't be wasting his time working for us at a hundred a day. Crap."

We pored over Landrum's notes and the reports to Busey that dealt with his surveillance of Margaret. He had said that he was afraid whoever killed her would be after him because he must have turned up something.

But he had not been able to spot what that something was, so his file came to us—for an additional fee, of course. "Hey, I put in time on this and it's my property —you didn't want in when you had the chance. Now you want to use my property, you got to pay for it."

"You're already being paid—and what have you given us so far?"

"I got a few leads! I'm talking to people. I'm out there knocking on doors, which is a hell of a lot more than you're doing sitting on your butt in this office!"

"Time's getting short, Vinny."

"Five hundred." He held up the manila folder, slightly soiled and leaking corners of paper. "Five hundred and you can have it. Otherwise, you can buss my buns."

"You've got the decimal point in the wrong place. You never did work worth five hundred bucks in your life. Make it fifty."

"Quality work, Bunchcroft! You wouldn't know quality work if it bit you. Two-fifty. That's it. Not a penny less."

"A hundred. Not a penny more."

"A couple a Jews—a Jewish tag-team, that's what I'm trying to do business with!"

"You can stop doing business right now if you want to. It's your choice, Vinny. I didn't want Dev to hire you in the first place because you just screw things up. You heard the man—a hundred bucks. Take it or leave."

"You bastard. You're still a fucking cop, aren't you? You really like pushing people around, don't you?"

"You're not people."

"You know I need the money, don't you? You bastards!"

"Come up with some information, Landrum, and we'll pay you for it. So far all you've done is take money and bring excuses. Here." I wrote a check for a hundred. "Now disappear."

Bunch watched the door close hotly behind him. "You're throwing good money down a rat hole, Dev. And that's the rat."

"It's a gamble," I admitted. "But he might come up with something yet."

We settled down to read through Vinny's file.

"You never spotted him when you were with Margaret Haas?"

"No."

"Well," Bunch said grudgingly, "maybe he's good at that, anyway. The damned sneak."

We were looking at the log sheet in his notes on Margaret's activities, the day-by-day and hour-by-hour notations of what she did, where she went, and who she was with. I stifled the anger I felt swelling as I thought of Landrum spying on her; after all, I had done the same thing to her husband, and there was supposed to be nothing personal about it. Just get the facts, ma'am, and turn the facts over to the person who was paying you to gather them. But illogically, when Landrum did it, it seemed worse in an unclean way, as if his notes and photographs were an attack on her.

"Here's a shot of Loomis."

The photograph showed the portly man talking to Margaret in front of a restaurant door. His mouth was open on a word and his right hand pointed a stiff finger at her as she smiled slightly behind sunglasses. The notes gave the date and time and named the restaurant —the Promenade—just off Larimer Square. I recognized a table edge with its fragment of umbrella partly in the frame, and the brick that walled its quiet sub-level patio.

"Maybe that's why Loomis's name was in Busey's purse. She wanted to know what he was talking to Margaret about."

That made as much sense as anything else we came up with. The other photographs showed her talking to a few people: a woman in a business suit as they stood beside Margaret's car, a store clerk helping her with a load of groceries in a supermarket parking lot, a smiling greeting to another woman as Margaret and the children strolled down the sidewalk. Many of the photographs were of me and her, sometimes with Austin and Shauna along, and I had to agree with Bunch that Landrum was good at this job. I could remember each place caught in the black-and-white frames, and, thinking back, recalled no sense of being watched and photographed. Of course my eyes and mind had been full of Margaret, and that was a good excuse. Still, for a security agent with any pride, it was an insult; and it was intensified by the thought that instead of Landrum it could easily have been one of Aegis's scumbags. None of which was helped by Bunch saying again, "Man, didn't you really know he was there?"

Only two of the photographs showed Margaret's house, which wasn't surprising, since Landrum would have a hard time loitering around inside the compound without being spotted. Most of the surveillance focused on the times she came out on various trips or errands, along with less routine trips: "01:44—return w/D. Kirk, kiss on porch. Enter alone. BR light out 02:18."

Thorough, the little bastard.

"I don't see a thing in any of this stuff, Dev. Except for you, there's not a suspicious face lurking anywhere."

Which was the way I felt, too. The investigation was of Margaret, and only by hints and implications could we get a slight sense of Carrie Busey's part in it, or her reactions to it. For one thing, she kept paying Landrum one way or another to stay on the job. For another, she was probably frustrated at the lack of any evidence. Perhaps she was even starting to come to the conclusion that there was no evidence to find, because the surveillance shifted from daily and complete to periodic—a check of Margaret's shopping routine and tailing her through that, and once-a-day surveys of the house. Another document in the folder showed a weekly pay record to the gatekeeper on the evening shift to list car licenses cleared to visit the Haas address. That was the widely smiling college lad who was working his way through school, and at this rate he could afford Harvard. And deserved it. There were a few license numbers that I didn't recognize, but most of them I did: mine for either the Healy or the Ford.

"I don't see anything either."

"That makes the score Ignorance, 1, Kirk and Associates, zip. Do you want to show this stuff to Margaret Haas?"

There were reasons not to. For one thing, it would drag up a lot of painful memories, and for another she might be upset to know how detailed a picture of her life Landrum had gathered. But it was also possible that she could see something where we didn't. "I suppose I'd better."

I arrived just after the kids were bathed and wrapped warm in their small robes and skittering their pajama feet across the rugs in hairy slippers made to look like rabbits and skunks. Shauna wore the rabbits, whose wagging ears were lined in pink rayon, and Austin wore the skunks.

"Because he stinks," giggled Shauna.

"No, I don't. And who wants silly old rabbits anyway!"

"Children—Devlin didn't come here to listen to you fuss."

That wasn't entirely true; it was good to see them, and even their fussing brought a smile, stirring memories of me and my cousins and giving a hint of the continuity of human character. Margaret wore her hair drawn back from her face in a French twist that heightened the delicacy of her profile and the slender lines of her neck. And when she looked at me, those green eyes —large and dark in the light of the room's scattered lamps—still held something of the depth and warmth that had filled them when we had been together last.

We settled the quarrel over slippers by laughing at what ifs—what if the slippers were turtles, or what if they were monkeys, or big fat hippopotamuses. That led to story time, and story time to bed, and finally Margaret and I could share a long and uninterrupted kiss before I mixed her a gin and tonic.

"I have something I'd like you to look at."

"What?"

"Nothing to be that happy about, I'm afraid. Some photographs taken by the detective Carrie Busey hired to follow you."

"Oh? Why?"

"There may be something in them that could shed some light on her murder."

"Devlin, I had absolutely nothing to do with that woman's death!"

"I know that—that's not the point."

"Well, it certainly seems to be the implication."

"It's not the implication at all." The welcoming warmth that had been in her eyes was replaced by a mixture of anger and hurt, and I tried to explain. "There may be something in the pictures that has nothing at all to do with you. But something that put her in danger because of what she knew or might figure out."

"Such as?"

"I don't know, Margaret. I really don't. Bunch and I are trying every angle we can think of to come up with a reason for her death. This is just one of them, and a long shot, at that. You don't have to look if you don't want to."

"What do you want from me?"

"Tell me who these people are. Bunch and I will

check them out and see if there's any possible connection between them and Busey." I spread the photographs out on the coffee table along with the list of her visitors. "Anything you can tell me about them."

"My God—was he watching me do all this?"

"It's not that hard with the right equipment. Even for Landrum."

"But so many! And I never suspected. . . ."

"There are a lot of you and me, and I didn't spot him, either. That hurts my professional pride."

"It makes me feel"—she shivered slightly—"as if I've been fondled in my sleep."

There wasn't much to say to wash away that feeling because she was right. In one view it could be fondling; but mostly it lacked even that quirk of passion. It was simply gathered data, factual and unemotional, and that antiseptic professionalism was supposed to sanitize any moral issue. "It was a business for him, Margaret. Just like a newspaper reporter."

"Or a concentration camp guard? Aren't there laws against this sort of thing? Invasion-of-privacy laws?"

"The pictures are all taken in public places. They show public, not private, behavior. Here's someone I recognize: Loomis."

"Yes—we met for lunch. I wanted to talk about going back to school. The market for MBAs isn't what it used to be, I found out."

"What can you tell me about these others?"

She went over the rest of the photographs, naming those she recognized. "This is just the grocery clerk who helped me with my bags. Did that detective think I was meeting him for some purpose?"

"He was making a record of all the people you spoke to."

"But why? I can understand him taking a picture of someone I went to lunch with or of someone I seemed to know. But why a store clerk?"

Most likely for the same reason I was sitting here with Margaret and looking at the pictures—a fishing expedition for anything at all that Carrie Busey might find useful. I explained that to her.

"That she might find useful! One shouldn't think ill of the dead, but I'm beginning to dislike Miss Busey."

I turned to the list of license plates that the gatekeeper had sold Landrum. He had his contacts in the motor vehicle division, too, and the numbers had been translated into owners. "Here's a list of names. Do you recognize any of them?"

"Well, yours, certainly. What list is this?"

"Visitors to your house."

"Did he go through my garbage as well?"

"He would have, except he couldn't get to it."

"It's sordid." She scanned the brief list. "Professor Loomis, again. He brought by some information on MBA programs. This is Beth, a friend whose husband works for McAllister. Sue Graham—she's one of the carpoolers for Austin's preschool. So is Anne. Edith Goodrich . . . oh yes, the real-estate woman." She glanced at me. "I wanted an appraisal on the house in case I do move out to San Francisco."

She hadn't mentioned that in a while and I felt a small stab at the thought that she was still considering it enough to have her house appraised. "Have you made up your mind about that?"

"No. But I want a clear picture of all my options. And Austin's parents have been more insistent lately—they've bought a place in Marin County. They keep telling me how wonderful it would be for little Austin and Shauna."

"I was hoping you'd stay here."

"I haven't made any decisions yet, Devlin. You understand that."

"And I haven't tried to pressure you for any."

"I know. And I'm grateful—I need to make up my

own mind about what's best for the children."

"What about you?"

"Yes. That too." Her fingers touched mine. "Lately, that's become a real puzzle." She turned back to the list, dismissing that topic. "This name, Mr. Whelan, is the plumber. It was when the disposal backed up." Her finger paused at the next one. "Efficiency Car Rental?"

"That's the vehicle's owner. We haven't yet traced who rented it."

"Oh." She went through the few remaining names, most of whom were mothers of children that Austin and Shauna played with or who shared the driving chores in the preschool carpool. The only unidentified number was the rental, and Margaret turned it over in her mind, finally giving up. "I can't place it at all. This car was supposed to have come to my home?"

"On the eleventh."

She shook her head again. "I have absolutely no idea who it could have been."

I drew a circle around that one and stacked the photographs and the list in the manila folder.

"Devlin . . ." She frowned slightly and gazed at the fireplace with its half-burned log hidden behind the screen. "Is this the kind of work you do? This," her hand gestured toward the folder, "photographing and note taking?"

"Sometimes it is. Most of my work is preventive security. But, yes, I sometimes do just what Landrum does: snoop on people."

She was quiet and I could see her weighing the words before saying them, so that when they did come, I knew they were considered. "I suppose it doesn't seem important to you. I suppose it wouldn't have seemed so important to me, either, except now I've been the victim of it. Now it does seem important."

"Bunch and I have argued over whether or not we're in the pornography business."

"Do you think it's a light question?"

"No. But I'm not sure of its relevance. Investigation is just that—there's nothing salacious about it. And, ninety percent of the time, there's nothing interesting about it, either."

"But it's an invasion . . . it's . . ." She tapped the folder. "When you saw yourself in these pictures, you said your professional pride was hurt. Wasn't your sense of humanness invaded, too? Didn't you resent having been spied on?"

"A little," I admitted. "I'd resent it more if I'd been doing something to be ashamed of."

"With or without shame, I resent it." She sipped at her drink and once more thought over her words before speaking. "How long do you think you can do that sort of work without becoming . . . sullied?"

"If you're asking me to defend my work, Margaret, I could make an analogy with a doctor or a lawyer. Both of those occupations deal with human misery; they both make their money off of human pain."

"But theirs is the attempt to alleviate it. Yours seems to contribute to it. I'm not trying to make you angry, Devlin. I'm just trying to understand. You told me that your uncle raised questions about my fitting in with your line of work, and I've been thinking of that. And now, well, this is an aspect of it I never considered."

"I work with people in trouble or people who want to prevent trouble. It's not a clean corner of the world and it's not always a clean business. Sometimes, in fact, it's pretty damned dirty and mean. But I do my best to keep that outside of me—on my skin so it can be washed off. And despite what the job calls for, there are some things I do my best to avoid. Maliciousness, for example. Or harm to those who don't deserve it. Maybe even help for those who do."

"You the jury?"

"Judge and jury, sometimes—if it's called for. I guess

what I'm trying awkwardly to say is that the dirt doesn't have to be eaten."

"And yet you," she selected the word, "investigated Austin before he committed suicide?"

"Yes. What I did might have contributed to his death. That's a fact, and I am truly sorry for that."

"But he was guilty, so it all balanced out in the jury's eyes? Is it fair to say that?"

"I don't know about the world's balances, just my own. He was in trouble, and he was getting other people in trouble. I was hired to find out what kind of trouble and how bad."

"But when you were hired, you didn't know that. You didn't know if he was innocent or guilty when you began investigating him."

"That's true. That was the thing I was supposed to find out."

"And so you took pictures of him and made lists of his visitors?"

"I also tapped his telephone and went through his papers."

"I see."

I wasn't sure what she saw. I hoped it wasn't a vision of saying good-bye to me. But I wasn't going to soften the facts; the work did involve a lot of things that weren't clean and nice and well mannered. There was no sense misleading her about that. She was trying to get a picture of her options, and if I was still one of them, I wanted that picture to be very clear. "There are some rights and wrongs we hold to despite the kind of work we do. Bunch has a good sense of them. I like to think that I do, too. Even someone like Landrum has a glimmering of them."

"You mean you're some sort of Robin Hoods?"

"Nothing so glamorous or fabled. But I've known some people who have very respectable jobs but whose private lives—and hearts—are cruel and greedy and petty. I like to believe that Bunch and I are the reverse of that. We work among the cruel and greedy and petty, but there are some moral standards we hold to —a sense of human dignity that's even more important because we see too many who are without it."

"I believe I understand. I mean, we pass judgments on people every day, don't we? But I'm still confused." She glanced at the folder on the coffee table. "And I'm still a bit shocked at what was done to me. And at how you explain the need for it. I have to think, Devlin. I want time to think."

I finished my drink and gathered up the papers. "While you're thinking, Margaret, please remember that I love you."

She nodded, silent, as I went to the door by myself.

"She's doing a lot better," said Bunch. "Did you hear that sentence? Three words—'I like it.'"

We had been driving Mrs. Faulk around on last-minute errands—she was to fly back to Des Moines for a few days to stitch up the fabric of that abruptly torn life, and then drive back to Denver in her own car. After that, we had gone by the hospital to visit Susan and that left Bunch in high spirits, reliving everything she said and did and finding reason for hope in each tiny change.

When the last aspect of our visit with Susan had been savored, Bunch asked me what Margaret had said about Landrum's file, and I told him that part of it which was relevant.

"There was a car she didn't recognize?"

"I talked to her again this morning. She still couldn't place it." But at least her voice no longer held that distant, musing tone that had chilled it last night. In fact, she sounded genuinely pleased when I asked her to a show at one of the local experimental theaters.

"So we've got two possibles: one unidentified and one repeat."

"A repeat? You mean Loomis?"

"I don't mean you, partner. He has two contacts with Margaret Haas and his name was in Busey's purse. In sleuth talk, that's a notable coincidence."

"It's not so notable if she was only going to ask him why he was talking to Margaret."

"But we'll never know that for certain, will we?" Bunch asked, "What do you have on the guy?"

"About the same as you do: he was my father's business partner, he's a consultant to and friend of McAllister, and he was Margaret's professor. That seems reason enough for him to keep turning up."

"Sure it does. But suppose you didn't know the guy? Wouldn't you check him out because he's a repeater?"

"Yeah. You're right."

"I'll flip you for it. Heads is Loomis, tails is the car rental."

I said heads and it came up Loomis. Bunch said "Ciao" and headed for the airport and the Efficiency Auto Rental office; my first call was to the private university that housed Loomis's business school. I explained that the *Denver Post* financial editor wanted me to do a story comparing the local business schools and asked the secretary if she would be kind enough to answer a few questions. I underestimated the press's power to tremble the ivied halls; with a breathless eagerness, she quickly turned me over to the dean, a fat voice that hovered around the first person singular and spelled its own name twice. Among the myriad facts, I learned about one of the finest programs of its kind in the state, about one of the finest faculties in the nation, about one of the finest administrations in the world. We approached the galaxy and the universe as I was told that, yes, Professor Loomis was an especially prized member of the faculty and an internationally recognized expert in his field of—and here the dean had to clear his throat—and that he had established very strong relations with the local business community, who often requested his consultation. The professor had been at the institution for several years, coming with the highest recommendations from—the dean believed, no, was certain—Columbia University. To facilitate my interviewing of Professor Loomis or any other of the outstanding faculty, the dean finally turned me over to the secretary who had a list of telephone numbers and office hours and who would be happy to assist in any way possible. And could I give her an idea of when the story would be coming out?

The next call was one of those that had to go through two or three operators and half-a-dozen secretaries before being halted by a female voice of crisp and authoritative officialdom. "Yes, Mr. Kirk. Professor Loomis was on our faculty. He resigned his position four years ago."

"Did you know him?"

"I did."

"Can you tell me something about him? Something I can use to fill in the human-interest side of my story?"

"I would prefer not to."

It seemed Columbia University never heard of the *Denver Post.* Or did I detect a faint aroma of animosity there? "Was he difficult to get along with?"

"I did not say that. In fact, I did not say anything. I do not gossip about faculty members, past or present."

"I see. Did the professor give any reason for his resignation?"

"You would have to ask the dean that. But I'm sorry he's not available."

"Can you tell me of any awards or grants he may have won?"

"You would have to ask the dean about that."

"How about publications while he was there? Or consultantships?"

"You would have to ask the dean that."

"Is this a recording?"

"I beg your pardon?"

"I said I'd like a recording of his triumphs and successes as seen by his peers and students. Can you recommend anyone I should speak with? Besides the dean, that is."

A pause. "Yes, Mr. Kirk, I do believe I can. If this is kept confidential."

"Of course."

"Then you might try Mr. Robert Sharabigian. I believe he works for Computer Electronics over in Newark. Good-bye."

She didn't wait to hear me say good-bye—too emotional a moment, perhaps. The call to directory assistance was even less helpful and left me with the slight suspicion of having been had: Computer Electronics wasn't listed in the greater Newark directory. And there turned out to be thirty-five Sharabigians in the New York region, a tribute to the perseverance of the Armenian nation. Nine of them were named Robert. One had not attended Columbia University, another had never heard of it, and the others either weren't home or weren't answering their telephones. That left me talking to the hearty quack of Percy Ahern, one of the reasons Kirk and Associates was in the plural.

"Devlin! Is it still snowing out there in Indian country, lad?"

"It's almost summer, Perce. We haven't had snow for at least two hours."

"Almost summer! Well for your sake I hope it comes on a long weekend this year. And what is it you want from me besides entertainment and wisdom?"

The only time Percy had flown out to Denver had been a quick trip one July to check on the investment and borrowing records of a creative financier who had purchased a bank in Albany, New York, apparently using the bank's own funds to make the down payment. As his plane landed, one of those heavy mountain storms had blown in and hung low and tattered among the skyscrapers and dropped an inch or two of crunchy snow across the city, to give the seersucker-clad Percy a shock that he never got over.

"I'm doing a background check on a Professor Michael Loomis who was at Columbia business school five years back. The only lead I have is one Robert Sharabigian, and I can't find him. Last address was the Computer Electronics Company in Newark. But it's not listed. Can you help me out?" I spelled all the names and gave him the numbers of the Sharabigians I had not been able to reach.

Percy would do it because I traded off by looking up things for him in this area—he preferred to stay out East where the seasons could be identified—and also because of the touch of nostalgia we shared for our days in the Service. He asked me a few more questions about Loomis and Sharabigian and when we'd finished telling each other about names from the past, he said he would call back as soon as he had something. "It might take a few days. You know how it goes."

The routine work of keeping the agency going ate up the next few hours. I logged in the tax-deductible items before they slipped away into unprovable obscurity, checked the mail with its bills and ads and—more importantly—responses from possible clients, had the satisfaction of tallying and mailing the final bill for the AeroLabs project, and began answering the calls on the recorder. Far down the answering machine's tape was a brief message from Vinny Landrum, "Kirk, give me a call. I got something."

He wasn't at his office, but the telephone clicked forward to the next number and Landrum answered.

"This is Kirk. What do you have?"

"It took you long enough, for Christ's sake. I thought you were so goddamn hot for this stuff."

"I just got your message, Vinny. You were way down at the end of the tape—sort of the story of your life."

"Funny guy. What's it worth?"

"How do I know until I hear it?"

He thought that over. "You said you'd pay a bonus for information. You said that, remember?"

"I remember, Vinny. And if it's any good, I will. Let's hear it."

"It's good. It's something the cops didn't come up with."

"Or perhaps didn't want?"

"It's good! Here it is: on the night that Carrie went up to my office and got herself shot, another female went up there too."

"A woman? With her?"

"No. Alone. Just after Carrie went up the stairs."

"You're sure?"

"Hell yes, I'm sure! I talked to this old guy lives across the alley from the office. A Mr. Svenson, 1650 Pearl. He was sitting on the crapper looking out the bathroom window and he sees her."

"How did he know it wasn't Busey?"

"He didn't know who it was, but she was wearing a tan coat like a raincoat, and a hat that came down around her face. Did Carrie have a hat? Tell me, smart-ass, did Carrie have a hat?"

No, she didn't, and her coat had been a dark, short one. "Why didn't he tell the cops this?"

"They asked him if he saw a woman go up the stairs at about that time. He said he did. But, man, the woman he saw wasn't who the cops were asking about. It was this other one."

"Did he see her face?"

"No, just the light brown coat and hat. That's why

he remembers. The hat. Nobody wears a hat no more."

"What time was it?"

"A couple minutes before seven."

"How's he so certain about the time?"

"He watches this program at seven. He was getting in his after-dinner crap before his program comes on."

That fit the time of death. "He saw her enter your office?"

"He saw her go up the stairs. He can't see my door from that angle, but she didn't come back down. So it figures she went in."

"But he didn't see her come out later?"

"No. He was at the TV. And he didn't think much of it anyway. When the cops asked him if he'd seen a woman go up the stairs at about that time, he said yeah. They thought he meant Carrie, but, man, he meant this other one. I asked him what'd she look like and he told me. I knew, man—that wasn't Carrie. So I went around to this other witness, the one who told the cops she saw Carrie, and had her describe the one she saw and it was Carrie. No hat and that dark jacket she had on. And this other witness figures the time at about quarter to seven. I figure this other one had a meet with Carrie for seven and then offed her."

"That's good work, Vinny."

"I know that, Kirk. I'm a damn good p.i.—the best. Now, what's it worth?"

CHAPTER 14

"I don't know who it was, Devlin. But I was terrified. It was no accident—it was deliberate!" Margaret's voice still had the tense, quivering note of fear and anger that verged on tears.

"Are you all right? The children?"

"Yes, we're all fine, thank God. We had our seatbelts on, and Austin and Shauna were in the back seat. I still don't know how we got out of it."

"You're at the police station now?"

"Yes. The officer said someone would give us a ride home."

"Stay there—I'll be right over."

Margaret's call had caught up with me in the Healy and I angled across the lanes crowded with six o'clock traffic and turned south. What she told me had been fragmented and disjointed, but I pieced it together to understand that a van had forced her car across the road toward incoming traffic on one of the high-speed arteries that sliced through the southeast corner of the city. Somehow she had managed to avoid the cars screaming toward her and skidded across both lanes to spin to a halt on the edge of the road, sitting in almost numb shock and trying to calm the now terrified children. The car's right front wheel was broken and the right side scraped and dented where the van had sideswiped them. It had disappeared somewhere during the frantic seconds she fought the steering wheel, and everything had happened so fast that all she saw was the black wall of steel and the heavily tinted glass of the driver's window.

District Three police headquarters was just off I-25, a flat-roofed, one-story building that had solid white walls and several parking lots scattered around it. One was reserved for visitors, and a walk led around the side of the building to the silvered glass of the main entry. A woman police officer sat behind the chest-high bench and glanced up as I came in; Margaret and the children were at one end of the oblong room.

"How are you doing?"

"Devlin!" She held me tightly and I could feel the quiver still in her body. Austin and Shauna, silent with eyes wide, sat side by side on the chairs drawn up to a small table where Margaret filled out the accident report form.

"You sure you're all right? You checked the children for bumps and bruises?"

"Yes. The officer . . . I was just sitting there—I couldn't believe it—he told me to look them over. They say they're all right and I didn't see anything."

I took a deep breath, suddenly aware of the tight feeling that must have clamped my lungs since Margaret's call. "I'm glad you're safe. All of you."

"We had an accident," said Shauna. "A big one!"

"This truck came right at us. I was scared. Shauna was too—she cried."

"I'd have been scared too." I knelt and wrapped my

arms around both small bodies and held them close for a moment, their warmth like fragile birds against my ribs. "I was scared when I heard about it."

"We were all scared," said Margaret. "And I'm still angry. The more I think about it, the angrier I get!"

I glanced over the long form with its sections for vehicle ownership information, insurance coverage, diagrams, and narratives. "Did the officer give you a ticket?"

"A ticket? What for? That van pushed us across the road—it wasn't my fault, Devlin!"

"I didn't say it was. I only asked if he gave you a ticket."

"No. He just made sure we were all right and brought us here."

"Did you get his name?"

She shook her head. "I've been on the telephone— the insurance company, a tow truck, you. And then filling out this damned form!"

"Mama said another bad word!"

"Okay—finish it up. You guys want a soft drink?"

They glanced at their mother and she nodded. I tumbled some quarters into the machine at the other end of the long room, the lounge end that held a few nondescript and tired-looking seats and couches scattered around a low table. I brought one to Margaret, too, who thanked me and drank as deeply as the kids. They were thirsty from the fright and nervousness, and I could see them relax as they drank. While Margaret finished the narrative, I went to the desk officer, who looked up with an official smile.

"Can you tell me the officer's name who brought in Mrs. Haas and her children?"

"Officer Dean."

"Is he around?"

"He's on patrol. He should be back at the end of the

shift." She glanced at the large clock. "About eleven tonight."

"Do you know of any witnesses to the accident?"

"No, I don't. I haven't seen the report yet."

"How about the black van? Did you put out a pickup on it?"

"We put out an alert."

I gave her one of my cards. "If anything comes in on it, would you call me? Anytime."

She glanced at it, the official pleasantness hardening slightly, and tucked it somewhere under the shelf that formed the top of the bench. "We'll try to remember." She turned back to the mound of paperwork that cluttered her desk. From the dispatcher's office came the steady rattle of radio voices. I went back to Margaret, who was finishing the last section of the form.

By the time we left the police station, the streetlights were just coming on, their glow a part of the sky's lingering twilight and almost invisible. Austin and Shauna, firmly anchored in the jump seat of the Healy, were telling me about their ride in the police car. Margaret sagged, drained now of the nervous energy that had buoyed her. With her head back against the seat, she watched the traffic flicker past.

I had a good idea who had been driving the black van, and between half-aware comments on Austin's story of what he saw in the police cruiser—a radio, a nightstick, even a big gun—I had images of Susan sitting in her fleece-lined wheelchair trying, with the help of a therapist, to recall the names of her friends and family as they went once more through the photograph album that Mrs. Faulk had brought from Des Moines. Now it could as easily be Margaret. Or the children. And it might not be a hospital they were lying in.

It wasn't until we had reached Margaret's home, and Austin and Shauna had buried their recent fright and excitement under the warmth and familiarity of dinner and the evening routine, that Margaret and I had the privacy to talk.

"Can you tell me anything at all about the van?"

"I've told you all that I can remember. It happened so fast, and once he hit us, I was trying to steer the car and all I saw were those other cars coming past us." She drew a shaky breath. "I don't think I had time to be frightened. And then I was too angry to be afraid. Now I'm scared."

"Too late now—it's over with. You missed your chance."

"Oh, Devlin! It's not funny."

"There's no sense dwelling on it, Margaret. It's like a bump in the road—you got past it and it's behind you. There's no sense hitting it over and over again."

"Is that what you do? In your line of work?"

"When it happens. Which isn't often."

She sipped her wine and smiled wearily. "I understand. What I don't understand is why. It was deliberate, Devlin, I know that. He had a clear road and he pulled up and swung over into my car. Not just once, but twice—hard. He was trying to kill us."

"Okay—one last time, and then I want you to forget about it. Just close your eyes and tell me what you see. Try to remember exactly what was there, exactly what happened. Anything and everything—just let your memory go."

She did, and as I listened, I watched her profile with its symmetry, the dark of her lashes pressed toward the smoothness of her cheeks, the fullness of her lips as she spoke, the glimpse of white, even teeth. Her eyes blinked open, feeling my gaze, and the instant of puzzlement in them changed to warmth as she smiled slightly and turned her face to mine. We kissed with a hunger spurred by the knowledge of how close death had been, and fed by the comforting—and then excit-ing—familiarity of our bodies pressing together. When Margaret finally leaned away to search my eyes with her own, she said, "I'm really frightened, Devlin. Why should someone want to kill us? And what if he tries again?"

I had wondered about that, too. What she told me offered nothing new: a black van with tinted windows. She had seen it once or twice in the rearview mirror, hanging back among the cars behind her. But that wasn't unusual and she hadn't made any effort to notice the driver. He was just a blurry figure in the small glass. Then suddenly it was beside the car and lunging at them, hitting solidly to swerve them over the center line.

"I don't think they were after you. I think they were trying to get me through you."

"Like . . . like Susan?"

"Yes."

"What are we going to do, Devlin? Shouldn't we tell the police? Isn't there something we can do to protect ourselves?"

"The police can't do much. They can't provide pro-tection." That was my business. "I know a good man. I want you to have him as a chauffeur and bodyguard."

"A bodyguard? Living here?"

"Just for a little while. The house has a guestroom he can use, right?"

"Yes, but a stranger in my home . . ."

"He's very competent. I've used him before. I'd like to do it myself, but I can't do that and chase the bad guys too."

"What's that mean? Chase the bad guys?"

"Just that. Not to worry." I stroked the long, smooth line of her cheek. "I want you to have protection, Mar-garet. You and the kids. For my sake, too."

"Won't that be expensive?"

"Special rate—won't cost you a thing. I'm the one who brought you the trouble."

"I'm willing to listen to a better idea, Bunch."

Framed by the arch of the office window, he scratched at the short hair curling toward his nape and then turned to look at me. "I want those scumbags, too, Dev. Maybe even more than you do. But too many things could go wrong this way."

"Too much has already gone wrong and we don't have any more time to futz around. We know why Susan's in the hospital. We know who tried to put Margaret and the children there. We don't know who they might try for next if we give them any more time."

"We've already rattled their chain. Through McAllister and Lewellen—the word got to them. Kaffey called us about it, remember?"

"I remember. And we've been sitting on our keesters waiting for something to come of it. What we got was a hit on Margaret. We shouldn't have left the initiative to them. Now we make them come to us only."

"They're not stupid, Dev. They'll figure just like we're figuring—that we've set them up. They'll know what's going on."

"But they'll have to do it anyway. They won't know whether it's true or not, and they can't take the chance." I added, "If we don't do something, they might go after Mrs. Faulk next. It's their style."

Bunch sighed. "All right—so do it."

I picked up the telephone and played the little wheedling tune for the Aegis offices, dialing the number that had been in Haas's desk. A man answered on the first ring with a familiar, "Yeah?"

"Mr. Neeley?"

"Who's this?"

"I have something that'll interest you."

"Like what?"

"Like evidence. Documents that link Austin Haas, the Aegis Corporation, and the Columbine project."

"The hell you do. There's no evidence because there's no link."

"I dialed you direct, Mr. Neeley—I didn't go through the switchboard. You can check it out. I have your private, unlisted number and it came from Haas's papers. I have some other things from those papers, too."

"Who is this?"

"I also have some information on Spilotro. Down in Vegas."

"Who the fuck is this?"

"Not over the phone, Mr. Neeley. Let's meet at Bear Creek Park. At the tennis courts out there." That was the site Bunch and I had discussed, one that offered a lot of visibility in all directions except one—the creek and the bike path—and that's where Bunch would be. I told Neeley what side of the courts and the day and time.

"Why should I meet you? What the hell do you want?"

"Money, Mr. Neeley. A lot of it."

That was a motive Neeley not only understood but didn't argue with. Bunch, listening at the telephone speaker, looked up when the line clicked into a steady buzz. "When you said 'Spilotro,' I thought that sucker was going to crawl through the phone."

"He'll be there."

"Or they will be—those two bastàrds."

"I don't expect them. Not this time."

"Why not?"

"What would you do in his place?"

Bunch nodded. "Find out what cards you were holding first. Then hit you."

"So let's stack the deck." I shuffled through one of the

drawers of the desk and pulled out a small packet of stationery with the McAllister Corporation logo. "What kind of evidence do you think Haas might put away as insurance?"

We spent a few hours thinking up the kind of documentation that an industrial thief might pocket to give himself some protection in case the payoff was held back. Then we checked names and dates and a few topical references, aged and foxed the papers a bit, and ran off Xerox copies of the originals. All together they made a handsome dossier that was close enough to the truth to pass a single reading. Bunch also thought of having a roll of used recording tape labeled "Aegis." With the help of Harry Goodman and his laboratory full of electronic wizardry, we dubbed in fragments of the tapes we had on file, including the last call to Neeley. With the tape of Haas's voice from our earlier taps on his phones, and the bits and pieces of Kaffey and Neeley, we came up with some coherent conversations: " 'It's me, Austin Haas.' 'Yeah?' 'When do we play?' 'I got a tee-off for four on Thursday.' " All together, the conversations weren't much—ninety, at most a hundred and twenty seconds. But we hoped it would be enough. Goodman just hoped it was legal.

"Are you certain you're not going to use this in any evidentiary way?"

"Hey, Prof, no sweat. We just want the guy to think we are. It won't get out of our hands, I swear."

By the time we finished, it was visiting hours at the hospital and we spent time with Susan who, despite her pallor, was regaining some weight. She was starting to remember more and more, too, but there were still those agonizing moments when her memory refused to fish up the word or name and she thumped the arm of her wheelchair in angry frustration. But she was walking some now, making carefully balanced steps along the carpet past the nurses' station where the bright faces smiled with friendly efficiency. The solarium was a favorite place and we spent a lot of time in that luminous room with its glass wall and scattering of green plants that rested the eye from the sterility of the remainder of the wing. Susan, as always, made friends; and among her fellow patients was an elderly woman who smiled through continual pain, and a youngster in his teens who had fallen in love with Susan and whose door was open an anxious crack whenever we walked her down the corridor. It was a separate, insular existence with its own relationships and intensities and special worries and topics. But it was removed from the life that took place outside in the sun, and it was a world into which Margaret and the children could so easily have been pushed. That thought nagged as Bunch and I periodically entered Susan's new world.

That evening, I led Dutch Peterson over to Margaret's. He was a stocky man with a round and slightly pudgy-looking build, not the kind of image that the term "bodyguard" brought to mind. But I had worked with him before and knew how that softness could harden into muscle when it was needed. More important, he was intelligent and quick and reliable—characteristics better than bulk alone. Most important, I trusted him.

Margaret tried to be matter-of-fact when she met us at the door, but she was still nervous and even a little embarrassed at the idea of having a bodyguard. Behind her, Austin and Shauna stared with curiosity at the stranger with the ruddy face and blond mustache who stood with a scuffed cloth suitcase and a garment bag over his shoulder. Margaret had told them they would have a visitor for awhile, but she didn't explain why. "I don't think it would be wise for Austin to tell the other children at preschool that we had a bodyguard." So she said only that Mr. Peterson would be staying for a few days.

They shook hands solemnly and then Margaret led the troop of us to the guestroom.

"This is very nice, Mrs. Haas. Very comfortable."

"Dutch will want to see the rest of the house, too, Margaret."

"Is he going to buy our house, Mama?"

Margaret laughed. "No, Austin. Mr. Peterson's just visiting for awhile." Her glance caught mine. "And we haven't decided whether or not we'll be moving, remember?"

"I want to see Grandpa and Grandma," said Shauna.

"We can see them without selling the house. Where would you like to start, Mr. Peterson?"

Touring the ground floor first, Peterson noted the doors and those windows that could serve as entry. He checked the locks and shook his head at a flimsy pair of french doors that opened from the dining area to the bricked patio outside. "Do you have a dog, Mrs. Haas?"

"Can we get one, Mama?"

"No!"

A dog wasn't a bad idea, and not just for security— kids and dogs went together. If things worked out the way I wanted, maybe Margaret could be talked into a puppy for the kids. A golden lab. One of those big, happy outdoor dogs that Austin could run and wrestle with.

"Could I see the upstairs?" asked Peterson.

"This way."

When the inside tour was over, Dutch and I walked around the house's perimeter.

"It's a big place. A lot of windows and doors."

"There's a residential alarm system that came with the house. It's not worth a damn."

"Right. Cut the phone line and it's dead."

"Suggestions?" I asked.

He ran a knuckle along one wing of his mustache and eyed the shrubbery that provided picturesque support to the artistic swoop of the roofline, and a well-concealed approach to the living-room windows. "We don't want to make them prisoners in their own home. But I'd feel better with a first-rate alarm system. It's not much, but it's something."

"I can get that done."

"Does she have a radio backup for the telephone?"

"You can use my mobile. I'll bring a unit over tomorrow."

"That's good—better than a CB. Do you know the neighbors?" He nodded toward the houses scattered discretely across the large and generally open lots.

"I don't; Margaret does. But I understand everyone stays pretty much to themselves."

"That's good, too. The less traffic to the house, the better." He took a deep breath like a man about to plunge into cold water. "Okay, Dev. Leave it to me."

"She's important to me, Dutch."

"I haven't lost a client yet. I don't aim to start now."

Bunch had a couple items to share when I made it to the office next morning. "That rental car—the one on the gatekeeper's list of license numbers—was leased to a Nora Challis, address: 14820 Alamo Road, Houston, Texas."

"Anything else on her?" I made a note to ask if the name meant anything to Margaret.

"Not yet. I put in a few phone calls and maybe something'll turn up." He glanced at his small notebook. "She rented it on the sixth and turned it in on the fifteenth. Milage, seven-two-eight."

"What time on the fifteenth?"

"Nine ten P.M."

"Busey was killed on the fifteenth. Around seven P.M."

"Yeah. I thought of that. Challis went through the

Belcaro Estates gate on the eleventh, she left on the night Busey was killed. It's possible." He added, "I called that Mr. Svenson—the one who saw another woman. He told me the same thing he told Vinny."

"Did you think Vinny might have lied about it?"

Bunch's shirt wrinked as he lifted his shoulders. "We got any reason to trust him? It checked out, anyway."

"Who'd you talk with in Houston?"

"Nelson."

Nelson Hunt, who retired from DPD five years ago and went to Texas to find a warm climate for his new skip-trace business. He wasn't a member of the oily Hunts, but it was a big family and he let people think what they would about his name. Sometimes they came to the wrong conclusion and it had paid off more than once. "Did you ask him to find out what he could about Challis?"

Bunch nodded. "He said he'd call back when he had something. I also got a call from a buddy down at the impound lot. The traffic division brought in a black van that had been reported stolen a couple weeks ago. It has heavy damage along the left side." He poured himself another cup of coffee from the glass pot and raised his eyebrows to ask me if I wanted some.

I held out my cup for a splash. "Any prints?"

"Too many. Mostly smeared and overlapping. It sat in the lot a long time before they made the connection with the Haas assault. I don't think they're going to get anything from it."

"Where was it stolen?"

"Over at City Park. Some picnickers left the key in it and when they finished their beer and Frisbee, lo— it had disappeared."

"No leads at all, then?"

"Only our well-founded suspicions."

"A stolen car and a hit-and-run—it does sound like a familiar m.o."

We were both thinking about the same thing: the meeting this afternoon with Neeley. The man would probably have someone with him—a driver, perhaps, who also provided muscle. But he had been told to come to the site alone. We'd picked the spot because it was a long, open walk away from the closest parking; and with Bunch a short pistol-shot away hidden in the bushes along the creek, there would not be any way to sneak up on me. I hoped. That part we would have to play as it came, and I could feel the nervousness begin to build in my taut neck and shoulders as I thought about it. Bunch must have felt the same way, because he stretched his back, his spine giving a muffled rattle of pops when he laced his fingers behind his head and pressed. But there was no sense worrying now; things had been set in motion, and time—measured by the tiny pulse of my watch—steadily passed. I made a call to one of the home security companies whose work I trusted and told them exactly what I wanted installed at Margaret's, and how soon. Then I turned to the day's paperwork and tried to focus on it. But I wasn't really successful, and it was a relief when the telephone broke into what could laughingly be called my concentration.

"Devlin, lad, it's Percy. How many feet of snow are you under this fine day?"

"It's barely up to the window, Perce. Of course we're on the second floor."

"Ah, it's not the snow that's piling up, but something else I think. I have some information on your Professor Michael Loomis, late of the hallowed halls of Columbia University. There's a bit of a story about the good professor, one that not too many people wanted to air to old Percy's ear."

I motioned to Bunch and flipped on the phone's speaker and tape recorder. "What'd you find out?"

"It seems the professor was something of an embarrassment to the grand institution, a bit of poison ivy, so to speak, and they were all too happy to give him a fine recommendation to be able to send him on his way to greener pastures. Saved embarrassment all around."

"What kind of embarrassment?"

"Apparently the gentleman used his classes as a means of industrial espionage—something along your line, Dev."

"Espionage?"

"Clever. Ingenious, in fact. Thoroughly admirable technique. It seems that the students in his graduate courses came from a variety of business backgrounds, and most of them were working and attending their classes at night. All Horatio Algers stuffing down the American Dream as promised in the *Wall Street Journal*, and burning the midnight oil in the pursuit of knowledge and self-betterment."

"I understand, Perce—I get the picture. What about Loomis?"

"Patience, Dev—you always were an impetuous lad. To fully understand the beauty of this scam, you have to envision these students: eager to grasp that next rung, anxious to please the good professor, proud of their achievements in the companies they served so well, wanting—in short—to do the best possible work in order to further their bright careers as administrators and managers and ultimately captains of their massive corporations."

"I envision them."

"Good. Now envision the professor: brilliant in his field, witty, very demanding but avuncular nonetheless. And oh so insistent on high-quality and up-to-date research. Insistent that the research be based on the real world—the world, in short, of the students' own occupations."

"He made them raid their companies?"

"Ah-ah—he guided their research, Dev. A pointed question here, a request for amplification and expan-

sion there, a well-done-but-couldn't-we-broaden-it-a-
bit now and then. They did the work for him, and he
picked their corporate brains like a branchful of plums.
Eager, they gave him the secrets of their companies,
and not one of the poor bastards realized what he was
doing. Not one, that is, except for that mad Armenian
you put me onto, Mr. Sharabigian."

"You found him?"

"Not without exercise. But when I did, he was a veri-
table volcano of information about Loomis, spewing
flaming epithets and hot nuggets of information. He
made crystal clear why such an important and busy and
richly successful collection of professors like the Columbia University School of Business was so eager to say
nothing about one of their cohorts. A little mud splashes
a long way, you understand."

"He did a paper for Loomis?"

"And what a paper! He did a market-and-develop-
ment analysis for a new patented formula that his pharmaceutical firm was working on. Sharabigian is a whiz
at computer programming, and he based his paper on
the work he was doing—as his professor requested. But
Professor Loomis didn't like the first draft. Too many
holes in it, he said. Not enough information about the
product in question, he said. Without a clear idea of
what was to be marketed, how could Mr. Sharabigian
design a marketing evaluation and strategy for it, he
said. So Mr. Sharabigian gave him more. And then
more. And before he could say diddly-squat, his firm
had lost its market because some Swiss pharmaceutical
outfit announced the sale of exactly the same product."

"Loomis stole it?"

"Sharabigian swears to it. Loomis, of course, swears
he didn't. Was very offended at the accusation, in fact,
and had Mr. Sharabigian dismissed from the university
on charges of moral turpitude. Nice touch, that. However, a decent period after all that died down, Professor

Loomis announced his resignation from the faculty to pursue more lucrative fields elsewhere—out West, where all our crooks flee to start their new lives."

"Did you find a link between Loomis and the Swiss firm?"

"I haven't, no. That would take a lot of time and not a little expense, Dev. Right now, Sharabigian's old company—he was fired by the pharmaceutical people and went to work for a computer firm that proceeded to go bust—and the Swiss company are fighting over the patent claims. Something might come out of that for you but it will take years. And most likely it'll be settled out of court anyway; all drug companies have skeletons that they prefer not to dangle in the public eye of the courtroom. But I did manage to get the names of some other students of Loomis from that secretary you talked to. She has a very harsh tongue, by the way. I wonder if she's related to my mother-in-law?"

"Did you talk to them?"

"A dozen or so. And two others had similar experiences, but it wasn't until I mentioned the papers they did for Loomis that the parts fell together in their little brains. They had been robbed and didn't even know it, and their companies had spent thousands looking for the industrial spy who somehow got the goodies. Needless to say, there were a few red faces and some very worried young executives who were eager that I not pursue the topic further."

I thanked Percy and offered to reimburse him for any expense. But he called it even for a favor I did him earlier. When the line clicked silent, I looked at Bunch, who stared back at me.

"What the hell do we have here, Dev?"

"A man who's not all he seems."

"Or more than he seems. Loomis . . . Busey . . . Haas. It makes a neat triangle, doesn't it?"

I picked up the telephone and called McAllister's

direct line. His personal secretary asked me to hold on while she found out if Mr. McAllister was available. A few seconds later, the strong, brusque voice barked hello. "What do you have, Kirk?"

"I'd like to ask you some questions about Professor Loomis, sir."

"Mike? What for?"

"Some background information. I don't know how relevant it might be."

"All right. But make it quick—I've got a plane waiting."

"How long have you known him?"

"About . . . four years now, I guess. I brought him in as a consultant in . . . May, four years ago. May seventh."

"Did he have anything to do with the Columbine or Lake Park projects?"

"He did a projection on their short-term market potential. His specialty's short-term growth analysis."

"Did he have access to the detailed plans?"

"No. Just the final numbers. That's all he needed for his work. What is this, Kirk? What are you fishing for?"

"Just a few more questions, sir. Was he good friends with Austin Haas?"

"They saw each other socially. He was Margaret's professor one time back in New York, I believe."

"Have you ever had occasion to be suspicious of the professor?"

"What?"

"Is it possible that he and Austin Haas worked together to get the plans to Aegis?"

"Hell no! What the hell are you trying to say, Kirk?"

"His name was found in Carrie Busey's purse, Mr. McAllister. I ran a routine check on him and found that he had been forced to resign from Columbia University because he was suspected of stealing corporate secrets from the papers his graduate students were writing for his classes. That's what's behind my questions."

There was a long silence and when McAllister finally spoke, his voice was low and taut with anger. "I know goddamned well what's behind your questions, Kirk. You don't like Loomis because you think he stole your father's business. He told me all about that before he even brought you to me. And he told me about his name being in Busey's purse, too. And, by God, he even told me about leaving Columbia because he felt the administration did not do enough to support him against some kind of accusation from a disgruntled student. He didn't know why his name was in Busey's purse, and I believe him. And I also believe he wouldn't have his present position in the school of business if there was the slightest chance those old accusations were true. Those people over there aren't fools, Kirk; they're businessmen. And I'm no fool either. Now, by God, I won't put up with anyone—you included—besmirching a man's reputation with slanted questions and innuendo. You think I can't judge a man? You think Mike or anyone else could blind-side me and I wouldn't see through it? I wouldn't be where the hell I am today if I was a pushover like that! By God, you've got another think coming, and here's something else you've got coming: you're fired. Your check will be in the mail for your services up to this second. Because as of now you are fired!"

"Devlin," sighed Bunch, "we've got to improve our customer relations."

Fired or not, we had Neeley to worry about now. Bunch and I drove slowly toward the west side of town where the long, narrow green of Bear Creek Park wound for miles between two major highways that flanked the small stream. On the north side was one of Denver's sprawling residential areas, block after block of single homes with their patches of front yard cushioning them from the streets. On the south, the suburbs of Bow Mar and Lakewood and even parts of unincorporated Jefferson County held the same kinds of houses and shopping centers and schools and churches. In the distance, the snow that highlighted the ragged skyline of the Front Range was shifting from glaring white to softer blue as the westering sun shadowed the steep faces of the peaks. And over all—the mountains, the distant rows of homes whose roofs followed the rolling prairie, the billows of low trees along the creek, and the green of the park's evenly mown grass—arced a clear blue sky that seemed both a short reach away and eternally deep. All in all, it wasn't the kind of setting one thought of for meeting with a potential murderer.

CHAPTER 15

I sat at one of the concrete picnic tables scattered across the field. From somewhere beyond the high, green-tinted mesh surrounding the tennis courts came the hard ping of rackets and the scuff and squeak of tennis shoes pacing one of those cerebral games that substituted a lot of lobs and corner shots for a strong serve. The unseen players were serious, too, because the only other sounds were "long" or "net" or "out" without any of the howls or laughter that accompanies a light-hearted game. In fact, I could feel the tension of the combatants in the long, ping-filled silences between calls. Or perhaps I was just projecting the tension I felt while I sat and idly traced the initials carved into the table's planks, and thought how nice it would be to run and sweat and worry only about reaching a spinning ball before it touched earth for the second time.

Across the asphalt bike path, a thick screen of brush marked the creek, and, here and there, the bushes

opened to muddy paths that led to the water, a shallow
and mild turmoil over its rocky bed. Bunch was somewhere in there, a pair of binoculars and self-powered
shotgun mike aimed at me. I had let him off a block
away and pulled slowly into the almost empty parking
lot by myself. Then, unhurried, I strolled around the
area, gave an eye to the few possible places a man could
hide, and looked to see if the tennis players seemed
honest about their purpose. Finally I meandered over
to the bench and settled at the table where I talked to
myself in a conversational voice and gave Bunch a
chance to test and adjust the mike against the screens
of the tennis courts that—we hoped—would block out
any background noise from the distant highway. And
now, listening to that game echo around the other vacant courts, I waited.

At precisely two minutes to the hour, a gray car
cruised slowly through the lot, paused, then just as
slowly pulled out again. The hour passed. Five after,
and I began to feel the hardness of the bench numb my
backside, while the warmth of early afternoon sun nib-
bled into my shoulders. At almost ten after, the same
car swung in again, this time purposefully, and a distant
figure got out to leave the vehicle empty. Neeley had
not brought the two thugs with him. And, as the man
came briskly toward me, I saw that Neeley had not
even brought himself. Instead it was Kaffey, whose
balding head glinted as he lifted his hat to rub at it with
a handkerchief.

"Kirk. We figured."

"Mister Neeley couldn't make it?"

"He could have if he wanted to. Now what's this
about you have . . . ?"

I lifted the briefcase from under the table. "Sit
down."

"You stand up first. I want to make sure . . ."

"Check my ears? Fingernails?" I stood while he

quickly patted me down. "A sad indication of your deep
distrust of human nature, Mr. Kaffey."

"It pays to be cautious. You don't carry a . . . ?"

"A weapon? Not if I don't have to. And certainly not
among gentlemen." Besides, a well-armed Bunch was
listening in.

"Right. They're a real pain." He ran his hands down
my hips and legs. When he was finished he gestured me
to sit and open the briefcase. "I want to make sure
you're not wired. You know: we keep things . . ."

"Confidential. I know. Who can hear us? Look
around."

"Right. It's a nice place. Now, you got . . . ?"

I opened the briefcase and he saw the portable tape
recorder among the papers.

"What's that?"

"A tape recorder. But it's for playing, not listening."
I set it on the table so he could see it wasn't turned on.
"It's some of the merchandise."

"All right. Let's . . ."

I handed him the Xeroxed pages that Bunch and I
had put together as a reconstruction of Haas's dealings
with Aegis. We had, I thought, done a pretty good job
in collating the dates of "tee-off" times in Haas's appointment book with entries in a newly invented diary.
We even had a couple of bogus memos requesting parts
of the Columbine and Lake Park files from the documents section, as well as a complete set of the plans on
disk, compliments of our late employer. Another document accompanying the disks held cryptic but suspicious notes outlining exactly what changes should be
factored into the violated plans.

Kaffey read them over quickly, scanning the papers
as if he were familiar with most of them and spending
more time on the personal notes that Haas might have
written if he'd had the foresight. Then he looked up.
"What's on the . . . ?"

I pressed the Play switch and Kaffey heard himself say hello followed by Haas spliced in and then his own answer. It was a voice from the past that seemed long ago now—a ghost that, as Bunch had once said, wouldn't stay buried; and for all his stony lack of expression, Kaffey was startled to hear it. I gave him the few more seconds of tape that included Neeley's voice spliced with Haas's, and then clicked it off and smiled. "There's a lot more, but that'll give you the idea. No sense boring you with the whole sordid tale."

The man chewed his lip for a long minute and stared sightlessly at the papers he still held. "None of this means shit, you know. In court, this stuff couldn't . . ."

"Maybe it couldn't, maybe it could. It's always a gamble to go to court, isn't it? Think about it, Mr. Kaffey— the strange coincidence of Aegis corporation's plans being almost exactly like the McAllister plans. Except for that little accounting discrepancy, of course—the one noted in Haas's files and dated before its discovery. And tapes of the voices of Haas and two chief executives of Aegis on their private, unlisted lines. And a suicide, of course, for heretofore undiscovered reasons. A judge might think it probable cause for a hearing. And you know how crowded the dockets are these days; it would take a long time to come to trial. In the meantime, the Aegis Group would get a lot of publicity over it. A lot. The kind Mr. Spilotro would not like."

"We never heard of . . . ," he said, but the response was automatic because his mind was on something else. "All right, just for discussion. This shake-down—how much?"

"Half a million."

"What?"

"Five hundred thousand."

He stared at me with his mouth open and his lips began to work around some unheard word, and for once his sentence trailed off at the front, " . . . crazy?"

"It could have been a lot cheaper except for the shit you've pulled, Kaffey. Those two gumballs you sent after me—running down women with cars, pushing one off the road with her kids in the car. That doubled the price, Kaffey, and if it happens again, there's no price you can pay."

". . . out of your mind!"

I took the papers from his shocked fingers and put them in the briefcase with the tape player and snapped its locks with two sharp clicks. "McAllister doesn't know about these yet. But if he finds out, it's a court case for sure."

"You said something about this guy Spilotro. You said you had something about him."

"That was just to get your attention, Kaffey. I'll let you worry about how I got his name."

He stood, frowning, and started to leave, then turned back. "What road? What kids?"

"You know what I'm talking about. And that's the price. Just think of it as overhead for the cost of your way of doing business."

"I got to talk to . . ."

"Better make it soon."

Bunch set his equipment on the back seat and, scraping mud from his shoes onto the park grass, slid in beside me. "It sounded like he bought it."

"It looked like it, too. You should have seen the bastard's eyes."

"I tried. But I didn't want to make too much noise. Muddier than hell along that creek. How come you always get the dry spots and I get the mud?"

"Evolution."

"Yeah? Well I'd like to get my primordial fingers around somebody's throat. Did you hear him ask 'What kids?' "

"I heard."

"He really choked when you said half a million."

"So will Neeley. They were thinking a few thousand —ten at most. Now they have no choice but to come after us."

Bunch cracked his knuckles. "I know."

At the office, I called Margaret to see how she was doing, and before hanging up asked to speak to Dutch. "Everything quiet?"

"The way I like it, Dev."

"Has the alarm company come out yet?"

"No. But they called to find out what time we'd be home this afternoon."

"All right. If he's not there by four, give me a ring and I'll get on them." I told him as much as he needed to know about the possibility of people wanting to do nasty things to Bunch and me. "Don't make any unnecessary trips for the next few days, and if there's anything at all suspicious, don't take a chance."

"Got you. You going to come by?"

"When I can. But if you need help, call. I'll get there." I hung up, a bit more comfortable knowing that Dutch was with Margaret and was forewarned. The next call was another try at reaching Loomis. But like the earlier times, the telephone rang unanswered.

Bunch prowled restlessly from the door to the large domed window spilling light into the office. "You should have told Kaffey he had only twenty-four hours. I don't like this waiting."

"We put him in a bind. He'll need time to talk it over with the big boys and figure out which way to go."

"Yeah, I know. But—" He paused, listening. "Somebody's outside the door."

Through the frosted glass I could see a hazy figure poised as if listening. Bunch moved quickly to the wall beside the door and I sank down slowly behind the thick wood of the desk. The knob turned and swung in and a moment later Vincent Landrum's face came around the frame. "What, you sleeping under the desk?"

"Just dropped a pencil, Vinny." I slid my pistol back into the holster that rode awkwardly on my kidney. "What brings you out in the daylight?"

"I like you, too, Kirk. That's why I'm going to do you a favor."

Bunch, holstering his weapon, came silently from behind the door to Landrum's back. "What's it cost?"

"Jesus, I hate it when you're off the leash, Bunchcroft. What the hell's with you guys? You act like you're waiting for the Indians to attack." He looked from Bunch to me. "Somebody finally catch up with you?"

"What's this favor you want to do us?"

"I don't know if I should. I come in here trying to do something for you guys and I get handed all this shit."

"You're used to it by now, Vinny. Like I said, how much?"

"It's worth something, Homer. It sure as hell is. You guys screw up my business and then toss a few peanuts my way when I come up with stuff that neither one of you could find out. And now I'm getting bad publicity about Carrie. Yesterday the goddamn newspapers said whose office she was found in. You're damned right it's worth something."

"If it is, you'll get something. What is it?"

"I got a call from somebody you know. This Professor Loomis. He's the guy whose name was in Carrie's purse, remember?"

"I remember. What did he want?"

"Anything I could tell him about Carrie. And about why she hired me. The guy was sweating, literally. I could hear it over the phone. He wanted to know everything about her—who her friends were, who she talked to. Everything."

"When?"

"Last night. I got this call at the office and at first I thought it's some guy selling insurance or something. Then he starts asking me about Carrie. When I told him I'd found a suspect, he just about shit."

"You told him that?"

"Well, I told him I'd come up with a good lead, yeah. Something nobody else has been able to dig up—the cops, nobody."

"And?"

"And he wanted to know who it was. I told him it was confidential."

"So he didn't find out we were looking for a woman?"

"I know how to keep my mouth shut, Kirk."

"That means he didn't offer you any money for it," said Bunch.

"Listen, I'm doing you a favor. You're not doing me one. I don't have to take your crap."

Loomis again. Suddenly, and in some way I hadn't expected, things seemed to be converging, and there at the point of convergence was not Aegis but Loomis. "Maybe we'd better call on the professor, Bunch."

"You think that's a good idea right now?"

"Why not? What are you guys covering up?"

"Out, pissant."

"Cut it! Get your goddamn paws off me, Bunchcroft!" The man's red face bobbed up over Bunch's shoulder. "Pay me, Kirk—damn it, Bunchcroft, wait a minute! I brought you something, Kirk—you owe me!"

"I'll send a check."

"How much?"

The door slammed on the writhing figure and I heard the iron steps clang heavily as something rattled on them. Then Bunch, his breath a pinched hiss through his broken nose, came back in. "I just took out the garbage."

"You should have wrapped it first." I finished dialing and a few seconds later the voice at my ear was saying that Professor Loomis wasn't at the university and that his classes had been canceled.

"Is he ill?"

"He was called out of town on an emergency."

"Can you tell me when he's expected back?"

"I'm sorry I can't. He telephoned this morning to cancel classes for the rest of the week. That's all I know."

I thanked her and settled the receiver in its cradle. "Let's go by his house."

We checked the car for tampering before getting in —a routine precaution against a routine style of greeting from people with Las Vegas connections—and caught the Valley Highway south to University Park and a brick and timber two-story that featured English cottage design. It was the kind of home one imagined a professor would live in, stately in a quiet way and private with its yard full of shrubbery and trees.

A rolled-up newspaper lay in the driveway as we pulled up the gravel strip to a porte-cochère and an open and empty garage beyond. Bunch walked to the back of the house while I went up the two wide brick stairs and rapped on the door arched beneath its concrete Gothic tracery. My knuckles made a pecking noise on the solid wood and I waited, trying to hear the sound of feet inside. Nothing. Invisible behind the shrubbery next door, a neighbor's dog continued to bark loudly at us, and on the other side of the yard, a car pulled slowly out of a driveway hidden behind a tall hedge. I rapped again. An answering rattle came from a chain behind the door and a moment later the latch clicked. The door swung back to show Bunch. "The place is ours."

"Was the back door open?"

"Almost." He folded his lock pick and dropped it in a pocket. "My guess is he's gone for good."

We wandered through the vacant rooms. In the

kitchen, dirty dishes half filled the washer, and the scraps of a hasty breakfast sat on a plate in the sink. The refrigerator held the usual collection of milk and vegetables and open cans that a single diner saved from one meal to the next. Upstairs, a towel lay on the floor of the master bedroom where the bed was tossed unmade and a clock radio glowed. The closets were half empty; the only clothes left were an overcoat and a couple of dark suits, as well as a number of shirts, slacks, and ties. In the bureau drawers, we found some sweaters, half a dozen pairs of socks, some underwear and handkerchiefs. The shelves of the bathroom cabinet were scraped clean, all the toiletries gone. Downstairs, in the study with its bay window opening into a small garden, the desk's contents had been cleaned from a couple of drawers and the others held the usual detritus of life's routines: bills to be paid, notes and documents for classes, correspondence, advertisements that for some reason had been kept.

"He was in a hurry, but it was planned," said Bunch. "If he'd panicked, this crap would be thrown all over hell and gone."

There was nothing among the papers and correspondence that dealt with Aegis or McAllister or, most important, personal finances. Checks, bankbooks, statements, all the expected signs of business transactions had been taken. That was, apparently, one aspect of his life he did not want to leave for inspection.

The rest of the house—other bedrooms and downstairs bath—was neat and generally unused. The living room had a scattering of financial periodicals and a week-old collection of the *Wall Street Journal,* as well as yesterday's *Denver Post* and *Rocky Mountain News.* The *News* lay open to an inside page and a small item in a lower corner that said "Murdered Woman Identified" and summarized the Carrie Busey case. It was the first article to identify the detective agency where she had been found, and that was how Loomis got Landrum's name.

I heard an electronic squiggle and turned to see Bunch rewinding the tape on the answering machine that sat beside the telephone.

"He forgot to erase this."

Bunch clicked the Play switch and, after a few hums and toots, the telephone computer's voice said, "If you'd like to make a call, please hang up and try again. If you need help, please hang up and dial your op—" The tape fell into scratchy emptiness and Bunch nudged the Fast Forward until he heard a garble of a voice and then reversed to pick it up from the first. Again it was the telephone voice starting to offer advice and then cut off as the leader ran out. Then another and still more. "Somebody wanted the prof pretty bad."

Finally Bunch reached a variation: "Loomis, it's me. I know you're there. You call me as soon as you hear this."

Beyond that, a few more squawks of computer voice, then a fragment of a woman's voice that had been partially run over by a later unanswered call: ". . . as soon as you can." Followed by the hiss of empty tape.

Bunch reversed the tape to the man's message and listened intently to it again. "Dev, that's Neeley."

"You're sure?" It was too brief, too twisted by the speaker for me to hear the things Bunch noticed.

"I've listened to him enough times. We can check it with Doc Goodman, but he's going to tell you the same damn thing: that's Neeley's voice. I know it." Snapping the cassette from the answering machine, he wagged it at me like a stubby ruler. "Loomis and Haas. Both of them tied to Neeley. They were both in on it, Dev—the son-of-a-bitch was doing his thing just like he did in New York: stealing corporate secrets."

To judge from the many unanswered calls that preceded it on the tape, Neeley—or someone, or a lot of someones—had been trying urgently to get a reply. "I can guess why Neeley wants to talk to him."

"To ask about us? To find out if Loomis is working with us to shake him down?"

"Maybe even to make sure he won't be able to."

Bunch gazed around the room with its lifeless scatter of magazines and books. "I think he skipped before Neeley could get him. He took too much with him."

I nodded, still hearing the echo of both of those voices on the tape. "My guess is the airport."

"With a different name. He wouldn't want Neeley following him. Or anyone else."

"We have that picture—the one Vinny took of him and Margaret talking. Stan can blow it up for us."

"Let's do it."

"You want just the man's face?" Stan Hupp, senior partner of Hupp and Twomey Photo Labs, Inc., adjusted the magnifier so that the negative swelled to picture only Loomis against the screen inside the bottom of the cramped hood.

"How tight can you make it and still have a clear picture?"

"That's about it. That okay?"

I stared at the face with its mouth open in speech. The magnification had caused the picture to become grainy, but the features were still identifiable. "It'll have to do."

With a set of glossy and still-damp prints, Bunch and I headed over to Stapleton Airport. It was possible that Loomis would have driven wherever he was headed, but my hunch told me he flew, and for good reasons. For one thing, he had been selective about what he took from his home—enough to fill maybe two suitcases rather than a whole car. For another, his Audi Quattro had license plates, and Bunch had already managed to

get the number on the wanted file that went out to the
Colorado Highway Patrol and to neighboring states.
And finally, I figured that if Neeley was after Loomis,
the professor wanted to cover as much distance as he
could in the shortest time possible.

"You think Loomis knew something about Busey?
You think that's why he ran?"

I pulled the ticket from the machine guarding the
airport parking ramp and the arm lifted to let us speed
up the concrete lane. "I think so. I think he and Busey
and Haas were all in this together. Now he's the only
one left alive and all of a sudden he's getting phone calls
from Neeley. If Loomis does know where the Aegis
payoff is stashed, or if Neeley thinks he's working with
us to shake him down, Loomis has a right to be worried."

"That's really funny, Dev. We shake the tree for the
scumbag boys, and one fat professor falls out. Birds of
a feather all on the same branch." Bunch grinned,
pleased at his metaphor. "Not all that bad for a cowboy,
right?"

"Not for one cowboy, anyway." I swung the car into
a dimly lit slot under the garage's low concrete sky.
Among the regularly spaced piers reaching up to the
next level, caged bulbs shone dully and glinted on the
domes of parked cars. Somewhere in the shadows tires
squealed on a ramp as Bunch and I hustled toward the
glassed bridge that crossed to the airport and its ticket
booths.

"I'll start at the south end." Bunch strode off the
slowly moving belt that carried us through the almost
deserted hallways. In the evenings or on a weekend, or
during ski season, the concourses would be jammed
with people and their luggage. But at this hour, before
the afternoon flights from both coasts began to stack up
in the approach paths, only a few travelers strayed
down the carpeted hall.

"See you at the escalator."

There were maybe thirty airline counters, including the commuters, and some of them did double duty by selling tickets for sister lines. But the question was the same for all of them: Did this man buy a ticket this morning? Ask each person behind the desk and make sure to include anyone on a coffee break. Occasionally someone would ask if I was police, and I'd flash my p.i. identification, but usually they just looked at the photo and shook their heads. I had hoped to get lucky at one of the big carriers, those that had direct flights to New York where Loomis had lived before coming to Colorado, but their answer was as negative as the others, and I was two-thirds down my half of the counters and hoping Bunch was having better luck when a large hand wrapped around my arm. Bunch's excited voice said, "Dev—I got him. He went out on United this morning. Ten o'clock flight to Mexico City."

"Mexico? You're sure?"

"No question about it—they remembered him. He came in at the last minute and booked for a no-show. He gave them a Canadian passport in the name of Edward Holtzmann and paid cash."

"Mexico." Or farther down. Someplace in South America that had no extradition.

"The plane stops in Houston and then goes straight to Mexico City. He didn't have a connecting flight, but he could get one there."

"Nora Challis. . . . Doesn't she live in Houston?" I glanced at my watch. If the plane was on time, he would now be somewhere over the Gulf of Mexico lounging back against the seat and sipping a glass of wine. Smiling, probably, as he thought about his unanswered telephone still ringing.

"Let's see if Nelson's found out anything yet."

At a pay phone, Bunch—his shoulders blocking the two adjoining booths—jabbed at the numbers for our office code and then for the Nelson Hunt Agency. After a series of rings he nodded at me and spoke into the mouthpiece. "Nellie? This is Bunch. Did you get anything on that female we asked about? Nora Challis?"

I watched while Bunch grunted answers and nodded as if the man on the other end of the line could see him.

"And that's it? Nothing else on her at all? Hang on a minute." He covered the mouthpiece. "He says she's clean. No record of arrests, no credit problems, nothing in the automobile files."

"Is she married? Single?"

Bunch asked the questions and then told me the answers. "Single. She's a sales rep for an encyclopedia company out of Chicago. He didn't get any closer than that because he didn't know if we wanted him to."

"Can he find out if Loomis got off the plane in Houston or if she got on?"

"Nellie? One more favor." Bunch explained it. "Yeah. United from Denver to Mexico City this morning." He gave him the flight number and our thanks and hung up. "He'll call our office as soon as he finds out."

"Okay." I dropped a quarter into one of the three telephones that Bunch vacated and dialed Margaret's number. She answered on the third ring, slightly breathless. "It's Devlin. How are you and Dutch getting along?"

"Fine. Actually, I don't see much of him. He's working outside in the yard right now—he said he feels stale unless he gets some exercise."

And he could keep a better eye on the neighborhood that way, as well. "Do you know a Nora Challis?"

"Challis? No, I can't place the name."

"She's the one who visited you in the rental car—on the eleventh."

The line was silent for a few breaths. Then, "Miss Challis! That was her name!"

"Whose name?"

"The encyclopedia salesman—saleswoman. I sent in one of those cards for information on a set of encyclopedias for Austin and Shauna. And then she showed up."

"She was selling encyclopedias?"

"Yes! I'd forgotten all about that—she came to the door and told me who she was and I told her I'd changed my mind and didn't want to see any samples. I was a bit irritated—they advertised that no salesman would call. I suppose technically they were right—it was a woman. But I remember being not at all certain that I wanted encyclopedias anyway, just a little more information. And then when the salesperson showed up I just said no thank you and closed the door." She asked, "Is it important?"

"I'm not sure. But your information fits what we have from Houston."

"Houston?"

"That's where she lives. That's why she had a rental car. Colorado's probably part of her sales territory."

"I'm sorry it's nothing more earth-shaking. But it completely slipped my mind."

"It still may turn out to be important if she's tied to Loomis. Or to Carrie Busey."

"Tied how?"

I wasn't sure how much she really wanted to know. Her husband's suicide was almost a year old by now, but the scar was, I knew, still tender. And here I was leading her to pick at the scab.

"How, Devlin? How do you mean they're tied?"

"May be tied. Just a distant possibility."

"I don't understand. And I want to."

"I think Loomis was involved with your husband in selling McAllister's plans to Aegis. He did the same thing back in New York, at Columbia. And I've found evidence tying him to one of Aegis's executives."

"My God!"

"You didn't hear of anything like that when you were his student?"

"No—and I'm not sure I believe it now. Are you certain, Devlin? Something like that—even a rumor—could ruin the man's life."

"There's not enough for a court case. But I'm certain."

"But . . . I mean—are you really sure you're being objective?"

"Because of my father?"

"Yes."

"I have evidence, Margaret. It has nothing to do with my father. I think the man ingratiated himself with your husband, made the proposition to him, and served as the go-between with Aegis."

"That means . . . that means I helped cause it. It was through me that he met Austin."

"Did you know what he was up to at Columbia?"

"Of course not!"

"Then don't blame yourself for his faults. Or your husband's. You trusted him and it turned out that he's a hypocrite and a thief. That's his responsibility, Margaret. Not yours."

"Yes. Of course. But it still makes me feel . . . an unwitting accomplice or something."

"You're not, and that's all there is to it. You dared to trust him—you dared to take him for what he said he was. It's the kind of daring my father used to say made the world worth living in."

"I . . . I suppose that's true. It's good to trust. And to love. But it's not so good when that's betrayed."

"But the betrayal doesn't diminish the quality of love and trust. Just of the person who betrayed it."

"Yes." The line was silent and I thought her mind was on her husband. But apparently it wasn't. "Then that explains where the payoff money is."

"You keep thinking like that, and I'll make you an associate in the firm. That's the way I see it, too: your husband's death came before he and Loomis split the money and Loomis kept it all. That's probably what he used to skip with. That and whatever else he had socked away from his other deals."

"Skip? You mean he's gone?"

"Last seen this A.M. heading for Mexico. In haste."

"Oh, my God . . . then it is true. All this you're telling me really is true!"

I could sense some of the remaining props of her familiar world melt and collapse. She'd heard what I'd been telling her, but it had not yet reached the center of belief. Now she believed. And once again the outside world was suddenly as unyielding as a flash of icy light, or a raw stench, or a heavy, cold stone. "It's true, Margaret."

"Of course it is. I'm sorry. It's just so shocking—it has so many implications."

"Not for you to be upset over. The man's gone, and I doubt that we'll be able to find him. Latin America's a big place, and a safe one for a man with that much money."

"Why do you want to find him?"

"For what he knows about Aegis. With him, McAllister could have a strong case against them. And I still think Loomis knows something about Busey's death."

"I thought you were off that."

"McAllister reduced our incentive, he sure did. But the woman's dead, and Loomis might be a link of some kind."

"You should let him go. Let him run and hide for the rest of his life—he deserves it!"

"He won't hide forever. When things simmer down, he'll come back to the States and get a new job. He'll con the university into giving him a clean record—

temporary insanity or a nervous breakdown—and they'll do it. And he'll start all over again."

"That's the university's worry—it's not yours or ours. Just let him go!"

"Hey, take it easy. There's not much I can do about it anyway."

"I'm sorry, Devlin. I'm just so disappointed—in him, in Austin. In myself for being so blind to what he was."

"He fooled a lot of people who trusted him, Margaret. It's nothing to blame yourself for."

We talked for another minute or two and I promised to come by as soon as I could. And I made her promise to stay where Dutch could keep an eye on them. When I hung up, Bunch was moving restlessly between the plate-glass windows that overlooked the increasing number of cars and limousines and vans that had begun to arrive for the afternoon flights.

"Visiting hours started about twenty minutes ago," he said. "I'd like to swing by the hospital before we head for the office."

"What the hell are you waiting for?"

The message on the office answering machine was terse and to the point. "Kirk, it's McAllister. I had an appointment with Loomis and he didn't show. Nobody knows where he is. You call me and tell me what the hell's going on."

"Maybe he'll put us back on the payroll again." Bunch poured a cup of coffee from the Silex pot and sniffed it gingerly. "I think we left this on too long."

"Just since yesterday." I dialed McAllister's private number and his secretary put me through immediately. "Well, Kirk? What can you tell me?"

I told him.

"Mexico? The son-of-a-bitch ran to Mexico?"

"Or points south. Under a different name and with a Canadian passport."

"I'll be damned. I'll be double-damned!" I could hear the hiss of McAllister's disgusted breath. "I suppose I should offer you an apology."

"Accepted."

"I said I should offer it, I didn't say I'd do it!" He added, "But I do." Then, "Do you have enough for a case against Aegis? Can we tie those bastards up in court?"

"Only if we get Loomis to testify. But I don't think he would even if we find him."

"I'll drop every charge against him. It's the bastards behind him that I want."

"They're the ones he's afraid of, not the law. He's worth a lot more to them dead than alive, now."

McAllister pondered that. "You think they would do it? Kill him?"

"Yes, sir. I do." I told him what I'd learned about Aegis.

"Good Lord. They have to be stopped."

"They haven't broken any laws that we can prove. So far, they're more or less legitimate businessmen."

"That galls!"

"If it makes you feel any better, the police have been notified about them and their connections. I think they'll make what they can out of the construction rip-offs and then sell off the projects or claim Chapter Eleven. The FBI, IRS, local police agencies—they'll all be camped on their doorstep if they stay."

"That does make me feel a little better. But the bastards should be behind bars—and they would be if it wasn't for the damned left-wing courts. Damned liberals soft on crime!" He sighed heavily. "Well, the older I get, the more limitations I seem to discover. As for Loomis, what the hell—let him go. I don't want anyone else dead because of this mess. Let him enjoy. . . . Cabo San Lucas! By God, that's where the bastard is: Los Cabos!"

"How do you know?"

"Two years—hell almost three years ago, now—we were talking deep-sea fishing. He mentioned he had a *finca* on the Mexican coast and that he could walk to the harbor where the charter boats docked. I asked him where it was and he said Cabo San Lucas!"

CHAPTER 16

The trip to Cabo San Lucas by Mexicana Air takes about three hours, and I was lucky enough to get the last single seat on a flight crowded with grinning tourists eagerly drinking the complimentary margaritas. The several fishing villages that make up the cape's scattered population form patches of dusty green at the tip of the thousand-mile finger of rocky waste that's the Baja California peninsula. The towns had been there for centuries, clinging like whelks to the meager subsistence that the sea and rocks provided, and much of the population was the offspring of pirates who had sheltered in the lee of barren, guano-streaked rocks to dart out and strike the Spanish ships that cruised the Pacific coast from Chile north, or that lumbered across the central Pacific to the isthmus with the riches of the Philippines in their holds. Now it was a newly discovered tourist mecca, but the ancient tradition of piracy was still alive in the fleets of drug runners who moored their glistening yachts in the small harbor behind the Arch and lounged in the sun while counting their money. Loomis would be right at home.

It was a long shot, but McAllister had insisted—putting us back on the payroll with a joke about having his accountant work overtime to fire us so he could hurry up and rehire us. It wouldn't take more than a day to be certain, and the chance to get Loomis was worth that. Make the offer, McAllister told me; find the man and make the offer.

Through the quivering window on one side of the plane, the flat, dead-looking waters of the Sea of Cortez gradually gained life, rippling like wrinkled aluminum foil with the Pacific surges that rolled into the sea's mouth from Tahiti or China. Through the other window, when the plane finally banked for its landing, the earth was a brown tumult scarred here and there by patches of gray green crops and meandering lines of arroyos that hid a little moisture from the tropic sun. On the steep glide down toward the new airport's single strip of black asphalt, I could see the small houses scattered among palm thickets and stiff cactus and linked by webs of unpaved roads and meandering dirt trails. As I bounced on the broken springs of the creaking taxi that carried me the thirty or so miles to the town of Cabo San Lucas, I glimpsed boxlike houses nestled in the saguaro and cholla and, occasionally, the sudden luxuriant green of carefully tended gardens and palm trees that marked hotels perched at the edge of the sea.

The territory of Baja California del Sur is controlled by the Federal Police based a hundred miles north in La Paz; but the several towns of Cabo have their own local police—municipals who patrol the highway and answer emergency calls in squad cars that look like the highway patrol vehicles in any number of states north of the border. They would be my last resort because they would have questions of their own. My guess was that someone in the village—shopkeeper, waiter, bartender—would know of the gringo whose picture I showed them. I also guessed that the harbor Loomis had told McAllister about was at San Lucas instead of one of the lesser indentations along the almost featureless stretches of sandy cliff and beach.

We lurched and swerved through low sandy hills tangled with sun-scorched shrubs and cactus, passing on blind curves with the faith of a devout Catholic. When we neared one of the billows of green palms, the driver would point and name the resort—"Calinda Aquamarina," "Palmilla"—and tell me what attractions each had: sport fishing, surfing, skindiving, a notable restaurant. Finally, dropping out of a last tangle of highway past skinny, long-horned cows that grazed on cactus, he pointed ahead to the spine of tan rock that sank into the sea beyond the glitter of distant white buildings. "El Cabo—the tip. Beyond that, splash!"

"That's the Arch?"

"Yes. Like a window. This side, the Sea of Cortez, that side, the Pacific. You must take the tour to Lover's Beach—swim in two oceans. Very nice—very cheap. You are looking for fishing?"

"No. I'm looking for a person."

"Oh?"

"An emergency. He's here on vacation, but I have important papers for him to sign."

The brown eyes in the rearview mirror looked at me without expression and I lifted from my briefcase the impressive sheaf of papers that made up the Columbine Project.

"You are maybe police?"

"No. I'm a lawyer. *Soy un abogado.*"

"Ah. The lawyers and the vultures," he said in Spanish. "They fly around in the same circles."

"But the lawyers can eat more than the vultures."

"Ha! Es verdad!"

The road suddenly ran out of pavement in a rattle and skid of gravel and a scattering of warning signs that marked construction.

"It's a drainage ditch around the city for the floods."

"You get that much rain here?"

He shrugged. "Maybe. Some day. But I don't think so."

The town's edge was a swirl of new highway construction that tangled the light traffic of cabs, tour vans, and the ubiquitous flatbed trucks that were used for everything from construction to family outings. The pop and sputter of small motorcycles filled the sun-washed streets as we slowed to a stop-and-go crawl past the bright façades of shops and restaurants. "Where does this man live?"

"I don't know where he's staying. I have to find him."

"Ah. He's a *Norteamericano*?"

"Canadian." I showed him Loomis's photograph. "Edward Holtzmann. He has a *finca* somewhere near the harbor."

"Okay—that's not so hard. We will look." His eyes snagged mine again in the rearview mirror. "I can be your guide, yes? I know Los Cabos—we will find him."

"That's fine."

Nothing said about money—that would come later; but McAllister could afford it. The driver, a greater happiness at the prospect of a day-long hire and a job out of the ordinary, turned completely around while he drove and held out a hand, "My name is Juan Rodriguez."

Our first stop was a cantina that faced across the main street to the harbor, where small boats of all kinds lay moored and pointing at the open sea. On the other side of the flat water, a large hotel jutted from a rise of high ground and overlooked the town; behind the cantina, the spine of gray-and-brown rock lifted steeply toward the pale and hazy sky. Scattered across its barren face, houses clung above the dusty heat of the village, propped by masonry arches and concrete pillars. "My friend owns this bar—he knows everything about San Lucas. You wish to come in? Good food, good drinks!"

"Perhaps after we find him."

Juan Rodriguez was only slightly disappointed. "Only a few minutes." He took the photograph with him and I strolled along the narrow walk past the tourist shops to gaze at the harbor and the open-air market that formed a cluster of thatched roofs. On the near horizon loomed the white massiveness of a cruise ship, and scratches of white marked the steady shuttle of barges going back and forth from the ship to the quay. From this angle, the Arch wasn't visible, but glass-bottomed boats and motor cruisers filled with brightly dressed tourists moved steadily from the harbor and back, rounding a shoulder of steep rock for the gap in the mole that protected the small harbor from the sea. Now and then, a fishing boat, its rods lifted high above the conning tower like a row of feelers, pushed slowly through the smaller skiffs and outboards that constantly crossed the glaring surface. Despite the smallness of the village, there was a sense of urbanity and congestion, the sudden boiling up of human activities that marked a crossroads in what was otherwise an alien wilderness of desert and empty ocean. It had a cosmopolitan note reinforced by the French and Spanish, the German and English that idly drifting clusters of tourists spoke as they strolled from one shop to another in the weighty midday heat. It was the kind of place that Loomis could comfortably be lost in—remote enough from the United States for safety, yet not isolated nor vacantly provincial. And his money would go a long way.

"Ah, there you are! My friend, he does not know this man personally but he has given me many places to ask for him."

"Where do we start?"

"The bakery—every man must have bread, yes? My cousin there will know if this man lives here."

"Let's start at the real-estate office." I pointed to the sign that dangled over a curving, narrow street that followed a gully leading up the mountainside. My other hand held a fifty-dollar bill under Juan's wide eyes. "If we find him within an hour, you get a bonus."

"Ah!"

It didn't take that long. The woman in the real-estate office, once she was convinced that I wasn't looking for a condominium with a magnificent view of both the Sea of Cortez and the blue Pacific Ocean, leafed through her records for Holtzmann's name. I had the feeling that she recognized the photograph Juan showed her, but she took the name from a Rolodex while an anxious Juan, glancing at his watch, hovered at her shoulder. The house was high up on Guerrero Street, a winding trail of gravel and dirt that climbed behind the town and narrowed so that even Juan had to slow to thread between steep cuts on one side and the railless plunge into the village hundreds of feet below. Finally the cab creaked to a halt at the fenced entry to what looked like a single-story, tile-roofed house and a wide expanse of concrete driveway.

"Forty-two minutes, *señor*. Less than one hour!"

I handed him the fifty which he studied for a moment. "I'll probably be here one hour. Can we make it to the airport for the afternoon flight?"

"Cómo no? No problema!"

Squealing and rumbling, the cab seesawed back and forth to turn on the narrow lane and head back down. I paused a moment in the wind that swirled dust and an occasional zinging insect; from this high, the ocean liner looked like a child's plaything, and the white marks of the barges seemed scarcely to move. Through a sharp V in the peaks, I made out the hazy line of the

Pacific horizon and a distant cloud bank that caught the light like a shred of dirty canvas. The bungalow showed no sign of life. I hoisted the briefcase and let myself through the metal gate, my shoes loud on the gritty concrete driveway. The house was one of those I had noticed from below, jutting out from the cliff like a mushroom growing on a tree trunk, and falling away in three or four stories below the ground-level entry. I clattered the iron knocker against the carved wood of the doorway. A few moments later came an answering rattle of a latch and the door opened a few inches to show a black-haired woman somewhere in her sixties who kept her hand across the opening and peeked over it. *"Sí, señor?"*

"Señor Holtzmann, por favor. Está aquí?"

"Momentito, señor."

Sandals padded away across the cool, dark tile and from somewhere in one of the neighboring houses a dog started barking—a single, halfhearted yap followed by time to regain its breath, then another perfunctory yap.

"Por favor, Señor Kirk." The woman unlatched the final chain and let me in to the soothing shadow of the room. I followed the pale bobbing of her polished heels toward a staircase that wound in a spiral down to the next level. There, in a shaded veranda that reached out over space, Loomis lay sprawled on a chaise longue, a book folded on one finger, and peered professorially over his glasses at me.

"Ah, Devlin—I've only arrived myself this morning. It certainly didn't take you long to find my little Shangri-la."

"McAllister remembered that you owned a place in Los Cabos."

"Good Lord, that man's memory! I shouldn't be surprised, I suppose, but that really was years ago." He glanced at my briefcase and smiled slightly. "And that must be the papers that you've come so far to have me sign. Sit down, please. Enjoy the view. Can María get you something cool to drink? I heartily recommend her mai tais."

"Why not?" I nodded to the woman. *"Un mai tai, por favor."*

She nodded back without showing any of her gold-lined teeth, and padded away into the house. Loomis grunted slightly as he hoisted himself to a higher sitting position and set the book on the glass table by his chair. Beyond him, a trickle of water fell down a low rock wall to form a small pool whose sound softened the heat and glare of the sky beyond the patio. Above, sunlight filtered in blurry spots of light through the thick bougainvillea vines that dangled orange and pink and purple blossoms.

"The real-estate woman called you?"

"We have an understanding. For a retainer, of course. Everything is for a fee—it's one of the few unchanging universals."

"This is a very nice hideout."

"Thank you. That wasn't its original intent. But as things turned out . . ."

"You left Denver in a hurry."

"It's not polite to overstay one's welcome."

"I thought you were quite popular. And growing more so."

"Ah well, fame isn't everything. And it's so fickle."

"If I found you, so will Neeley."

"I'm aware of that. And I'm grateful that you used your own name with Señora Castro—it saved me some strenuous effort, which, in this heat, is a blessing." He yawned and quickly covered his mouth with a polite hand. "Pardon me—it's siesta time. A very sane custom in the tropics, and I've been traveling a great deal in the past twenty-four hours. For all the good my circuitous route did me. Tell me," he changed the subject, "how is our pompous and arrogant friend taking all this?"

"McAllister? When I first told him about you, he wouldn't believe it."

María's sandals slapped across the tiles and wordlessly she handed me a large, cold glass filled with juices and fruits. Then she padded away again into the dimness.

"He wouldn't believe it," Loomis repeated to himself and sipped his own drink. "You mean he wouldn't admit that I had outsmarted him?"

"If you want to call it that."

"Oh, I do. And I did. All's fair, my boy, all's fair; and if you don't know by now that the corporate world is aflame with war—nasty, brutish, and not very short wars—then this segment of your education has garnered you nothing, has it?"

"My education? Is that why you brought me into this? To educate me to the corporate wars?"

Loomis's mouth, framed by the two deep lines dropping from its corners to his jaw, lifted in an angelic bow. Once again I noticed how, when he talked, only that lower jaw between those two lines moved up and down without changing the rest of his face. "Part of the reason. It was indeed. I still have affection for your father. He was a very rare thing, Devlin, very rare: an honest businessman."

"And you outsmarted him."

"No. As a matter of fact, I didn't. I tried to, but he was as brilliant as he was honest." That bow of a smile again. "Perhaps that's why he was honest. But in the end, of course, none of it made any difference. He saw to that." He sipped deeply. "Drink up, my boy. María will think you don't like her handiwork."

"So you were just doing the son of your old partner a small favor."

"In part, certainly. And I was doing myself a favor,

too. I much preferred to have a man on the case to whom I had access, rather than a stranger who might tell me nothing."

"So you used me."

"We used each other, Devlin, as is the usual arrangement between people. Your business is quite successful now—thanks to the opportunity I gave you to work for McAllister Enterprises."

"And through me you found out what you needed to know about the Haas case."

"Enough to keep abreast of events. It was a fair exchange—quid pro quo. Cheers."

"Have you ever worn drag, Professor?"

"Have I what?"

"Drag. Worn a dress as a disguise."

"What on earth for?"

"Carrie Busey."

"Ah—I see. No, I haven't. And I've told you before, Devlin, I have no knowledge at all of Miss Busey. I never met the woman, nor, as far as I know, have I ever spoken with her. And I am not the woman who was seen going into the office of that conceited ass of a detective."

"He told you about that?"

"For a promise of the customary fee." His head lolled back against his chair and he gazed up through the vine-covered lattice at the soft blue above. "I never understood her role in all this."

"She and Haas were lovers."

"Ah—of course." The large head rocked down and he eyed me. "That does explain it, doesn't it?"

"What?"

"Her role in all this, of course. And now you are looking for another woman or someone dressed as a woman. *Cherchez la femme manqué,* eh?"

"I thought Haas and Busey were both in it with you."

"Haas was, certainly. If he included Busey, it was at

his own discretion—and would have been against my advice had I known of it. As a matter of fact, her death caused me far more problems than her life did. After all," his hand, palm up, moved in a slow circle at the hacienda around him. "Without all the excitement and perturbation that caused, I wouldn't be in such painful exile, would I?"

"Why did you run?"

He shrugged. "At first I thought Neeley and his people had killed her. And that I would be next. A matter of economics, you see—cheaper to pay an assassin's fee than a lawyer's fee if McAllister brought a case. But when that unpleasant detective told me about the suspect woman, I decided it was time to go anyway." He called María and rattled the ice cubes loudly. Her cracked voice called *"Sí,"* a squawk from somewhere in the cool gloom like a caged bird, and a few minutes later the pad of slippers brought out two filled glasses. "I still know a few more things about the affair than you do, Devlin. I'll be happy to share them with you if you have the time to listen to an old man ramble on."

That was his way of saying he wanted to brag—which was fine with me; I wanted to know. "Such as?"

But he wasn't going to waste the savor by answering directly. "You've met with Neeley by now?"

"With Kaffey. Neeley's the shy type."

"Yes. He has that propensity. But Kaffey speaks for him. Tell me, are their feelings toward me animose?"

"I think they'd be happy if you disappeared forever. They're afraid of McAllister. You're still the star witness."

The head nodded.

"In fact, McAllister wants me to tell you that if you testify, he'll drop all charges against you."

"Yes, well, that's most generous. But I'm not interested at all—Neeley and his people tend to be thoughtlessly vindictive." His soft mouth lifted, deepening the lines that ran down to his chin. "You could tell them you've seen me, when you return."

"Why should I?"

"To put them on my trail. Or to assure them that I have no intention of ever causing them embarrassment."

"They probably want their own guarantee."

"A risk, certainly. And one I've considered very carefully, believe me. But I really don't know what my alternatives are. So I must plead with you, dear boy, for your assistance: when you get back, please just a telephone call to tell Neeley that I intend to retire outside the United States and that they have nothing at all to fear from me. Would you do that for me, my boy? As a sort of trade for the information I'm about to give you?"

"What information?"

"It begins with that anonymous call to McAllister so long ago concerning Haas. The one that started all this and drew you into it."

"You did that?"

"The promise, my boy. The quid pro quo."

"All right—it's a deal."

The mouth between the carved lines turned up cherubically. "You are like your father—I know I can trust you. Cheers." He raised his glass. "Yes, I made that call. Or caused the call to be made, to be exact. A few dollars to a chap who read the message from a piece of paper."

"Why? Why would you want to tip McAllister to something you were involved in?"

"Several reasons. First, McAllister knew his plans had been taken and was determined to investigate; I decided it would be better to be an insider to the investigation than an outsider wondering what was going on. Second, Haas had threatened to go to McAllister and confess. He felt remorse, or fear of being caught—

which are the same things, aren't they? So I decided to strike first—to erode his credibility with McAllister. That way, if he didn't keep his mouth shut, not everything he said would be believed."

"You were still taking a big chance."

Loomis's smile was hidden behind the leafy top of his mai tai. "Fortunately, he died."

"And before you divided the payoff with him."

"Yes—very astute of you! That was a vital part of the arrangement: that I would be the one to receive payment from Neeley. My reasoning was that although I provided the initial link between Haas and Neeley, once they were in touch with each other, there would be no need for me anymore, would there? Consequently, I insisted that the payoff be through me."

"And you still have it."

"I banked it. Outside the United States. A normal arrangement in such cases, as I'm sure you know."

"Weren't you afraid Haas would go straight to McAllister as soon as he heard about the suspicion?"

"The risk was small."

"Why?"

His heavy torso heaved and he fished in a watch pocket for a key that he held out to me. "You'll find the answer here. It's the key," he smiled and lifted his glass, "to the puzzle."

"A locker key?"

"The bus depot. I was planning ahead, you see. And I must congratulate you again—I didn't expect to have to use it so soon."

Before I left, he reminded me of my promise to telephone his peace offering to Neeley, and he urged me to do it as soon as possible. "They are so impetuous."

The flight brought me into Denver in late afternoon and I just had time to make the call to Aegis before their

offices closed; a deal is a deal, even with someone like
Loomis. The familiar nasal voice of Kaffey answered.

"Kirk. Now what."

"I've been talking with Loomis."

"Loomis." Then he remembered, "Who's . . . ?"

"Right, you never heard of him. He wants me to tell
you that he's not planning to come back to the States
—that you don't have anything to be afraid of from
him." So much for my promise. "But I know where he
is, Kaffey. If I have to, I can bring him back." That
wasn't true, of course. By now Loomis was already on
his way to some deeper cover elsewhere in Mexico or
South America, and probably with still another alias.
But Kaffey didn't need to know that.

"It takes some time, Kirk. You asked for a lot."

"You've had your time. I don't want it to slip your
mind."

"We ain't forgot. Believe me, we ain't forgot."

Which naturally gave a spurt to the adrenaline. I
made a quick call to Margaret to make sure she was all
right and to let her and Dutch know I was back, and as
I drove across town toward my office, I kept one eye on
the rearview mirror.

Bunch was clambering down the stairs as I came up.
"Dev! Come on, man—I'm on my way over to the hospital. They're letting Susan out—Mrs. Faulk just
called."

"You want to hear what I found out?"

"On the way over, man! She'll be an outpatient, but
at least she'll be away from that place and back in her
own apartment. They had to run some tests to be sure
it was okay, and I don't want her to spend another night
in that place. She's really wired about going home."

During the ride, I told him about Loomis, but he was
too excited to listen closely, and finally I shut up. We
found Susan waiting in a wheelchair, her suitcase
packed and set by the door and a couple of plastic

shopping bags full of plants and magazines and stray gear. The wheelchair was hospital policy but when we got to the entry, she insisted on walking from the door to the Ford, pausing to breathe deeply the warm spring air and to look at the trees whose new leaves were a delicate tracery against the clear sky of early evening. Bunch half held her with one arm and gathered a suitcase in his other hand while Mrs. Faulk and I came behind carrying the rest.

"Nice!"

"It sure is, Suze! Come on, let's get you in and we'll go celebrate."

Mrs. Faulk took one load of plants and said she'd meet us at the apartment; Bunch helped Susan into the front seat while I tossed the luggage into the trunk. Piling into the back, he leaned over the seat with a grin almost as wide as his shoulders. "You really look great, Suze—hey, your mother's fixing up a little surprise at the apartment, too. I guess I'm not supposed to say anything but I did, and I'm not going to tell you what it is until we get there."

I drove; Bunch, hanging over the seat, kept laughing and talking with Susan while she, a bit of color bringing warmth to her pale cheeks, answered him as best she could and stared hungrily at the world passing the windows. It wasn't until we had turned north on Downing that I noticed the car hovering behind to follow our turns. I gradually slowed to let traffic pass in the left lane, then sped up to pull away, but the car stayed where it was. Bunch finally stopped talking and looked at me and he knew.

"Behind us?"

I kept my voice as calm as possible. "Looks that way. Are you armed?" I wasn't. My pistol was still back at the office where I'd left it before going through airport security.

"Yeah. But we can't take any chances with Susan."

She turned from gazing out the window. "What?"

"Nothing, honey—I just remembered something I forgot about. Hey, look at that: a whole line of geese heading toward the river!"

The car, a dark sedan whose headlights were not yet turned on, moved closer and I could see two silhouetted figures; one, when its head turned, showed a ponytail of hair gathered at the back. Bunch glanced over his shoulder and then searched the highway ahead of us. Scattered traffic dotted the four lanes and when the Evans Avenue traffic light stopped us, the sedan pulled bumper close. They weren't afraid of being noticed, now. In the mirror I used the glare of my brake lights to make out the mustached face driving, and the round, fleshy face of the ponytailed one.

"Bunch, can you use the car phone without them seeing it?"

"Nine-one-one?"

"It's worth a try." Maybe the dispatcher would think a report of one car following another car on a busy highway would be important enough for a police response. Maybe.

"Goddamn them, why now?"

"Because we're vulnerable."

"We've got to get her someplace safe, Dev."

The light changed and I pulled away close behind the car in front. The sedan stayed with us, its lights now shining hotly into the cab as Bunch shielded his arm with his body and dialed the radiophone.

I half listened to him argue with the dispatcher while I tried to think of a place where Susan could get safely out of the car. It would take time; she couldn't move quickly, and not even Bunch could carry her fast enough to escape the two who stayed on us like bees at a flower. Up to the overpass across I-25 and its river of traffic and through the series of stoplights that governed the freeway ramps.

Bunch shoved the phone back disgustedly. "She said she'd notify cars along the route. Shit—they don't even know where we are!"

"They're just tailing us right now—they're waiting to get a good shot." The gleaming headlights hung in the mirror. "If we make it downtown, we can pull in to the police garage. It's got concrete all around it and room for only one car at a time."

"That's a long way."

It was that; halfway across the city. But the other district headquarters had open parking lots and no protected approach. Trying to get Susan out of the car in one of them would be like pulling into a supermarket parking lot. "Maybe a patrol car will spot us before then."

Ahead, on the right side, streetlights paced the mile-long darkness of Washington Park. As traffic strung out from the stoplight, the headlights behind suddenly swerved to the inside lane. In the side mirror, I glimpsed an arm hanging out the rider's window, a pistol aimed skyward and ready to drop down when they pulled beside us.

"Grab Susan!"

Swinging hard to the right, we careened toward the gated entry to the park, the lights became a sudden swirl of dodging cars as the sedan veered after us through the scream of tires and angry horns. Occasional street lamps shone down on the tangle of meandering roads through the park, but mostly it was dark, and whipping out of the blackness on each side of the tarmac, the startled faces of joggers shouted for us to slow down. The narrow lane turned sharply left, toward the east entry of the park, and I leaned the car hard through the turn, but the faster headlights behind cut inside and hooked our rear fender.

"Hang on, Bunch!"

We slid sideways toward the curbless grass and thudded solidly into a towering spruce tree; Susan, crying now, tried to cover her face from the windshield as the seatbelt yanked hard against her. The sedan knifed across our front to pin us against the tree and I flung the door open and tumbled in a roll toward the dust cloud that swirled into the still bobbing headlights. Behind me I heard Bunch shout at Susan to get down and then the spurt of pistol fire told me where they were.

One shadow loomed against the headlights, its arm lifted toward our car where Bunch fought to get out of the back door and the lights glared into his eyes and into the open front seat where Susan, hands clutched in her hair, cowered against the dash. Another shot whipped something past my ear and then I had him.

We tumbled into blackness, the jolt of sandy earth hard against my shoulder. I clamped my hand tight around the man's wrist as I twisted and it folded back against the elbow. Something thudded my back and shoulders and in the darkness I made out his shoe swinging past my face in a savage jab. I groped for his eyes, my fingers snagging in soft flesh somewhere, and a moment later his teeth came down hard on my knuckle in a grinding gnaw. Shoving hard against the wrist, I yanked my finger away when he screamed and I drove the blade of my hand at his throat. It hit solidly and the scream choked off and the man sagged as if a string snapped. I rolled over to press against him hard and began to pound his head against the earth with long, solid, methodical swings. Then he was still.

Behind me, I heard Bunch's voice in a steady, almost gentle chorus, and I turned in time to see, silhouetted against the oddly angled headlights of our car, two figures, one massive and standing like a grizzly with forearms raised, and in them, clamped in his hands, the writhing, kicking shape of a man silent with the effort to buck free. Then the arms flung the man against the steel of the automobile. A heavy sound—like an animal bumping under a car's frame—then only the noise of Susan's deep, hoarse sobs.

"There, honey; it's okay now—it's okay now, Suze."

"Jesus, did you see that? Those guys were shooting at them!" From the surrounding darkness a cluster of faces—joggers, bicyclists—hovered with shiny, startled eyes and stared at the tangle of cars and oddly twisted bodies.

"An ambulance? You need an ambulance?"

"The cops are on their way! Somebody called the cops already!"

Bunch was cradling Susan against him, his voice a steady murmur under her jolting sobs. I felt for a pulse in the limp arm of the one sprawled on the edge of the asphalt. He wasn't dead, but he wasn't quite alive, either; the other one, moaning and wagging a knee slowly back and forth, lay wadded beside the dented car door.

"Can you hear me?"

"Uh." It was the fat-faced one, the one with the ponytail and the gun.

I lifted his head clear of the ground by the throat and his eyes popped open in a hoarse scream. "My shoulder!" The words were squeaky through my fingers. "God—!"

"Can you hear me!"

"Yes—goddamn—stop—!"

"Listen good: if anything happens to Margaret Haas —anywhere, anytime—you are dog meat. I'll kill you, do you hear?"

"I hear!" Then, "Who?"

"The woman you ran off the road two days ago."

"What . . . ? I didn't. . . . Goddamn, man, we weren't even here two days ago. Vegas. We just came in."

I stared at his face shadowed by darkness and blood. "It was Neeley, wasn't it? He wanted her hit."

"Never heard· of Neeley. Ow! You—you were the hit!"

"Who hit her?"

"I don't know—goddamn you, stop it—I don't know!"

The whine of the siren grew into a pulsing wail, and flashes of red, white, and blue emergency lights began to dance through the night to lift the grass blades out of darkness. The man stared back at me with eyes stretched by pain and fear, his face a pinched triangle between my fists. "We never hit on her. I swear! Just you—you were the hit."

"Neeley?"

"Fuck you. Ow! Yes—but just you!"

"All right, what's going down—leave that man alone, there!" A flashlight shone over us and the creaking bulk of a policeman loomed against the dark sky. "What's going on here?"

Bunch had been shot in the fleshy part of the neck, a clean wound just above the collarbone and a fraction from the artery. He was lucky. Susan was less so. A ricochet caught her low in the side of the abdomen. Those are the worst kind. The slug hits something and gets knocked into a ragged shape and begins spinning so that when it hits, it tears and chews a wide path through the flesh. There's a lot of bleeding, much of it internal from so much ripping, and the victim needs help as quickly as possible. Susan, crying and stunned, slipping into shock and still unable to speak clearly through the damage to her brain, couldn't tell us anything except "Hurt," and it was too long before anyone noticed the blood seeping under the side of her blouse and down into the crack of the car's front seat, so she died.

It happened sometime in the early morning to the accompaniment of the hiss and ping of pressure tubes and monitors, and the support systems that work so many miracles. Bunch, taped and with an angry nurse fluttering behind, sat at one side of the bed and held her hand. Mrs. Faulk held the other. When they started disconnecting the wires and tubes, I went out and left them. Sergeant Whelan from Crimes Against Persons was waiting.

"I need to fill in the gaps, Mr. Kirk. I'm sorry."

"It's all right."

"Can you tell me more about this Neeley and why those two assaulted you?"

"It was a professional hit. Neeley ordered it. Have either of them told you anything?"

"No. The one who could talk, Dunahay, asked for his lawyer and that was it." Whelan added, "He has a broken clavicle and some cracked ribs, and he was damned lucky to get off with just that. Bunchcroft used to be with DPD, didn't he?"

"Yes."

The sergeant wagged his head. "He's tough."

"What about the other one?"

"Jones is in a coma. Severe brain damage. If he makes it, he'll be a changed man."

"Good."

"We could be talking a manslaughter charge on that, Mr. Kirk. I have to inform you of your rights."

"We're talking self-defense."

That might be true, but he was a cop who'd seen a lot of weird things come out of the courts, and he read me the Miranda as a matter of policy. Then he got as much as he could about Neeley and Aegis. But without an admission from Dunahay, the most he could do would be to question Neeley about his alleged involvement. And Dunahay would not admit anything; he would do the right thing—do his time like a good soldier and when he got out in eight or ten years, would find a job waiting for him.

"That's it?" Whelan asked.

"Compare notes with Lewellen in the White Collar section. He'll have some background for you."

"Thanks."

Denver General sits right downtown, and when you come out in the morning you can hear the rush and clatter of the new day's traffic from the surrounding streets, and from one corner of the building you can look across to the gleam of the state capitol's gold dome on the high ridge above downtown. You can see the birds fluttering in the trees along Cherry Creek Boulevard, but during the rush hour you can't hear them, and of course the fragrance from the flowers spotted around the hospital and parkway grounds is buried under the spew of traffic. I left the dented Ford for Bunch to use when he finally felt like it and caught a cab back to the office. Then I drove the Healy over to my place and stood for a long, long time in the shower.

At nine, I called Margaret to give her the news about Susan. When that was over, I called Neeley. The police had already questioned him. I told him that I wouldn't turn the papers over to McAllister but I'd keep them in a safe place for insurance and McAllister would get them automatically if anything happened to me or mine.

The line was silent for a breath or two. "If I knew what you were talking about, I'd call it a deal." Then he added, "But I don't, so you can just sweat, you son-of-a-bitch."

Which told me that he was pulling out. Aegis would still be around, and Neeley would still be in the distant background. But with the heat from the shooting and their fear of what McAllister could do with those papers and tapes, they were going to stay quiet and dump the properties and move to a cooler frying pan. Which got Loomis off their hook, too, because now he wasn't worth bothering about.

In the pockets of my stained and torn trousers, I found the key that he had given me. I'd forgotten about it, and I stared at the worn brass disk with weariness. But I wasn't going to sleep, I knew that, so I might as well spend the time wrapping up the loose ends.

The locker was in the Trailways terminal on Nineteenth, and it didn't take much detection to count down the numbers until I came to the one matching the key. The only thing inside was an unaddressed large envelope lying on the scuffed plywood floor, and inside that a packet of papers that began somewhat smugly, "If you are reading this it is because I want you to." They went on to say why Loomis had written the contents. The main reason, he admitted, was insurance; it might pay to have this story written down if he needed something to trade. The second reason was revenge and he wasn't certain at the time of writing whether the holder of the key had received it personally from him or had it mailed to him. Either way, the conclusion said, there was no sense trying to find Loomis because by now he had disappeared into a world that offered abundant shelter to those with enough money. And, it added, he had enough now.

Between salutation and conclusion, he said who the revenge was on and why, and I read it several times with a kind of sick numbness until I could almost quote the words from memory.

CHAPTER 17

Peterson answered the door. He had heard from Margaret about Susan and Bunch, and there wasn't much to say. "I'm sorry, Dev."

My father had told me something about the distance between a man's wants and what life allowed —its capricious ironies in answering his pleas, as if some malevolent god delighted in twisting painful fates out of those pleas. "But the thing is, Devlin, I don't believe there is a malevolent god. And there's a good possibility there's nothing—that we're on our own, and somehow that's even worse than being subject to a demon. But if so, that's where we have to spin our web of faith, Dev —out of ourselves. It's all we have to hold ourselves up with, and maybe to hold up God, too." But his faith had not been a strong enough support; and even if I could now understand its weakness, that didn't make it any less bitter. I gave Dutch his final assignment and told him he could pack up. "Send me your bill. I'll get your check in the mail."

"Sure. I'll get my gear."

Margaret was waiting for me in the living room, and, wordless, she stared at my face that had a numb and stiff feeling. "Oh, Dev!"

Everything was familiar about the way she felt against me. The fragrance of her perfume and hair, the small, strong grip of her hands on my back pressing me tightly against the yield and softness of her body. And then the slight stiffening as she leaned back to study my face again.

"You haven't slept all night, have you? Would you like some coffee?"

"Where's Shauna?" Austin would be in preschool by now.

"Upstairs cleaning her room. Why?"

"I found Loomis yesterday."

"Oh." She backed away, her arms hugging her own ribs. Somewhere upstairs a piece of furniture rumbled clumsily, and then came the distant, muted whir of a vacuum cleaner as Shauna busily straightened her room. "What did he tell you?"

I don't know what I expected her to say. Something that would prove Loomis a liar by showing puzzlement or shock or even disbelief. But she wasn't surprised; she was waiting. "It wasn't what he said, it's what he wrote. Along with some documentation."

"What was it?"

So I told her what she already knew: about the deal between her and Loomis and Aegis, and how the two of them convinced her husband to steal McAllister's proposals. About Loomis making the telephone call to McAllister to establish a reason for Austin's suicide. I told her about Loomis keeping the payoff money after Austin was dead and how she borrowed a trick from him by hiring me to look into the theft in order to frighten Loomis into paying her share—two-thirds of a half million dollars. When it was paid, she would take me off the case. Then I began the guessing, but it was right, too: I told her that the telephone number for Neeley that I "found" in that envelope containing her husband's effects had been planted there, and that Loomis's name in Busey's purse had been put there, too, so I would be led closer to the professor. And I told her the names were planted by the same person—the one who killed Busey.

"You're accusing me?"

"Yes."

"You can't prove it. You can't prove anything!"

"We have a witness who saw another woman follow Busey up to Landrum's office. And I called Tammy, your babysitter. She says she sat for the children from six to eight on the night Busey was killed. Where did you go?"

The green eyes gazed toward me, not seeing but thinking hard. Upstairs, the vacuum cleaner fell silent and a moment later Shauna's legs flickered down the banistered stairs with light thumps as she hopped, rabbitlike, until she saw me. "Devlin! Hi, Devlin!" And then she ran, her fine hair like a light gauze behind her. "Hi!" Reaching her arms up to be swung and I lifted her, lighter than my heart, high and giggling and happy almost to the ceiling and she stretched to touch it with a finger. "When is Dutch going? He won't let me play outside unless he's along. He says I have to stay where he can see me. Where've you been?"

"Shauna, calm down. Go in the other room. Mr. Kirk and I have to talk."

The girl looked at her mother and suddenly sagged to be let back to earth. "What's the matter, Mama?"

"Nothing," I said. "We just have some business to talk over."

She looked at me across a new distance, aware, now, that her mother, too, had withdrawn from me, and an edge of fright knifed into her glance.

"Go on now," said Margaret more gently. "I'll be in soon and then we'll go shopping. Just the two of us. Without Dutch or anyone else. Just us. And we'll buy lots of things."

At the door, Shauna turned to look back at me, a mixture of puzzlement and acceptance, and a new knowledge—uncomprehended but real, that we were saying good-bye to each other. And to something else, too. Then she was gone.

"Loomis was driving the van."

"What?"

"The van that ran you off the road. It was Loomis. When it didn't work, he ran."

"He told you?"

"No. But it fits. With everything else."

Margaret stared at me. She did not ask why he had tried to kill her.

"You knew about Carrie Busey and your husband."

"Yes! Yes, I knew. That slut. Both of them . . ." The rage still in her eyes, she glared hotly at me. "You said you were judge and jury, Devlin. You said you were that in your work. So was I—it wasn't any different from what you would have done!"

"Loomis described how you killed your husband. The first bullet in his head. Then reload. The second one fired with his own hand to leave powder residue on it. You wore a pair of disposable rubber gloves, and that's what little Austin meant when he heard the second shot and thought he dreamed that you were peeling the skin off your hands." Behind her, the large rubber tree stood like a healthy sapling, its broad leaves dark with food and light. "Is the second bullet still in there? In the dirt?"

"They got what they deserved. Both of them."

I gazed back at those wide, green eyes. "You killed

your husband because he was going to McAllister, not because of Carrie Busey. You killed her because she was investigating his death."

"They deserved to die! There were a lot of reasons they deserved it!"

"And I was your tool to force Loomis into paying your share."

"At first, Devlin, yes. But not later. It wasn't for money . . . that woman. That wasn't for money. I was afraid—there was so much, and then she . . . I was afraid!" Margaret stepped toward me, her eyes glistening with sudden tears. "I tried not to love you. I tried to make you see that I couldn't love you. But it didn't work, Devlin. We do love each other. No matter how hard I tried not to, I fell in love with you, and you loved me."

"I still love you."

"I still love you, too! We can still be married! What's happened is over—nobody has to know about it."

I doubted whether she ever loved me or anyone else —whether she even knew what it meant to love someone else. She loved herself, and she liked those who shared that love and enhanced it. And she needed me, which was close enough to love for her. But I did not know if any feeling she had went beyond that. And the argument was pointless, anyway. "I still love you, Margaret. But I don't like you."

Her hands ran quickly through the black hair above her temples. "There's no proof. I dug up that bullet and it's gone. You can't prove anything!"

"Loomis's statement is enough to open your husband's death. And enough to bring charges against you for Busey's death, too."

"You would do that?"

"Yes."

"Even if we love each other?"

The answer was the same, though it took a little longer to get it out.

"You fool."

That could well be true, but it changed nothing and I remained silent.

"You're a fool for listening to Loomis and a fool for letting him go."

"There was no reason to bring him back."

The tears had dried and now her eyes held the mocking heat of contempt. "No reason? You fool—how do you think he knew how Austin died? How do you think he knew?"

Somewhere in the back of my mind I had been asking that, but there had been too many other thoughts tumbling through my skull to focus on that one. And besides, he hadn't been here—I knew; I had been watching her house. "You did it alone; you told him how it was done."

"You fool! Who do you think told me how to do it? Who do you think told me how it could be done?"

"Loomis?"

"Yes! And how do you think he knew it would work?"

She waited until I said it, my voice a dry croak. "My father?"

"Yes. Your father. The same way."

I stared at her as the words sank in, but it wasn't Margaret's face I saw. It was Loomis's: the angelic smile, the mai tai lifted in toast, his benediction as I left, "I know you will do the right thing with the information, dear boy—you and your father are so much alike."

"He's gone now, isn't he? You let him go! He has all the money and he ruined me and he's laughing at you, too!"

"Loomis killed my father?"

"Yes! And he got away with it—all of it. The money, the killing, everything. And so did I—I would have. I still can: it's only your word against mine and I'll swear I never admitted a thing to you and that every word Loomis wrote is a lie!"

The green eyes had hardened into ice and they dominated the white hatred of her face. "He's a thief and a liar and he won't come back to testify! No one will believe that piece of paper! Go on—call the police—see how far it gets you!"

"I won't call," I said. "Dutch can."

Behind her, from the half-open door of the study, a short, slightly pudgy figure pocketed the small tape recorder and plodded heavily toward the telephone.

FOR THE BEST IN PAPERBACKS, LOOK FOR THE

In every corner of the world, on every subject under the sun, Penguin represents quality and variety – the very best in publishing today.

For complete information about books available from Penguin – including Pelicans, Puffins, Peregrines and Penguin Classics – and how to order them, write to us at the appropriate address below. Please note that for copyright reasons the selection of books varies from country to country.

In the United Kingdom: For a complete list of books available from Penguin in the U.K., please write to *Dept E.P., Penguin Books Ltd, Harmondsworth, Middlesex, UB7 0DA*

In the United States: For a complete list of books available from Penguin in the U.S., please write to *Dept BA, Penguin, 299 Murray Hill Parkway, East Rutherford, New Jersey 07073*

In Canada: For a complete list of books available from Penguin in Canada, please write to *Penguin Books Canada Ltd, 2801 John Street, Markham, Ontario L3R 1B4*

In Australia: For a complete list of books available from Penguin in Australia, please write to the *Marketing Department, Penguin Books Australia Ltd, P.O. Box 257, Ringwood, Victoria 3134*

In New Zealand: For a complete list of books available from Penguin in New Zealand, please write to the *Marketing Department, Penguin Books (NZ) Ltd, Private Bag, Takapuna, Auckland 9*

In India: For a complete list of books available from Penguin, please write to *Penguin Overseas Ltd, 706 Eros Apartments, 56 Nehru Place, New Delhi, 110019*

In Holland: For a complete list of books available from Penguin in Holland, please write to *Penguin Books Nederland B.V., Postbus 195, NL–1380AD Weesp, Netherlands*

In Germany: For a complete list of books available from Penguin, please write to *Penguin Books Ltd, Friedrichstrasse 10 – 12, D–6000 Frankfurt Main 1, Federal Republic of Germany*

In Spain: For a complete list of books available from Penguin in Spain, please write to *Longman Penguin España, Calle San Nicolas 15, E–28013 Madrid, Spain*

CRIME AND MYSTERY IN PENGUINS

Deep Water Patricia Highsmith

Portrait of a psychopath, from the first faint outline to the full horrors of schizophrenia. 'If you read crime stories at all, or perhaps especially if you don't, you should read *Deep Water*' – Julian Symons in the *Sunday Times*

Farewell My Lovely Raymond Chandler

Moose Malloy was a big man but not more than six feet five inches tall and not wider than a beer truck. He looked about as inconspicuous as a tarantula on a slice of angel food. Marlowe's greatest case. Chandler's greatest book.

God Save the Child Robert B. Parker

When young Kevin Bartlett disappears, everyone assumes he's run away . . . until the comic strip ransom note arrives . . . 'In classic wisecracking and handfighting tradition, Spenser sorts out the case and wins the love of a fine-boned Jewish Lady . . . who even shares his taste for iced red wine' – Francis Goff in the *Sunday Telegraph*

The Daughter of Time Josephine Tey

Josephine Tey again delves into history to reconstruct a crime. This time it is a crime committed in the tumultuous fifteenth century. 'Most people will find *The Daughter of Time* as interesting and enjoyable a book as they will meet in a month of Sundays' – Marghanita Laski in the *Observer*

The Michael Innes Omnibus

Three tensely exhilarating novels. 'A master – he constructs a plot that twists and turns like an electric eel: it gives you shock upon shock and you cannot let go' – *The Times Literary Supplement*

Killer's Choice Ed McBain

Who killed Annie Boone? Employer, lover, ex-husband, girlfriend? This is a tense, terrifying and tautly written novel from the author of *The Mugger*, *The Pusher*, *Lady Killer* and a dozen other first class thrillers.